SHADOW GUARD

REILY GARRETT

Acknowledgments

To Siobhan Caughey, for reading through my rough drafts. Your perceptions are spot-on and always appreciated in delving into a character's mind. First drafts are always the roughest, but is also where changes in a character's direction take root.

To Rosie Amber for an in-depth assessment of character and plot, thank you for all your help. You can find her blog and services at rosieamber.wordpress.com/beta-reading-service.

To RE Hargrave, for editing. Thank you for spotting the loopholes and answering endless grammar questions.

To my readers, each one of you who selects and reads one of my books, thank you for the opportunity to share my work. If you've enjoyed it, please consider leaving a review. They are the best way to help your author share her work.

Chapter One

Dani watched as Dr. Carari breezed through the reception area with purse and keys in hand, smiling at the last client preparing to check out.

"Thanks for closing up today, Daniele. Kevin's soccer match starts in fifteen. With a bit of luck, I can make the kickoff."

"No problem. Tell him to score one for me."

If only life were so simple. Work, household chores, and a little time to relax—shouldn't that compose the bulk of everyone's day?

Instead, Dani spent much of her life looking over her shoulder for a gun pointed her way or a stalker wielding a garrote.

"Will do. See you on Monday, kiddo. Have a great weekend." The vet waved to the last client in passing. "Good luck with the trial tomorrow, Marc. Give us a call Monday and let us know how he did."

A whispered *eek* signaled the door closing behind her boss, leaving Dani alone with the man she planned to exploit.

Marc nodded but kept his gaze on Dani. The long-coat shepherd by his side echoed his calm demeanor, waiting for his human companion to finish.

He'd requested the day's last appointment due to his schedule, which meant Dani could concentrate on her objective. Every time the private investigator brought in one of his dogs, he began their verbal sparring with a side order of flirtation. She'd kept him at arm's length for a reason. Concentration remained key to keeping her wits about her.

It'd obviously become a game to him, but she cultivated the tenuous bond without crossing her line in the sand. It was the only road to survival.

Not one to leave anything to chance, she'd researched his business, learning everything available to the point of donning a disguise and entering the busy night club he and his brothers owned. She'd discovered many ways to snoop. Extreme focus and a quirk of genetics had allowed her to investigate without getting caught.

If he discovered her past, the tone of their conversations would change, and not for the better. It wasn't her fault life forced her into impossible situations, compelling her to kill or die.

Above all else, she'd learned to survive.

A self-conscious tug on her sweater insured consequences of past escapades didn't collide with future plans.

She counted on him knowing someone who could forge a new ID. It wouldn't have to be top notch work as she kept a low profile and did her best to stay out of trouble. Her time was running short, and she needed a fresh start—elsewhere.

Seeing his golden eyes alight with the sharp intellect of a top-notch, ex-military private investigator encouraged her to convince him of her genuine need—without getting him killed.

A burnished lock of inky black hair fell across his chiseled features while a silent chuckle accompanied the small twitch at the corner of his mouth, not hidden by his dark mustache.

"I appreciate you getting Darius in today. His trial tomorrow includes scaling a five-foot A frame, and I wanted to make sure he's solid."

"No problem, and good luck. I'm sure he'll pass with flying colors. He's always a perfect gentleman." To keep focus on her objective, she avoided eye contact.

The time had come to make her move. Each night, she sensed the hounds of hell closing in. If she didn't flee the area soon, previous captors would catch her once again.

"So, this is the second of three tests for Darius in his Schutzhund training, right?" Her fingers shook as she reorganized the chart's papers into their proper order.

"Yeah, at Kober's farm outside of town." Darius nudged his dad's leg in impatience.

Dani accepted Marc's debit card over the bi-level counter, placing her other hand square over the book she'd started reading. If she couldn't live a fairytale life, she could read about one.

The brush of his fingers against hers stirred a shudder from neck to waist, each vertebra energized from the detective's intense and focused magnetism. She hoped he didn't perceive her sudden intake of breath.

A furtive glance declared otherwise.

One thick brow lifted. Tiny crinkles around his eyes and slightly flaring nostrils demonstrated his acknowledgment of their unusual connection. If she weren't in such dire straits, she might've accepted the invitation written in his gaze.

Damn it. He doesn't understand what's at stake.

"That'll be th-thirty, um, thirty-four dollars today, Mr. Crof– uh, Crofton."

She recognized the opening but couldn't form the words to assure success of her objective. Her thoughts dissolved into a quagmire of a thousand what-ifs.

"Call me Marc, just one syllable." The slightest twitch of his lips betrayed the suppressed humor dancing in his gaze.

Sure, he was handsome, but what choked her thought processes included images of her enemies slitting Marc's throat then dumping his chopped-up body in the ocean. He had no idea what skeletons cavorted in her closet, always ready to come out and wreak havoc.

Three attempts at sliding the plastic card through the reader proved excessive but unavoidable due to the moisture accumulating on her palms. Guttural rumbles in her throat betrayed her ultimate craving for the need to appear normal in the face of an everyday situation. These humiliating reactions never occurred during her mental prep. She wiped her brow.

His grin widened.

Dear God. He's teasing me.

He didn't comprehend the consequences of his actions, but she did. Was she willing to put his life at risk?

"Have you ever been to the Schutzhund trials, Daniele?" A half grin displayed his amusement, his voice edged with hope, but also something else, undefined.

Finally!

Her goal was at hand if her mental prodding had nudged him in the right direction.

"*Um*, no. Not yet." Words stumbled through tightened lips, tangled and refusing to fall into a coherent order. Shaking her head was safer than trying to dislodge the failed filter of her brain.

"Do your friends call you Dani?"

What if Ray or Tucker kidnaps him to leverage against me?

"*Um,* I don't have any... well, of course I have friends. But, well, yes, they call me Dani. And no, I've never been to the trials, but I've read they're quite exciting." She couldn't continue to travel two divergent pathways of conversations.

Pick one.

"Why don't you come tomorrow? You'd have a great time."

"Thanks, I just might." *She* needed a muzzle.

Chimes over the front door offered a small semblance of relief. The *whoosh* of cool air blew in another large dog with an equally large handler.

Shepherds of the world, unite.

"Hi, is Dr. Carari in? I think my boy here's getting a hot spot on his paw." The stranger's lean, muscular build accentuated his blond and blue-eyed good looks, an allure he'd use to full advantage based on his blatant perusal.

On closer inspection, he emitted a tightly wound sense of awareness she associated with hidden agendas and subversive objectives.

The man had something specific on his mind, and it wasn't just a date.

She felt it in her soul without having to concentrate on his body language or trying to perceive his intentions. Her flustered mind couldn't process anything significant. Marc's distraction doomed her to metaphorical drooling.

Seeing there wouldn't be conflict between the dogs, Daniele swiveled her chair to view the computer's schedule.

"No. I'm afraid you just missed her, but I can schedule you for Monday morning, if that's all right?" Although handsome, the newcomer didn't stir the least bit of interest.

"Sure, darlin'. What time is good for you?" Leaning over the bi-level counter allowed him visual access to her organized space. "*Ah,* I see you read hot romance novels. My sister writes for a large New York publisher."

Her fingers couldn't move fast enough to hide the book's graphics, a bare-chested man kissing a scantily clad woman. In her haste to hide the cover, Dani skid the book off the counter, where it landed several feet to Marc's side.

Of course. Where else would it go?

His swift reflexes resulted in scooping up the embarrassing material. After a quick perusal of the book jacket, he tilted his head back and forth, as if judging the merits of the scene depicted and finding it lacking in some specific way.

Something inside her dictated he'd return the book—for a price. Fiery heat blazed up her neck to engulf her face, becoming an inferno worthy of a three-alarm fire. His shaking shoulders did nothing for her composure.

"I have Monday morning at ten-thirty. Your name, sir?"

After fumbling the appointment card, she placed it on the counter and grabbed the nearby pen. Panic swelled to become a palpable pressure in her chest. This wasn't how she'd planned the morning.

"Clayton Hutson, and that sounds great, darlin'. I'll see you then. Unless... you'd let me take you to dinner tonight."

"Sorry, Mr. Hutson, I have plans." *I think I'll just call you Slick.*

"Well, how about lunch tomorrow?"

Something in Hutson's distinct and intense scrutiny scared her breathless—a foreboding she hadn't endured in three years. Prickling along her nape and arms never occurred without just cause.

Blood drained from her face to leave her shaken at the sight of his rough hands on the counter. Those calloused hands could wield a garrote with expertise.

Could he be the serial killer responsible for the string of recent murders?

The fact he stood before her, overshadowing and transmitting bad vibes ensured she wouldn't feel safe for a long time, even if he just saw her as a sexual conquest.

Under normal circumstances, discerning the level of honesty in someone's stated goals equaled child's play. To her dismay, Marc's overwhelming effect on her mindset obliterated the ability to pick up Slick's intent.

A suggestive throat clearing transferred her attention to Marc, whose demeanor revealed no evidence of the earlier carefree banter.

"No, Hutson. The lady's with me." Marc's expression had lost all signs of levity as he crowded closer to her workspace, edging the other man out. "I'll pick you up tomorrow morning at ten, Dani. Okay?"

Darius' combination whine-growl elicited a like response in the other dog. Each shepherd's attunement to his handler's emotions occurred in a flash.

Hutson's face broadcast a tangle of warning signs she'd label aggressive if expressed in canine form. Non-blinking, direct eye contact, a hardened jaw, and his predator's grin equaled a trifecta forecasting trouble.

Her well-planned intentions evaporated like seawater meeting magma, the haze formed smothering the intricate workings of her mind. At this point, mangled words were a useless commodity. She merely nodded to Marc.

"Here's your reminder." Turning back to Hutson, she handed him the appointment card.

"Have a good day, Mr. Hutson." Marc's conspicuous dismissal resulted in a low groan and insincere apology.

"Sorry, man. Didn't know she was taken. It's not like she's wearing a ring. Nice dog, by the way. I watched him track in his first trial. Good nose in bad weather and difficult cover." A calculating gaze bore into Marc as if gauging the likelihood of winning a dirty, no-holds-barred fight. The shark's grin hid nothing.

Hutson's departure allowed her to draw a slow lungful of toxin-purging air. "Thank you, Marc. He made me a bit nervous for some reason."

"Anytime, and you're welcome. He kicked my sixth sense into overdrive, too. You all right? You turned white as a sheet. Do you know him from somewhere?"

Darius whined and chuffed, pulling on his leash until Marc let go. "What's up, boy? You never misbehave—"

Barreling around the counter to rub against her thigh, Darius rumbled low when Dani buried her face in the long hair at his neck.

"Aw, sweetie. It's all right. You're such a good boy." His fur smelled of oatmeal and vanilla shampoo, the same type she used when giving dog baths in the back. "I've never seen that guy before, but he sure gave me the creeps."

"We'll hang around until you leave." More a command than offer, his statement and expression brooked no argument.

"Thanks. Something was definitely off about him." The soft fur against her cheek imbued a soothing calm unattainable through any other means.

"Yeah, I agree. Anyway, about tomorrow, give me your address and I'll pick you up."

"Oh. I thought you just said that to get me off the hook with Hutson. You really don't need to bother." Intervention via reality proved a bitch. She stood no chance of holding her own with this man. Which begged the question, how would she con him into helping her with a new identity?

"No trouble at all. That way I can check and make sure you're all right."

"How 'bout I meet you there?" she countered. Anonymity plus meeting in public equaled safety. Dangerous in his own way, Marc Crofton embodied thoughts of a future she could never have.

"Sure. I look forward to earning your trust. Perhaps after a day at the trials, you'll join me for dinner." He didn't just set the book down on her workspace. No, he had to make a meal of it, placing it and then giving the cover a conspicuous pat.

"Oh, I-I don't date."

Crap. He'd misinterpreted her intentions.

"That's fine. I'm not ready for a date, either. Good thing we cleared that up. We'll just grab a bite to eat. I'd hate to keep you out all day then return you home tired and hungry. Very bad manners. I'd like to say my parents raised me to know better." His gaze combined interest, concern, and a sincerity she couldn't deny.

"I-I know what you're thinking. Y-you don't have to be a mind reader." If he thought she'd want to recreate the scene depicted on the book cover, he was wrong.

How did all the air get sucked out of the room? Again, her thoughts went off on the wrong tangent.

Long-standing feelings of frustration consumed her, feelings she'd sought to overcome in Marc's presence yet failed each time he entered the office. She didn't intend to risk any more lives.

Besides, men that handsome only wanted one thing from women, genetically contaminated or not. Good looks, hypnotic charm, and innate confidence declared he seldom heard the word no.

Yet she had to find a workaround, a way to obtain her goal.

"And I don't need a psych degree to know you're curious. See you tomorrow morning, Dani. It's time to indulge." His smile said it all, but his gaze held a challenge, daring her to step outside her comfort zone.

Damn it. She needed his help to survive, plain and simple. However, maintaining an even keel with him present was a pipe dream. She should've known better.

He didn't say another word before turning to leave. Perhaps he flashed Darius a hand signal she hadn't seen. The dog's tail wagging and jaunty gait celebrated his master's victory, saying it all.

Holy hell.

Pictures formed in her mind from the pages she'd read earlier about a man who took what he wanted but gave back tenfold. A tickless silence of the frozen-geared universe filled her mind and saturated her numb thoughts, both biting and piercing in a mixture of horror and wonder.

What just happened?

Had she lost both the battle and the war? Marc misunderstood her interest, at least in part. Hutson could be in league with those sent to kill or capture her.

Chapter Two

Marc leaned against the building's corner, out of Daniele's sight line.

"Finally, after months of inane conversations, I win by default. What d'ya think, Darius? Take a victory however you can and under any circumstance?"

Brisk cool wind ruffled the dog's fur as Darius cocked his head, his expressive eyes declaring the obvious.

"I think so. I'd bet my PI license she's a spitfire underneath it all. Not to mention, she's at least curious about us. Might take a bit to figure out her baggage, but it'll be worth it. Hell, I think she's one part imp and two parts pixie underneath her veritable shields. The quiet ones have the greatest depth of character."

He'd never met anyone who connected with dogs better, understanding their needs and quieting their fears. The first time he'd taken one of his pups for a physical, Dani stepped in front of a charging mixed breed who'd slipped his leash. In a voice lacking fear she'd commanded the dog and settled him without a second's hesitation.

He'd worked with dogs for better than ten years and had never seen the likes of her ability.

Her combination of beauty and brains sealed his fate.

Though she'd seldom rested her gaze on him, he'd caught a glimmer of elfin sprite underneath the nervous and aloof façade. He loved the way her mouth started driving before her brain got in the car.

"I'll bet her neurologic meridian runs straight to her core."

Nothing but high-necked knit tops or buttoned shirts entailed her wardrobe, perhaps hiding a surgical scar or childhood injury. That insecurity entailed one of many he'd smash through to find the treasure held within.

"Damn, Darius. I know she's inexperienced, but how'd she reach adulthood without someone snatching her up?"

Perhaps no one had invested the time to forge a connection with the beautiful but skittish filly. If the records he'd run were correct, he had several years on her but damned if that would stop his pursuit.

Everything about her screamed innocence, something always avoided. Yet from their first meeting, he'd baited and courted, coaxed and teased, always shut down until she saw him as an escape.

His mind conjured the jokes of perversion his brothers would serve up since his general preference entailed a different type of woman for companionship. If the law considered her an adult, who was he to argue? A deep breath cleared the tangled emotions inspired by long, glossy waves and powder-blue eyes.

From his vantage point, the asphalt parking area hugged the brick building on two sides, sloping to the south. A long, winding lane cleaved the wooded barrier to the lonely highway beyond to complete the idyllic country setting.

Light reflecting off something shiny flashed across his face, the blip startling him even as it disappeared. Seventy-five yards west, a small movement among the pine trees caught his eye.

Last time he'd trekked through the woods, squirrels weren't using light-reflecting materials or spying on their neighbors.

Even if Daniele were so inclined to teach the woodland creatures the wonders of high-tech equipment, she'd instill proper manners. Considering her way with animals, she probably could.

Why is someone keeping tabs on the clinic?

A multitude of possibilities ranged from the normal drugs a vet would stock to catching a young woman leaving the office alone.

Darius alerted to Marc's reaction and the stranger's presence, sniffing the air to catch the voyeur's scent. Crouched and ready to spring, the shepherd's tight posture balanced aggression and self-discipline that could uncoil in a second's notice.

"Darius, *sook*! Find him, boy."

Various scenarios warped previous fantasies until his anger's slow burn urged him faster toward the woods. The prior night's snow continued to melt and created a slippery surface.

With such a strong lead, the intruder would make it to the highway before Darius brought him down. Of all the Schutzhund dogs he'd trained, this shepherd held the most promise, but remained limited by the force with which his paws could strike the ground. His air-scenting ability had dazzled judges and trainers alike during his first trial. At least, now, he had the bastard's scent.

If the slick operator who just hit on Dani doubled as a stalker, Marc would take pleasure in *educating* the man. If they couldn't catch him, he'd escort Dani home and ensure she had a decent security system, then return on Monday for a cozy one-on-one with Hutson.

"Darius, *gib laut*!"

Come on, boy. Tell me where you are.

After the dog's initial flash through thick underbrush, Marc followed the trail of moving briars and brambles until the shepherd advanced out of sight.

A deep-throated growl directed Marc's course adjustment down a small gorge through thick briars and tangles of vines, over fallen trees, and the small, slow-moving stream.

Marshy water splashed his jeans at the water's edge, the soft, muddy ground sucking at his booted heel. Balance became a precious commodity after stepping on a black snake.

Ahead, the slam of a vehicle's door acknowledged his prey finding safety as the steep incline slowed his progress. Squealing tires coincided with an engine's roar.

Yelling the command, "Darius, *platz,*" didn't guarantee his dog would obey and lay down instead of chasing the vehicle.

By the time Marc crested the hill at the wood's edge, Darius sat quietly by the road, huffing and whining his frustration.

"Damn it, didn't even get a look at the truck. At least you got the bastard's scent. We'll find him." Bending down, he rubbed his canine's chest. "Let's get back and see Dani home. I'll let Dr. Carari know something here has peaked a dirtball's interest."

Darius circled to heel despite continued glances down the one-lane road. Intermittent rumbles from his chest declared his job unfinished.

"Wonder if that was Hutson? He didn't strike me as stupid or incompetent. I think I'll do some digging this afternoon and see if I can find him. Damn thing is, he came in after us and left before we did, so all I have is a name, not his ride. Little to go on if he used a fake identity. Shame the vet's office doesn't have security cameras." Something he intended to mention during his next talk with the good doctor.

When he returned to the office, Dani's car was pulling off the lot. Considering her cornered and spooked demeanor, he wondered if she'd show at the dog trial.

"Damn and double damn. I'll crack her shell yet. At least I know the creep didn't follow her home. Wish I could swing by her house without her thinking *I'm* a stalker."

When she'd sparked his interest months prior, he ran her tags and a background check, curious to learn more. Seldom did he come up with mere framework of someone's life due to military scrubbing or WITSEC protection. He found no trails from either, which left him more bewildered and interested than ever.

Whatever she was hiding, he'd uncover. At last, he'd found a chink in her virtual shield and could delve through her darkest secrets. It'd take time, but he'd wipe that constant edge of fear from her gaze.

Chapter Three

Sleeping in her car confirmed Dani's new status as hobo, yet she still inhaled fresh air versus the stale waft pumped through subterranean pipes. She'd parked behind an abandoned shopping center and thanked heaven for moderate temperatures. The drive to Kober's farm lifted her spirits; she was that much closer to freedom.

Before stepping into bright morning sunshine, she took a moment to savor the freedom. Had she gone home the prior night, she could've already been confined to a twelve-by-sixteen cell.

This time, when she faced Marc, she'd hold to her plan and succeed. Her life depended on it.

Thinking of a similar genetic oddity's situation ensured caution in all endeavors. If not free, she couldn't investigate the power-hungry Washington official spearheading an elite organization. The task to imprison and harness talents of unique prodigies had begun years ago.

Ray McMillin, recruited in Maryland, had transferred to Minnesota to head one of several institutions throughout the country. Dani's perseverance and determination led to one young woman's release, but not without collateral damage. Deaths of the intermediary contact and support personnel weighed heavy on her conscience.

Franklin never made it out of the facility. His friend Daryl died in front of her during a late-night rendezvous. They gunned Jake down before he could spirit Callie to safety. Now, the killers hunted her. Shudders racked her body at the thought of an unmarked grave as her next bed.

A deep breath to settle her mind. Another to give her strength.

I'm going to watch the competition then ask Marc for help. New ID equals a new life in a distant part of the country.

A narrow path wound through the copse of pines leading from parking lot to trial field while low-hanging branches gave her a piecemeal view beyond. The rich scent of sap and wild onion lifted her spirits as only nature could. She'd miss a lot of things about Maryland, most of all, the chance to see Marc.

The prerequisite case of nerves when in his proximity prevented her from discerning the intentions of surrounding spectators. Coming to the trial was risky, considering she could've put five hundred miles between her and the men who wanted her at any cost.

So careful. She'd been so careful all these years yet would never regret her part in freeing Callie from the institution. No one should grow up in a not-so-gilded cage.

A tic at her right temple accompanied sweaty palms, excitement, and trepidation, all warring for supremacy over her body's reactions.

Schutzhund trials were always exciting with near-perfect harmony between dogs and handlers. Unlike TV shows, one could enjoy the quiet communing, allowing the scene to touch and enthrall the senses. Circling the field, she drew warm and admiring glances from a few spectators until dropping her gaze.

Marc stood between his two shepherds, each focused on his every move. Long, lean, and muscular, he wore jeans, chamois shirt, and a blue ball cap, the perfect picture of a relaxed alpha male on his day off. His presence felt like a weird cast of safety, excitement, and danger all rolled into one mesmerizing package.

Mere yards separated their two worlds. In closing the distance, she'd combine madness and sanity in an irrevocable twist involving serial killers, elite government forces, and, least of all, her heart.

"Hey, Marc." Her thin voice gained his attention and offered proof of his constant awareness, reminding her of a great predatory cat.

A smile both innocent and evocative flashed a small dimple in his chin. Short stubble added to the rugged looks keeping her attention riveted on his face.

"Hey, Dani, I was hoping you'd come today. Good to see you." With a natural and effortless grace, he closed the distance, his arms out to give her a light hug.

It was another slice of heaven.

Her mind stuttered. Lightning strikes contained less heat than his gaze. A light dotting of perspiration on her forehead added to her anguish as fire migrated from her face and disseminated through her body.

He didn't react. His welcoming expression remained a study in smooth, tranquil neutrality. She was unable to connect with the gaze capable of piercing diamonds like a tightly focused laser.

"Seriously? I've always wanted to watch this part of the competition.

I love seeing the fur kids so focused on their partners." The last word stuck in her mouth as the thought of Marc's likely *partners* came to mind. She pictured a beautiful, intelligent woman on his arm.

"My brother bailed on me at the last minute. You mind watching Pete while Darius is working the trial?"

Dani smiled. "Sure. We're good friends." As soon as she knelt, both shepherds whined then bounded around her with Marc's verbal release.

Nothing in the world dissolved stress as completely as dogs could. Dani accepted her due of pup kisses amid Marc's chuckle.

Shepherds, Malinoises, rottweilers, and bouviers dotted the perimeter along with the handlers wearing identifying arm bands. Various obstacles in the field, including a five-foot A-frame, moderate-sized jump, and a scaling wall tested each dog's agility, training, and willingness to work.

"Actually, I was kinda hoping to talk to you about something. After your boys finish, of course."

Yesterday's fiasco instigated a new page in her bid for continued freedom when Marc and Darius took off through the woods. As soon as Marc left the building, she'd sensed the stalker's presence, then stood at the bay window while dog and handler raced across the side yard.

"Sure. We can talk over lunch at Marty's. He loves my dogs. It's a great day to sit on the patio and eat." Intense curiosity lit his gaze.

The emergency bag stashed in her small subcompact contained everything she needed for life on the run. Instead of fleeing after her run-in with Hutson, she'd stayed in hopes of the possibility for more, if only a brief moment in time. What could a few hours hurt?

Months of Marc's harmless flirting had led to an innocent, if fragile trust as she grew to know more about his private investigative work and military training. Convincing him of her need for a new identity while keeping him in the dark would require a clever and shrewd conversation. She'd rehearsed it hundreds of times over the prior months. It always came off without a hitch.

Accepting his help necessitated treading a fine line between truth and personal space. A line that grayed each time in his presence.

"Sounds great. Darius and Pete ready?"

"Yep, they're both raring to go. We start as soon as the judge gives us the signal." Behind his calm and controlled façade, myriad questions burned in the depths of his gaze. This man was a multitasking puzzle solver.

Providence gave her a break with the start of the trial.

Darius heeled through a crowd of boisterous men without signs of distraction. Watching the shepherd work lightened her heart, his pure spirit and devotion visible in both gaze and step.

Phase two entailed navigating various jumps, walls, and other obstacles before finding the hidden object in the blind at the field's end. The strong-willed dog remained attentive to Marc and never faltered or veered from his course by his master's side. Conclusion of the performance earned verbal admiration from spectators.

The tug-of-war reward ended with a play bow and Darius' signature hop skip toward the sidelines. She could feel Marc's energy swelling with each stride.

"He did wonderful, listened to your every command along with your nonverbal." The shy smile she offered elicited one of Marc's sexy grins.

"Thanks. Pete here is a little more experienced. I think he'll do even better." Marc's hand signal prompted Pete's immediate response to heeling position.

Like Darius, Pete's steady concentration didn't falter, following his handler's orders and direction with precision and confidence. Considering Marc's line of work, she knew the dogs wouldn't shy from gunshots fired in a test of stability.

She didn't fare as well. It took all her strength not to buckle when the judge fired his trial shots.

Memories shook her entire frame and threatened her ability to stand. Concentrating on slow, even breaths helped her regain equilibrium and emotional control.

I'm too close to freedom to lose it now. This is daytime, not deep in the woods late at night. No one's going to die here.

The final part of the trial, a blind search, marked the handler's special training skills. Like Darius, Pete tracked an invisible scent trail to his target and earned the crowd's immediate approval and respect.

Security companies all over the country vied for the chance to own a dog trained by Marc Crofton. He'd worked hard and earned his reputation.

Sudden low growls grew in volume and disrupted the idyllic scene. With ears perked, Darius broke from his down stay and crouched beside her, ready to spring.

Kneeling down, she placed her hand on his neck to steady him.

Forward leaning posture and bunching hind muscles signaled his agitation amid low snarls which shocked nearby onlookers.

"What's the matter, Darius?" Such uncharacteristic behavior forced her to follow his gaze to the opposite side of the field where Clayton Hutson stood partially hidden by a man in a black business suit.

The shock knocked her flat on her butt.

Whether he reacted to the suit or Hutson didn't matter. Either could spell trouble.

Dani scooted closer to the dog and sifted her fingers through his fur.

This is so *not good.*

She had no chance of losing a tail now. Skilled in the art of evasive driving, she was not.

Marc's attention followed his dog's line of sight. Baring teeth and cracking knuckles preceded the rolling of his shoulders as if in preparation for a fight. The hard, flinty expression was something she'd not witnessed. Hutson's surprised countenance leeched anxiety as he returned Darius' stare.

"Darius, *sitz.*" Marc glared at Hutson as Pete heeled by his master's side to the finish mark, signaling the end of the trial.

Darius quivered with rage, the rumbling from his chest causing others to back away. The unpredicted outburst would cost him points, probably a failure, because of her. Her connection with the canine plus the prior day's catastrophe added up to the dog's protective streak shooting into overdrive.

Still, she stood, waiting, watching with a now unobstructed view of Hutson. Spectators on the opposite side of the field dispersed. Not many cared for growling dogs focused in their direction.

"Dani, stay there." The look Marc shot over his shoulder warned her not to move. "Darius, *hier.*" The dog zipped forward as if shot from a cannon. Though he headed for his master, his attention focused on the copse of trees, his constant growl filling the air.

Curses drifted back as Hutson ran, angling toward the parking lot. The back of his loose t-shirt bulked over something at his waistband, a swath of shine visible seconds before he disappeared through the trees. Hutson carried a gun.

If I leave now, there's no coming back, no seeking help from Marc, no new identity, and little chance of survival.

In addition, Marc just established himself as a target but wouldn't understand why unless she explained. She couldn't leave him vulnerable with no understanding of the danger.

From the end of the field, Marc ran with his shepherds on either side. Barely restrained rage radiated from Darius, the contagion spreading to Pete, who now echoed his thunderous fury as they zipped past Marc and down the footpath to the parking lot.

Seconds passed as Dani stood rooted to her spot. Handler and dogs were swallowed by the shadows, but Marc wouldn't give up even if his prey made it to a vehicle's relative safety. She knew he'd dig until reaching the bottom of the whole sordid mess.

Reputation and months of flirting confirmed his focus and single-minded pursuit of something he wanted. She'd trapped herself in a world of fate's design, a life of guns and death, betrayal and deceit.

Confused by such an irregular and frustrating display, the judge standing on the sideline frowned and shrugged his shoulders before calling out the next competitor. A Malinois heeled beside his handler to the starting position.

Dani waited, fear seizing every muscle in silent agony. A loud bark of a different kind froze the breath in her lungs.

A gunshot. Not from the judge's trial gun.

Cursing. Squealing wheels.

Neatly trimmed grass held the remnants of last night's dew as she bolted across the field, heedless of the competition. By the time she reached the parking area, her mind had already conjured Marc dead due to her inability to make a decision and act sooner.

He didn't deserve it. No one did.

She'd brought this stygian, treacherous world to his door.

"Marc? Marc! Where are you?" Row after row of cars, vans, and SUVs blocked her sightline, most containing wire crates and other training paraphernalia.

Tears flowed as her heart kicked hard against its cage, trying to find tranquility in a world of insanity. In the distance, she heard other voices behind her but ignored them.

"Over here, Dani. Shit."

The pain in his tone induced enough guilt to rip a hole in her chest. The disaster, instigated from her secret purgatory, now encompassed innocents without giving the advantage of seeing its approach. Marc stood by the hood of a parked car with blood soaking his shirt.

"Oh, God, he shot you." Stumbling over a large grassy clump, she landed on her hands and knees in the center aisle between two rows of parked vehicles. By the time she pushed up then rounded on his position, sobs choked her throat.

"No. Not me, Darius. His shoulder." Marc crouched to pick up the hundred-pound shepherd as if he weighed nothing. "Help me get him to the vet."

Without looking back, he strode toward his vehicle. "Pete, *fuss*. Let's go."

The black-and-gold dog whined and sidestepped to keep an eye on Marc along with his surrounding area.

"I'll get the door." Guilt cemented any further words in her throat as she opened the door. A whole new and terrible scenario laid out before her as she slid over the camouflaged seat cover. Marc settled Darius beside her with the dog's head in her lap.

Several confused minutes later, she held pressure with the cloth torn from Marc's shirt against fur stained with crimson. Pete hopped behind her on the folded-down section, his panting breath warm on her neck.

"Why would anyone hurt Darius? Did you get a look at the shooter's face?" In her heart, she knew the truth, but begged fate to provide an alternative, to have mercy just once.

"I saw someone at the vet's office yesterday. They took off when Darius started barking. Too bad your boss doesn't have video surveillance in or around the building." Marc gunned the engine, speeding between rows of parked vehicles before skidding onto the dirt road leading to the highway.

"I'm so sorry, Darius." Crooning in the dog's ear, she couldn't stop the tears from coating the dog's fur. "This is all my fault."

"Dani, you can't control other people's actions, only your own. I'll catch the bastard." Marc opened his cell and thumbed the screen. Years of training expedited the cliff-notes version of his close encounter.

With emergency arrangements made, the chime of his cell startled her. He looked at the text then secured the device.

"Dani. I wasn't sure yesterday if that bastard was after you, or perhaps drugs in the vet's office, or even me. Today, it seems pretty clear he's focused on you."

Marc glanced out the window as he took a deep breath. When his gaze swung back and met hers in the rearview, she couldn't look away despite guilt radiating from every sweat gland now working overtime.

"Hon, after we get Darius settled, I'm gonna take you to my home. You'll be safe there."

"What about Darius? What if they come back for him?" With her past racing to imprison her, the present in chaos, and the future in doubt, how could she in good conscience further embroil Marc?

"I have three brothers. Conner will stay at the vet's office until Darius is stable and ready to come home."

Jesus. Now I'm going to endanger his family too?

"The bleeding has stopped with pressure. He's been shot but his elbow hurts, also. Make sure you ask Dr. Carari to take a look at it."

Fear infused each cell of her gray matter, transcending her ability to organize thoughts.

"How do you know that?" His gaze in the rearview took on a probing quality.

"Um, just the way he's holding his leg. You pick up things like that working for a veterinarian."

I need a gag.

If she didn't pull herself together, she'd end up in a not-so-nice concrete cell, the type other prodigies called home.

The rest of the ride passed in strained silence. Would Marc offer protection if he knew about her past and connection to the Think Tank geniuses hunting her, or would he turn her over to the military?

Sweat beaded her upper lip and forehead, her nerves tethered to the cyclonic pressure building in her mind. Her bid to join thoughts and form a cohesive picture was denied.

Chapter Four

Skidding tires flung loose gravel in the parking lot with their abrupt stop. Marc cut the engine and pocketed his keys while Dani scanned the perimeter to make certain no one lay in wait.

He wasted no time in circling the vehicle and snatching the door open.

As Marc lifted his dog, two more SUVs ground to a halt on either side of them. The drivers' doors opened to reveal similar versions of Marc, each with the muscle and stocky build of a linebacker.

"What've you gotten into now, Marc? Seems I'm always bailing you guys out of one scrape or another." From his demeanor and Marc's prior descriptions, this was Conner, assuming responsibility for his younger brother's welfare.

"Looks like the bastard from yesterday shot him." Marc's tight expression echoed in both siblings. "Dani, my brothers Conner and Julien. Guys, this is Dani."

Both armed men nodded absently as Marc carried Darius toward the front door. Pete hopped down from the back seat and stayed close.

"Pick the lock, Julien. I don't wanna wait—" The roar of another engine drowned out the end of Marc's sentence. "Never mind, she's here."

Dr. Carari bounded out of her car, keys in hand. "Hi, Marc. Let's get him inside and see what we've got."

"Pete, *achtung*!"

Instant attention to the perimeter signified the dog's understanding and obedience.

Shifting shadows sent an ominous chill to circle Dani's spine as she followed Marc and her boss through the waiting room and into the back.

"I'll turn on the x-ray, Dr. Carari." Sidestepping Marc, she hurried to grab the clipboard in preparation for the long and harried experience ahead. Her mind's eye reversed the roles, with Marc bleeding out and her worthless apologies falling on dead ears.

"Julien, go with Dani, I'll stay with Marc and the doc." Conner's command received no rebuttal as Julien shadowed her movements.

"Sorry to meet you under such dire circumstances." Julien's voice, though polite, held the distraction of one solving a problem on the fly. "Have you known Marc long?"

"A few months."

A few months of procrastinating. And yes, this could all have been avoided.

Under such perilous conditions, giving as little information as possible might save a life. In fact, it might save all their lives.

"Hmm." He canted his head to the side, his brow furrowed.

With no time to decipher his thoughts or motives, she decided that trusting Marc's family proved her best option. Setting the controls on the x-ray machine, she watched through the glass partition as the veterinarian tried to position Darius under the cone's light after listening to his heart and lungs.

"Dani, switch places. He's too antsy and has too much pain to hold still. I need you to calm him down, so I don't have to sedate him before surgery."

Marc used his weight to hold Darius, who continued to struggle on the cold steel table.

"Hold on, Marc. Let me handle him. He knows me." Dani moved to the head of the table, placing her hands on either side of the dog's face and leaning in close. Resting her forehead against the dog's, she murmured softly, rubbing her face back and forth.

Marc took a step back as his dog whined then lay quietly. "Damn. Never seen the likes of that before. How do you do it?"

Now wasn't the time for confessions or self-recriminations. Without hesitation, she shrugged, smoothing the dog's coat and whispering in his ear.

"Okay, I'm ready to snap the shot," Dr. Carari said as Darius lay still and in position.

The low buzz signaled exposure. After two more shots, Darius was ready for surgical prep.

"Get him settled in the OR and start setting up, Dani. I'll be there shortly after examining the x-rays." Despite her sometimes abrupt manner—compassion, knowledge, and skill more than compensated for Sarah Carari's lack of tact. Her hands remained steady and smooth when it came time to work.

Setting up and observing surgeries didn't give Dani experience in assisting, which now put her out of her element. "Marc, carry him back here to the operating room, and we'll get him ready. I'll need to shave some of his fur."

A gnarled gut and bloody flashbacks reminded her why she avoided entanglements of all kinds, free of emotional vulnerability—until panic had forced her to accept Marc's offer. She hadn't shown him the decency of forewarning. The evil hunting her not only carried weapons but now enjoyed using them regardless of location or others present.

The next two hours passed in nervous apprehension as Marc, Conner, and Julien watched her boss from a discreet distance. The wound was dissected and the bullet removed from the shepherd's shoulder. A tinny *plink* as it landed on the surgical tray reminded Dani the next one was meant for her if she didn't run. Fast.

"Looks like a thirty-two caliber. Close range?" Julien glanced at his older brother.

"Didn't see the shooter, but I'm guessing twenty yards." Marc shook his head, his hands clenching and unclenching at his sides.

"Yesterday's bastard, or do you think this ties in with Nate?" Conner's probing visual exam could dissect a person's thoughts if they stood still long enough.

Dani squirmed under his scrutiny, shuffling her weight from one foot to the other.

"Dunno, but Darius will pick him out without a problem." Anger and a thirst for payback echoed in Marc's bared teeth and slightly flaring nostrils. Marc glanced from Dani to Conner, then to Julien before frowning. "Ease up on Dani, guys. This isn't her fault."

The admonishment granted her a little reprieve as Conner again focused on Darius.

Julien placed the offending metal in a small baggie. "It's gonna take time to get the results back. Any way to track your shooter?"

"No, didn't see his vehicle either."

"Hell, man, what good are you?" Conner's sympathetic expression softened the words.

"Not much, it seems." A subdued voice and heavy sigh delineated Marc's weariness.

Touching another human in recent years normally produced a shudder she couldn't control, but Marc's unearned self-disgust prompted her to move close and place her arm around his waist.

"I'm sorry, Marc. I really am."

His response, though distracted, was to pivot and hug her tight before his lips brushed her forehead. She pulled back, awed to have initiated a comforting touch, one offered and received with such tenderness.

He hadn't shivered with disgust or drawn his eyebrows together in a fierce frown before declaring her unfit to be considered human.

Julien and Conner exchanged smirks until Marc cleared his throat.

Dr. Carari's calm, efficient manner complemented her tone and the organized mind analyzing facts as presented. "It'll take a few hours for him to wake up enough to leave. I'll stay here with him, but I do have to report this to the police. Marc, I know you're a private investigator. Any ideas on this?"

"I've no problem talking to the police. We might need their help before this is over. The more eyes searching for the bastard, the sooner we find him." Marc stepped forward and let his light touch flow over his beloved canine, smoothing the hair in place like a loving parent.

"I'll do the meet-and-greet for now, Marc. How about you talk to them after you get Dani settled somewhere. I assume she'll be staying at your house temporarily?" Conner hesitated on the last word.

"Guys. I appreciate the offer, but I think maybe I should be going—"

"Yes, she'll be staying with me." Marc's assurance seemed to settle Conner and Julien's minds, their expressions declaring the topic closed.

"What if...?" She couldn't let anyone else get hurt.

All because nature's design flaw decided to zing me with a weird DNA sequence.

"Dani, we'll handle it." With a last loving stroke of the shepherd's neck, Marc ushered her out of the office and into the unknown. So contrary to the carefree, charismatic enigma during his dogs' appointments, he was now all business.

Her presence put them all at risk. She hadn't spoken up to warn them of encroaching danger. Hence, she deserved to take Darius' place.

The stalkers were just winding up and would kill anyone in their path. They'd proven that much, time and again.

Chapter Five

"It's better for you all if I leave now, Marc. I don't want anyone else hurt. Please, just take me to my car. I've already got a bag packed. I've taken care of myself for years."

Dani's profile offered a view that squeezed Marc's heart. A tear slid down her cheek before she glanced out the SUV's window and swept it away.

Her responses were too automatic and occurred without hesitation, rehearsed lines to the most obvious questions. He sensed they'd just scratched the surface of the situation, her stalker the beginning of a convoluted nightmare.

His instincts usually proved spot-on.

Her reflected gaze lowered and avoided his attempts to decipher the guilt in their depths, a swirling chasm of hidden information, a chapter concealed as she shunned the world. Pete jumped forward to the second-row seat and nuzzled her neck.

"That means you were prepared for this eventuality and have an idea about what's going on. Is there a crazy ex-boyfriend in your background?"

He'd never seen his dogs take to anyone the way they doted on the young woman, aloof with people but immediate friend to animals. It was affection returned without hesitation, every time.

The way she'd settled Darius prior to surgery instilled equal parts confusion and awe.

"No. I swear I've never seen that man before yesterday. I have no idea who he is." Her version of omitting a subtle truth entailed her gaze sliding away toward the stroboscopic effect of the telephone poles. *I didn't ask the right question*.

"But you do know what he wants... elsewise, why have a bag packed? Listen, you're in some kind of trouble. You know I'm a private investigator. I'll help you, but I need to know what I'm facing." He let his tone radiate authority, insinuating he'd ask questions until delving to the core of the matter.

Another tear slipped down her cheek. "Marc, I don't want you involved in this hell. Dr. Carari called last night after you talked with her. She's heard the news stations report the latest victim of a serial killer. I was afraid it was Hutson—that he'd set his sights on me and knew where I lived." She pulled at the collar of her mock-neck sweater.

Marc linked her half-truth to the high-collared tops she seemed to prefer.

"Obviously, I'm already involved. Moreover, the chance of today's shooter being the serial killer is unlikely. The MOs are radically different." He sighed, knowing he'd missed some vital point.

"Look. You're wearing the same jeans and top you had on yesterday, so it's safe to say you didn't go home last night. Let me guess, you slept in your car. Dani, what the hell is going on? And who else *is* involved." The façade she'd built for public disclosure hadn't fooled him and didn't sit well.

Her virtual clone in the window revealed the contradiction in tightening around her mouth and slumping shoulders, making him wonder how long she'd been in hiding and from whom? Why?

Marc had learned to cut through bullshit and excise facts and feelings with little effort through extensive training. Even now, he knew she wasn't ready to let him in, ask for help, or accept his protection. Instead, she wanted to take off and live in the shadows, probably what she'd done for years.

No freaking way.

"What have I gotten myself into?" Her mumbled words defied clarity of their situation.

"We'll figure this out, together."

Her gaze jerked up to meet his. "It isn't fair to get you involved in my trouble."

"Don't worry about it. You heard my older brother. It's my nature to bask in it whenever and wherever possible."

A half hour of quiet riding helped formulate a plan, if lacking particulars. He didn't know her well enough to push specific buttons, but he devised a way to find them. By the time he'd turned off route 34 to his home, he had the makings of a solid strategy. His quiet enigma had kept her face averted, another thing he'd soon change.

"You have a house on the beach." The statement lacked inflection, as if she'd known and already been inside. He wondered what research she'd done on him, either from curiosity or the desire for something more.

"I do."

His SUV rolled to a stop in front of the bifurcated brick walkway leading to his front and back porch. All the while, he tested certain puzzle pieces in various configurations, looking for a fit, a beginning. The mental tally of facts didn't add up to the smallest snippet of the whole picture.

She'd already stated she needed help. Their tenuous relationship formed after casual conversations had paved the way. So, why hadn't she already approached him? On the other hand, maybe she'd knocked on his door one day but hadn't followed through.

It gave him pause to wonder what else she knew about him. With enough time, he could manipulate her interest and curiosity to his advantage while gaining access to the darkest reaches of her mind. The question remained, did they have the time?

Using his knowledge and training, he'd uncover whatever horrific experiences engendered her guarded demeanor and determination to blend into the background.

Afterward, he'd take satisfaction in helping her develop a new way of life, a new way of thinking and perceiving those around her. He'd waited months for this break and intended to make the most of it. She intrigued him on so many levels.

Dani didn't wait for him to open the passenger door, clearly not accustomed to being treated as a lady—another thing he'd obliterate, that and exchanging her baggy jeans and sweaters for soft knits to accentuate the shapely body which lay beneath.

An attempt to escort her along the brick pathway with a hand at her waist elicited her sidestep when he reached out. She waited beside the bottom step, frowning at the back door.

"Problem?" He asked.

"Oh, ah, no. Um, just trying to picture you in here with two huge dogs."

Her mind's wheels must've spun like a racecar skidding over the rumble strip with no brakes, no cello foam barrier, and no firewall. When she started to climb the steps, he halted her with a hand out.

"Pete will search the house before we enter."

"No need. It's clear."

Despite the absolute confidence in her tone, her answer made little sense. "How do you know that?"

"Ah, oh. I just figured so because the door is intact." Her gaze ventured over the backyard, to the small waves lapping at the short beach. Would the sounds soothe her troubled dreams?

Keeping his movements slow and steady, he opened the door. After a quick hand signal, Pete darted into the kitchen, ears pricked and tail out. Search mode.

After padding throughout the home, he returned and sat by his handler's side sporting a wide doggy grin. Without attempting to touch her, Marc gestured to enter, observing the different expressions lighting her face.

A grin slid into place when cataloguing his kitchen.

No, she's not been inside before.

Instead of sideling against his knee, Pete rubbed Dani's leg and whined. In response, she sank cross-legged to the floor beside the kitchen island. Though sheets of black silky curls covered her expression, Pete tunneled through the mass to lick at her face, determined to commune with a friend.

"It's gonna be all right, boy. You've got the weight of the world on your shoulders now, but Darius is gonna be fine, home soon with you and your dad." She didn't look at Marc. Guilt was a heavy burden etched in every line of her body.

"You know, you're the only person beside my brothers who can get close to him without my command. Not to mention the fact you are the *only* one whose emotions he responds to with such enthusiasm."

"I like animals. They usually like me, too."

"All right, then. I'll fix us a couple sandwiches. We can sit on the back porch and figure out our next step. It's protected from the north wind and perfect for a cool afternoon."

Knowing what I intend to do and getting you to agree to it might be tricky.

Either way, he'd keep her safe.

"Considering the way animals respond to you, I'm surprised you don't have a dog of your own."

"I move around too much." Her words came out in a rush while still avoiding eye contact.

And still hiding...

"But you have a cat?"

Her mouth formed an O as she briefly glanced up.

She couldn't lie worth a damn. Even the simplest questions brought up her defensive walls. Soon he'd not allow her to hide, be it through cuddling his dogs or shielded by the raven's wing of lustrous curls.

"Well, actually... no. No, I don't. I said that to avoid getting you too involved in my problems." Gazing down, she let her hair slide forward like a rolling cloud of silk.

Bingo.

Right on schedule. If she possessed memories of a time not having to look over her shoulder, current circumstances scattered those recollections to obscure regions of her soul. He intended to find each fragment, however miniscule, and piece them together, negating the desire to conceal who or what she was.

"Hm." Among the scant available records he'd found, her house was titled to an offshore corporation. His brother was still trying to hack documents to locate the owner.

After failing to catch the intruder the prior day, Marc had driven by her lane leading to a small, modest bungalow tucked deep on an isolated wooded lot.

"What type of dog would you like?" Opening the fridge revealed several lidded containers stacked on the middle shelf, along with bottled water, sodas, and tea above.

"I'd love a golden retriever, but any dog would be wonderful. They're so honest, so open and compassionate. I kinda fostered one overnight a few months ago. What an incredible feeling to have him sleep on my bed."

A small rumble echoed in Pete's chest as he bowled her over on her back to play.

The ensuing grapple and wrestling reminded him of how the dogs played with him, and only him. "They've never tumbled with anyone else like that. You really do have a way with them. No wonder Dr. Carari loves you."

"He's hungry. Can I give him some food?"

How does she know that?

"Sure. I only gave him a light breakfast this morning."

"Figured you wouldn't fill his belly before the trial. I'll give it to him." The ear-to-ear grin was the first to reach her eyes.

Focusing on Marc, she tilted her head. The clarity of her gaze seemed to allow a thorough inspection of his thoughts, as if she examined each one in turn, determining if he was worthy of her trust.

"I feed raw. There are two covered bowls in the bottom of the fridge. Grab yourself a soda or bottled water while you're there." He set the mayonnaise aside to watch her snuggle one last time with Pete.

With a dancer's grace, she stood and pivoted as he cut the turkey sandwiches in half. "Sorry it's not a nicer meal. Wasn't expecting company."

The pop of the soda can surprised him given his expectation to see a water bottle in hand. Watching her bend over to grab the dog's bowl, he admired the view.

Not cool.

Metal ringing on the tile floor accompanied her choking and scrambling to retrieve the dropped bowl. Immediately, she hurried to set it down in the corner for Pete, her awkward movements and forehead's pink tinge revealing embarrassment before she ducked her head.

"You all right?" Again, she left him confused.

"Yeah."

Another round of coughing accompanied by a groan made him wonder. "You sure? Take a sip of your drink."

"Absolutely. I should've known better than to try to do two things at once. Not a good multi-tasker." Several gaps in the curtain of her hair framed her red-tinged visage.

"All right, let's eat."

He'd been deciphering her nonverbal cues since their first meeting. Dani turned skittish each time he touched her, yet offered comfort without hesitation. She liked to read hot romance books, but her manner screamed inexperience. Eye contact remained minimal unless engaged in conversations about animals.

He wondered if she'd suffered a period of abuse, then grew a hardened protective shell. The way she kept her neck covered could suggest physical assault, yet sheer determination dominated it all.

Time to earn her trust.

Marc expected the flinch when his fingers brushed hers ever so lightly in offering the plate.

As he headed to the back porch, a glance over his shoulder made him wonder, *how'd she know where Pete normally ate?* He'd picked up the dogs' mats before leaving the house and hadn't replaced them.

She stumbled over the threshold.

"Watch your step." Curiosity made him stop after stepping down in the cool afternoon air, pausing to see where she'd sit. "Ladies first."

Two wrought-iron sofas with thick padding and a matching round table for six gave her a choice of seats, little surprise she picked the far end of a sofa. Taking a seat beside her, he watched her square her shoulders and wondered what truths she hid from herself and at what age she'd developed such virtual armor.

Inane pleasantries flowed easily throughout the meal with the afternoon sun warming their cheeks. The slight breeze rustling through her hair made him wish she weren't so aloof. He longed to feel its silken mass slide through his fingers.

Her throat worked as if swallowing a large lump. "Went down the wrong way," said after choking and reaching for her drink.

Speaking in the broadest terms, she gave away little to nothing of her personal life. When asked direct questions, deflections rose with a question of her own. Her skill in conversation rivaled any good interrogator. He knew little more than when they'd first met.

"Okay, Dani, time to come clean. What's going on? I need to know in order to help." Taking her plate, he made light contact before leaning to set them both on the wicker table.

A quiet inhalation. She turned her face to the side, gazing toward the budding camellia bushes. The napkin suffering her fingers' restless energy took a beating. Small pieces of shredded paper littered the area by her feet.

"Okay. I—"

The cartoon jingle of his cell phone stopped the rest of her sentence. "Hold on, it's Conner. Probably has an update on Darius. I'll take our plates in and be right back."

A small rush of air from closing the kitchen door brushed his hair forward. Immediate settling of his stomach indicated how much her close proximity affected him.

"Hey, bro, how's Darius?" A niggling doubt kept surfacing since his shepherd's x-ray. Dani had known about the elbow injury in the vehicle. The load of crap spouted in the car hadn't made sense. Her presence had the immediate effect of quieting Darius, despite the dog's pain. There existed a sense, or aura about her he could neither explain or deny.

"He's awake and gonna be fine. Lots of rest, no steps, yada, yada. Want me to take him home for now?" Conner's offer came as no surprise.

"No, drop him by on your way. Caring for him will give Dani something to do. Any luck with her car?"

"Nothing there worth noting. It's registered to the same offshore account as the house, which I'm sure you already knew. Haven't gotten anything further. We've not been able to hack those records, tighter than a witch's ass."

A long lecture usually followed the deep sigh whistling through the wire, so Marc waited in silence.

"Marc, we don't have forensics back, but the bullet was the same caliber used to kill the other women who've gone missing in this area. Police haven't located all the bodies."

"O—kay. It is a fairly common bore. Could be a coincidence." The tangled knot of sour dread lodged in his stomach earlier now jumped to his throat.

"Not when you factor in each victim is estimated to be in her early twenties with long black hair, thin frame, and stood between five-six and five-eight."

"Shit."

"Each woman had been tortured for days before they were killed. Somebody's looking for information."

"Double shit."

"Yeah, not so much coincidence now, huh? Who is she tangled with? Mob?"

"Don't know yet, but I'll find out." His brother's last question shifted one of the puzzle pieces he'd juggled for months. The question was, did it fit?

Dani spoke fondly of a dog who'd only spent one night with her, yet gave comfort. The manner in which she'd talked suggested the night held great significance, maybe great tragedy. She didn't accept solace from people the same as she did from dogs.

Dani seemed to share traits with his brother Nate's significant other. Both were quiet, unassuming, and secretive. It made him wonder if they were alike in other ways.

A former black-ops teammate was murdered several months ago. It could be another coincidence that Jake was killed around the same time Dani experience some significant trauma. Since then, women began disappearing, all bearing resemblance to Dani. A coincidence of timing?

Just because the shapes were right didn't mean the pieces fit in the way he suspected.

"Figure this out sooner rather than later. We don't know what kind of reach the Think Tank administrator has, or how many reinforcements wait at their disposal. Nate gets edgy when Callie's in danger."

"Dani mentioned the serial killer."

"I've talked with Jasers, who's assigned to the murders. He asked us for canine help if there's another body. If we dig up anything else, he's gonna want to know about your girl. I didn't give him her description... for now."

"Definitely in her best interest to stay here until we find out more." Marc again wondered how someone as quiet and sedate as Dani wound up in so much trouble.

"Don't waste time. I'll be by in 'bout an hour." Conner disconnected on a heavy sigh.

Snapping the cell in its case cemented Marc's resolve. It was time to forge ahead to keep Dani safe.

She hadn't moved, but Pete lay beside her and rested his head on her lap. If she thought to use him as a buffer, it wasn't going to happen.

Once seated, he gestured toward Pete. "He's not permitted on the furniture." Allowing just a little roughness to infuse his voice brought her gaze up in confusion and surprise.

"Oh, ah, sorry. I saw some dog hair on... sorry."

With no command spoken, Pete jumped off the sofa and avoided looking in Marc's direction. Considering how many times both animals sat there on *his* lap, Pete's normal response should've resembled something of a yawn.

Again, odd. "Okay, Dani... or should I call you *Penny*?"

"Wh-what?" The sudden inhalation combined with widened eyes and dropped jaw confirmed his suspicion.

"I thought so. Now I need specifics." He gentled his voice as if talking to a stubborn child, recognizing the mental wall erected on the fly.

"H-how'd you know?"

"Doesn't matter. I'm going to help, but you have to be up front and honest."

"If I talk, they'll kill you." Hands fisted on her thighs before scrubbing one over her eyes.

"They've already shot Darius. You think they won't try for me next?"

"Oh, God. This can't be happening. I have to leave. I'm so sorry I got you involved, Marc." Brushing the hair from her face, she pushed to her feet.

In one swift movement, he grasped her hips and gently tugged her down beside him, but slid one hand around her waist in a subtle degree of invasion.

She froze, solid as a rock.

"No, you need to tell me what's going on. I don't want you hurt."

"Ah..."

"The women murdered by the serial killer—do you realize they all bear a resemblance to you?"

"I've heard that, yes."

"Someone's looking for information."

"How do you know?"

"It hasn't been released to the media yet, but each woman was tortured."

"And you'd know that because you work closely with the police?"

"Yes."

"I didn't have anything to do with those murders."

"Of course not, Dani, but you are connected, however loosely."

"I've never gone hurt anyone except in self-defense." Dani squirmed and looked away."

"Wouldn't suspect you would. I do, however, find it amazing just how many character traits you bear in common with a friend. In fact, I bet Callie *is* a mutual friend."

"Callie?" Dani's face paled, her jaw slackened to form a perfect O.

"Yeah, the young woman you helped escape from the Think Tank." A statement more than a question, it opened the door and invited her to expound. He prayed he was right and that she'd pick up where he left off.

"Well, kinda, in a way."

"How do you know her?" He let his fingers stroke her back over the knit material in hopes of loosening muscles tighter than a board.

She eyed the exits like a cornered animal. "Actually, I've never met her."

He arched a brow and waited. "Really?"

"I met Franklin online. He's one of the men who helped her escape from the institution. He put me in touch with his friend, Daryl, who died soon afterward." Cornered prey displayed less wariness.

"Hmm, convenient that I can't talk to either since they're both dead, don't you think?"

After twining her fingers for the hundredth time, she fisted her hands until her knuckles bleached white.

"So, how did you find Franklin? How did you help? I know you weren't 'with' him. He was a dedicated, married man."

Tears brimmed in her eyes when she met his gaze. "Now he's dead, and his wife is all alone because of me."

"His wife died in a car accident. It looked like someone tampered with her brakes."

"Oh, God. No, no, no. I never meant for any of that to happen. I just wanted Callie to be free. She deserves that much, doesn't she?" Sudden spasms of her abdomen threatened the reappearance of a half-digested lunch.

"Deep breaths, sweetheart. Take it easy." Marc softened his tone, caressing her with his voice and willing her to calm. Even through her thick fall of hair he felt the thinness of her frame. She couldn't afford to lose the calories.

Tears brimming her eyes were too much to bear as they damned his soul for pushing. "We're just going to sit here for now. You're safe."

"Damn it. Damn it all to hell."

"How did you know Callie was a prisoner? And don't tell me Franklin. He wouldn't have divulged such information." The firm statement was based on a growing conviction rooted in observation and intuition, like when watching a suspenseful movie and the music swelled to a crescendo, the audience waiting with tensed muscles and dry mouth for something terrible to happen.

"It's kind of a long story."

"We've got all day."

"I—you're not the only one who likes to snoop. I 've run across a guy, a political power player who heads up an organization overseeing various facilities."

"Facilities that hold specific prodigies?"

"Yes. I found out where he lived and snooped through his stuff. He was responsible for hiring administrators at each institution."

"He hired Ray."

"Yes. Ray lived on his parents' farm here in Maryland after they died, but he moved to Minnesota for the job. He comes back intermittently for meetings and vacation."

"That's dangerous work, Dani."

"Yeah, I almost got caught, then decided to lay low for a while."

"What's the name of this CEO?"

"Holland Freeman. From there, I discovered information about Ray, Callie, and the men hired to watch her. Then I found Jake and Franklin through Ray's digital records, at least, what there was of them."

"How'd you know Franklin would free Callie?"

"Leap of faith."

"Do you share Callie's gift on the keyboard?"

"Gift? What gift? I'm adequate, but no genius. I've learned a few specific tricks over the years."

"Okay, how and when did you meet with Franklin?"

"Never. Everything was digital, anonymous."

"And Ray?"

"Is one scary bastard. I've met several like him in my life avoid them at all cost." A firmness about her lips telegraphed a fortification of the mental barricade sliding into place.

Another half-truth.

"Why not go to the police?" He offered his handkerchief when she sneezed. What he wanted was to hold her and give comfort the same way she'd settled Darius when in pain.

"They killed Daryl. Right. In. Front of me. I-I was scared. He told me to run..." A broken sob followed by dry heaving prevented her from continuing.

While her story stretched the limits of his imagination, her heartfelt tears and sincerity in helping others validated her objective.

His brother Nate described how a young woman had helped Callie escape the Think Tank bastards *and* tried to warn his brother's ex-teammate, Jake, to watch his step. That meeting had ended in the friend's assassination and the murderer hunting Dani.

"So, is Penny or Daniele your real name?"

"I'm not sure what my name is. I was adopted. I like Dani." She nibbled a corner of her lip then stopped before meeting his gaze.

"So, they're trying to get Callie back and silence you for witnessing Daryl's murder. Those bastards at the institution don't give up. They must have seen you."

"We were in the woods. It was dark. I didn't think they'd gotten a good look at me. I thought it'd be a safe place. Then Jake... He was ex-Special Forces, like you and your brothers... I'm so sorry." A deep stillness created a cocooning effect despite the chilling ramifications of her confession.

"You've outrun assassins twice. Not many people live to say that."

"Doesn't matter. They won't stop coming. Someone's searching for me now, but I'm not sure if it's the Think Tank bastards or not."

"You haven't felt safe for quite a while, have you? I'm thinking long before intervening on Callie's behalf."

"True, and I'm tired of looking over my shoulder."

As he massaged her back and sifted his fingers through the fine satin of her hair, it occurred to him that after months of attempting to forge a connection, she'd landed in his lap because of a threat to them both.

Still, the depth of her eyes held information her mouth refused to vocalize. Earning her trust and bridging the gap between them would require time and a special skill set. Fate held the reins on the former. He'd spent years acquiring the latter. He'd probe until reaching the bottom of the nightmare.

Judging by her partial thaw toward him, he surmised two things. Up to some point she'd lived a relatively normal life, considering her ability to offer and receive comfort. If evil lay beneath a caring façade, he'd sense it. His instincts seldom proved wrong.

Some type of trauma or brutal betrayal resulted in suppressed emotions buried so deep she feared life itself, forcing both a physical and mental retreat.

That formed the base of his working hypothesis. Time would see it proven or revised.

The quiet stretched out as he contemplated what little he knew of her past and present circumstances. To call her complicated was an understatement, worthy of a politician glossing over catastrophic events.

“I can’t imagine you slept much in your car last night. Why don’t you lean back and close your eyes for a bit?” Looking at her now, he wondered what other horrors she’d survived. Her aloofness was born of long-standing practice, unlike the jumpy fear one experienced from a new threat.

It was obvious now why she’d researched him and his private investigations firm. She wanted to run and hide. He wouldn’t let her do that, but was grateful she’d laid the ground work which formed a measure of trust.

It wasn’t long before her breathing evened out in sleep. No doubt, she hadn’t slept much since Hutson left the vet’s office.

Not wanting to disturb her rest, he texted Conner to come in quietly with Darius while continuing to formulate his plan.

Chapter Six

A gun held to the stranger's temple clicked with the cocking of its hammer. Its front sight left a round, red imprint against pale flesh. Death was imminent.

They'd woken the husband then bound and gagged his wife before forcing him to kneel before the psychopath.

"Please, please don't kill him. He didn't do anything wrong," Dani cried as she focused on the man's eyes, the gaze begging her to help. From her kneeling position, she reached forward to push the barrel away. "I'll do it!"

Her entire body jerked with the sudden blast as if the projectile had thrown her back. Warm sticky blood spattered her clothes and face. The force of the shot hurtled the bound man against the bed before he crumbled to the floor, dead.

The terrified wife screamed behind her gag even as the next shots slammed into her chest. Crimson pooled in a widening circle between her breasts. Her pleading gaze denied understanding of what approached before lifeless, glassy eyes stared at the ceiling.

Dani screamed.

Dropping the gun, her tormentor picked up his next weapon of choice. A garrote.

It was her turn. She couldn't move.

Strong hands yanked her upper arms back and held her still as the killer circled behind for a better position.

His weapon consisted of a double-looped guitar string with each end knotted in the middle of a short wooden handle. Dani struggled to free a hand and pull one side loose.

Above her, the killer's sadistic grin radiated vicious glee in the face of her approaching demise. In the distance, several dogs' ferocious barking grew dim. She couldn't draw breath to scream.

Suddenly, he had hands everywhere, restricting her movement, choking her, pulling her fingers from her neck.

"Dani! Damn it, wake up." That voice could command death itself. "Come on. Open your eyes. See me. It's Marc."

"Oh, God. It's not real. It's not real."

"You're safe. No one's going to get you."

Marc's smooth baritone penetrated the thick haze of her panic. Soothing strokes of his touch glided over her forehead, down her cheek then back to her scalp. Combined with his softened tone, it dispelled the clinging vestiges of her torment.

"You fell asleep, sweetheart. Tell me about your nightmare."

Again, his voice reached to the very depths of her soul to insulate her from the horrific images assaulting her mind.

"Who was choking you?" Sliding her collar down, he exposed the scar on her neck even as she attempted to cover the puckered skin with trembling fingers. "Son of a bitch!"

"Someone from my past." Her heart thundered like mini explosions while he pushed her hand aside to examine the disfigurement. She couldn't think straight between the remnants of her nightmare and the fear of Marc learning her darkest secret.

"Who?"

"Please." Her frantic gaze scanned the area, seeking safety in anything that could harbor a terrified spirit.

"No Dani. It's time to face this. Head on."

"He scares me to death. He used a guitar string to strangle me. He'd kill you without thinking twice, and nobody would find your body. He knows from experience how to hide them."

"You're safe here, Dani. No one's gonna get to you." Marc brushed the back of his fingers down her cheek. "He won't get to us."

A soft whine brought her gaze to Darius nestled on blankets in the corner of the porch. "When did Conner bring him home?"

Her mind sought any method of distraction.

Awake from her slumberous demise, she looked around for evidence of demons from hell seeking sanctuary in the smallest shadows under the sofa or behind a side table, waiting to drag her back into the abyss she'd escaped.

"About a half hour ago. He's gonna be all right." His tone deepened, smoothed, and lost its sharp edge. "Take some slow, deep breaths for me, sweetheart."

"And his elbow?"

"Strain. The doc told Conner it should be healed by the time his shoulder is better."

"Thank God." The effects of his calm manner lulled her into a false sense of safety, accepted for now. It'd been so long since she'd felt it, this feeling of security. Warmth suffused her chest with the following slow deep breaths.

"How'd you get the scar, Dani?" Gone was the dominant interrogator, replaced with a sympathetic ear.

The change didn't fool her for a second. He could switch hats, but determination radiated throughout his aura. He wouldn't stand for injustice of any kind.

With her back against a virtual wall, she pushed his arm away. "Don't. It was a long time ago." Regardless of Marc's tenacious pursuit of the truth, she sensed in him no wish to use force, reassuring if not combined with innate persistence.

Still, nothing could stop the warmth from her pressing against his flank. This sense of safety occurred on such rare occasions. "Of all the people I've met, I've never felt this comfortable around anyone."

"All right, we'll revisit that subject later. It's time to set priorities. Considering what you've told me so far, I think it'd be prudent to talk to my ex-boss who has extensive resources that can help us figure out this mess." Marc didn't press for further information.

Relaxing back against the sofa allowed her to sort out the intention written on his face.

"Colonel Kenson?"

Kenson was the military man she had to avoid at all cost. A different branch of the government had imprisoned Callie, but would Kenson share the same viewpoint? The commander still didn't know the extent of Callie's abilities.

Like a cat about to pounce, Marc tensed. The way he pursed his lips declared his understanding that she withheld something.

"Yeah, my former boss can give us access to more records in an expedient amount of time. He's also in a unique position as someone who could safeguard extraordinary individuals."

Her breath rushed in on a muffled *whoosh* as his stare continued to ravage her senses. "I haven't met him either, Marc."

I don't have Callie's psychic ability, but the colonel would keep equal tabs on me if he understood what I can do.

"What about the Koreans who kidnapped Callie? Did you have any contact with them?"

His deep and sensual timbre skated along her skin then slid deep inside to fill her heart. His tone could do this regardless of the words spoken.

"Never ran afoul of them." Her breath came a little harsher, forcing her eyes closed in order to read him.

Intuition warned that despite the gentle tone, time would stress their emotional connection the longer she hoarded pertinent information. Each tick of the imaginary clock lengthened the distance between them.

Marc's trust in her would slip out of reach if she waited too long. If she couldn't get it back, she'd never ferret out a way to freedom, and Ray would hunt her to the end of time. When they caught her, she'd never see the light of day again.

"Marc, I—it's complicated."

"Always is, sweetheart. Always is. You're gonna have to trust someone, sometime. How long have you been on your own? Hell, I'm not even sure how old you are."

"I'm twenty-three. I've been on my own for three years."

"How'd you end up in a house held by an offshore corporation?"

"Stroke of luck." Looking away from his intense gaze, she didn't want to go into details.

"This breeze is cooling off. Let's relocate inside before we continue." Patting her upper arm lightly, he smiled, according her a minute to catch her breath.

"You're very self-reliant." Approval and respect shone in his gaze.

He held out a hand to help her up, the warmth both soothing and exciting. Perhaps a little distance would be a good thing.

"If you have some extra blankets, I could make a comfortable bed for Darius."

Without your hands on me, I have a better chance of staying focused on solving my problem and not on your touch.

"Sounds good. Closet in the hallway has extra linens. Meanwhile, I've got some phone calls to make."

"You have a beautiful home. May I explore?"

In a moment of doubt, she thought he'd refuse, but he merely shrugged a shoulder. "Sure, help yourself." His wolfish grin contained more secrets than she held.

As she padded away, his genuine interest warmed all the places her recent nightmare had left frightened and chilled. She'd recognized his sincerity in the offer for help but hadn't expected concern bordering on unrelenting insistence despite the angled approach.

The man radiated determination. Except, hadn't life taught her that truth was best approached sideways? Attempting a front tackle often saw it skittering away like the tail of a kite caught in a swift updraft. Marc was adept in many methods of interrogation.

French doors led back into a kitchen consisting of gleaming stainless steel appliances and cool granite countertops. A massive island with a vegetable sink indicated one who enjoyed cooking and could use the large space to full advantage. Aged brick arched over the alcove containing a six-burner cooktop and a built-in grill, a gourmet chef's dream.

"Your kitchen is beautiful." No sound issued from behind, but she'd felt his presence. To turn around now and face him would dissolve her into a puddle of longing for which he'd take full advantage—with more questions. He was a cagey bugger.

"Thanks. I'll carry Darius in after I'm finished on the phone."

The open floor plan appeared well-thought-out and designed for comfort. A casual, cozy combination of hardwood floors, overstuffed sofas, and floor-to-ceiling windows seemed tailor made to watch the late-afternoon sun melt into the ocean.

Off to the left, a rounded archway framed the rich interior of a masculine yet comfortable study with lots of wood molding. The scene beckoned one and all to enjoy a relaxing afternoon among hundreds of books lining the wall-to-wall shelves. She wondered what he liked to read.

To the right, a six-foot wide hall harbored bifold doors on either side. After retrieving several blankets, she noticed four possible exits. Two on either side would offer more insight into Marc's world.

She couldn't resist.

Pushing forward granted a jaw-dropping view framed by French doors and more large windows. Beyond the sand dunes, an offshore breeze stirred dazzling white caps as far as the eye could see. Each wave's backwash created filaments floating on restless air currents above tumultuous waters.

A massive, ornate iron headboard stood against the far wall. Woodsmen-style bedspread and pillow shams covered the king-size bed, the perfect stage for exciting nighttime activities.

Her life, like the cottage she'd occupied, remained Spartan and utilitarian, unlike this room designed for a man with particular tastes and who could afford the best.

Several steps in, she stumbled over a plush rug of geometric shapes in neutral shades, thicker than anything she'd ever felt.

The entire scene left her speechless. Yet, she should have expected it all. He co-owned Ambrosia, a night club, and this was an extension of his tastes.

No wonder he unnerves me.

How long she stood there, she didn't know. Soft footfalls announced his advance and jarred her back to the moment, and still, her feet wouldn't budge. It wouldn't do to have him witness her gawking like a star-struck kid.

Refolding the blankets let her resize them for the injured shepherd. In hurried motions, she arranged a comfortable bed in the corner.

"Hey, looks good. Thanks. Do you mind bringing in his water bowl? The vet said to ae sure he stays hydrated."

Despite holding Darius in his arms, Nate radiated a combination of potent virility in what she imagined to be a well-used bedroom. It stretched her nerves beyond capacity for clear thinking.

"S-sure. Be right back."

Slight hiking of his lips on one side drew her entire focus before she staggered back, turned, and stumbled away. Claustrophobia wasn't an issue in the great room without Marc's presence.

Two ceramic bowls sat on either side of the kitchen's alcove, one blue, the other green. Each bore black paw prints and had a chew bone and ball beside it.

The chew toy and rubber ball slipped from her grasp twice before she'd secured it along with the blue and black dish.

Filling the bowl two-thirds full ensured she wouldn't spill as she made her way back to his bedroom.

Instinct warned it the last place she should go.

Chapter Seven

"Here we go." Setting the bowl in front of Darius, she groaned as a little water sloshed over the side. He opened one eye, licked her fingers, then settled back to sleep. She couldn't resist a slow caress of his soft coat after setting his bone and rubber ball beside the bed within easy reach.

"I'm so sorry you got hurt, boy." When she stood and pivoted, Marc loomed above her, his overwhelming presence knocking both her mental and physical balance out of whack. "I brought his rubber ball."

"Yes, I see. Thank you. He likes having that close."

He took a small step forward, leaving a few scant inches separating them.

Again, his infuriating smile let her know he realized, and exploited, his arousing effect.

Interrogation, round two.

Knowing what was coming didn't clear her mind.

"You don't give them tennis balls. I'm glad because the felt is extremely abrasive to their teeth. It contains a glue."

"Yes. I've read about the adhesive used by manufacturers." Another half step closer.

He's trying to knock me off kilter. Let's see how he likes role reversal.

The ruggedly handsome man didn't realize she held an edge. Two could play the game.

Maybe.

She couldn't keep her breaths even, but it didn't matter when the predator's smile widened. Her timing would have to be perfect.

"I-I've seen canine teeth worn down to nubs before the owners got a clue. They worry and wonder, but don't bring the dogs in to figure out what's causing it."

"Yep, I believe it." His warm breath fanned across her cheek, minty from the candy he seemed to favor.

They shared the same space, the same air, intimate in a way previously unknown.

"I, um, I'm glad you take good care of your balls, ah, your dogs."

"I always take care of what's mine." His eyes could command the devil himself.

Her focus returned to his gaze like a moth drawn to light. Once done, her intended action couldn't be *undone.* Not to mention the repercussions it could cause. Her heart was the least of her concerns.

She gulped, trying to find another way, another path. He'd proven a master at manipulation. Could she outshine the teacher?

His close proximity blocked out everything, including her ability to think or decipher anything other than the intense hunger disseminating from him in waves.

Maybe spontaneous orgasms aren't a myth.

Revealing her weakness and insecurity had worked to her advantage, not that she'd planned it this way.

Then again, maybe not. Did her weakness encourage the predator in him?

"Dani, how did you know which bowl Darius uses?"

"Um, j-just a lucky guess? Please... you're backing me into a corner."

"*Mhmm.* And how did you know where Darius likes to sleep? In *this* room and in *that* spot."

The low murmur vibrating in his throat liquefied her desires to one option—counterstrike.

"Uh, there was dog hair in the corner." Her eyelids closed with his soft graze of her cheek.

Now or never.

He held his breath when she slid her hands over his chest and up his shoulders. Amber eyes widened then narrowed on her face, as if suspecting her ploy.

Before he could verify his suspicion, she closed the gap and hooked her hands behind his neck, drawing him down. His mustache grazed her upper lip as she kissed him, tentative at first, searching for the right response. She had no experience, only desire.

His fingers tangled in her hair and pressed her closer, his lips nipping before lifting to whisper in her ear. "I know you didn't open either of the other doors, but I appreciate your distraction."

She couldn't think, couldn't form a plan other than offering the diversion. "What makes you say that?"

Contact was explosive as he nuzzled a spot behind her ear and inhaled her scent deep into his lungs.

"Because they both emit a telltale squeak."

The whispered words vibrated in her chest, the warm, moist air bathing her face as his heat spread down her neck. She'd never known passion as a physical sensation. Nothing else mattered but his closeness, this connection.

"I guess I'm just lucky." The mental trap he'd sprung registered in the distant portions of her mind even as the figurative noose tightened around her neck.

His breath quickened, but she felt his iron will to get to the truth. He'd distracted her with the sensual touch of his fingers and the caressing warmth of his voice, his breath, the heat of his hard, muscled chest.

His sensual assault was more effective than her own.

"*Hmm*, I wonder..." His words drifted off as he nuzzled her neck.

Pete's whine and wet nose against her thigh shocked a small semblance of sanity within her chaotic mind.

Dogs always came to her rescue, but taking a step back didn't clear her thoughts, until she witnessed the determination in his gaze. If anything, she'd fanned the flames of his curiosity.

"Would you like to see the rest of the house?" His tone signaled the end of the sensual interrogation.

In her heart, she knew he'd use anything in his arsenal to get to the truth.

"Yes, please." Shaking her head, she took a quick step sideways and collided with the wall. As if her face wasn't flaming already, more heat spread the distance to her hairline. "I'd love to see your house. Let's take a tour."

Dear God, he's gonna figure me out. I'll end up in a six-by-twelve cell for the rest of my life.

Stepping away gave her a little space and the ability to take a deep breath. This time she was careful not to trip over the rug on her way out.

"Across the hall is my home office."

She wouldn't have rushed in if he hadn't reached around her to open the door and brushed her back with his arm. Like his library, one wall contained nothing but shelves full of books. Another displayed dozens of pictures of military men in dress uniforms, camouflage outfits, scuba, and skydiving gear.

A large triple window showcased the woodland scene bordering the sea, the stiff offshore breeze rubbing naked branches against each other as if attempting to chase the chill from the air.

"What do you like to read?" She needed a safe subject and prayed he didn't detail books about war, torture, or interrogation techniques.

There was no sound as he closed the distance until only his breath on the back of her neck slid between them.

"Pretty much an eclectic taste. I like to sample all sorts of things."

Dear God. He's not going to give up.

She could hear his smile. Lurching forward, she ran her fingers across the fine grain of the mahogany desk. Massive didn't come close to describing it. Like the man himself, it was neat, contained, and free of clutter.

In a pool of distracted and helpless frustration, her spirit sought solace in anything that offered a respite from Marc's overwhelming presence. Her gaze slipped outside to the ocean's wide expanse.

She couldn't ignore the beautiful view, a moment of madness. The sound of distant waves crashing against the short beach likened to the rush of sensations washing over her mind and body, endless in their persistence and eventually eroding the substrate. Likewise, he'd wear her down until he discovered all her secrets.

She had to escape. "How about the other rooms?"

"Those? They're just guest bedrooms. I don't think you'd be interested in them."

"Don't be silly, I love rooms."

And my IQ just dropped fifty points.

Without hesitation, she skirted him like a guppy attempting to outmaneuver a shark. In respect of his penchant for close proximity, she stood back to allow space for moving around her, noting his wolfish grin when he cleared his throat. A nonverbal warning of things to come perhaps.

The guest bedrooms appeared just as neat and orderly as the rest of the home. She'd expected the neutral color palate and thick rug on hardwood flooring.

His insightful manipulations negated her ability to sort her thoughts but offered an anchor, a tether against the whims of fate which tossed her world into anarchy. All she had to do was grab hold—and survive.

"Your house is gorgeous."

Leading her back to the great room, he waited until she sat, and then settled beside her.

"Thank you. Now, tell me how you know Colonel Kenson." Again, he'd pushed her off balance before striking.

"You did that on purpose." Knowing his tactics didn't provide a viable defense. She had no way to organize her dissipating defense.

"You tried the same tactic."

"But it didn't work." Self-control had never been one of her shortcomings.

"You're smart, but you have little experience with men, unless I miss my guess," he said as Pete sat between their feet and laid his head on her thigh.

"Obviously not smart enough. I'm afraid if I tell you, you'll get hurt."

"Like Franklin?" An arched brow declared he'd wait, but not long.

"Y-yes. Franklin died in freeing Callie." Tingling in her lips accompanied the shiver racing along her spine. Lightheadedness didn't make a good base during interrogation.

"He chose his own path, Dani."

"But— you're going down the same road."

"You're not responsible for other people's decisions." The lower timbre emerged as if it pained him to speak the words, "You… dealt with Sebastian?"

She couldn't hold back the sob as she struggled to get up.

Marc guided her to sit in his lap. "*Shh*. It's all right, Dani. Whatever happened will stay between us. I swear. If not for you, Callie and several of my brothers would be dead now. This conversation goes nowhere else unless you decide differently. Sebastian was a traitor who would've seen them all killed."

Marc's demeanor changed, no longer taunting or sexual in nature. "Sorry I had to throw you off balance before, but lives are at stake, people I care about. That includes you, in case you have any doubt."

"I—I just wanted Callie to be free. Sebastian sold her to those bastards. He also did some kind of surgical procedure. If she hadn't escaped the institution that night, the North Koreans would've had her and done much worse."

"So, you set up her escape through Franklin, with codes you got from the organization's CEO?"

"I... Franklin was still in Minnesota. I'd contacted him by phone. He asked me to meet with his friend, Daryl, as an intermediary. I guess he wanted Daryl to make sure I was on their side."

"For your help, I will be forever grateful. What happened?"

"Daryl was killed in the woods. It was awful."

"I'm sorry for what you've been through."

"When I contacted Jake, he asked me to meet him. I went, but they were there. I heard something from the road and was afraid to come out. They shot him in cold blood." Dani took a halting breath, then continued.

"Sebastian owned a house, but it was his lover who found me first. He was pure evil. He attacked me—and I defended myself, to his death."

"And in Sebastian's apartment?"

"Yeah, that was me, too. Do you know what he did to Callie, what he sold her into?"

"Yes, but why did you go to his apartment?"

"I needed answers. Since Sebastian had helped her escape, I thought his partner had betrayed him. Things weren't adding up. I'm the worst snoop in the world. Everything ends with death. Do you understand now why I don't want you involved?"

Marc surged forward to keep her vested in the conversation. "Sebastian was part of the team protecting Callie, but we found that instead of helping her, he'd sold out to the foreigners. Not only did he turn on his old squad, he was a traitor to this country."

She should've seen this interrogation coming, the incisive, intrusive questions after smashing her equilibrium. She'd given away too much. Her only hope lay in revealing as little as possible and praying he didn't decipher the rest. Now, more than ever, she needed his help to escape.

"Stop evading, tell me about Sebastian."

"I snuck into his apartment to look for clues concerning Callie's whereabouts. I couldn't find her anywhere. I'd panicked when I couldn't find much. Sebastian arrived and cornered me. I didn't know much about him, never met him. Turns out he was crazy, too."

"He fooled us all, Dani."

"I knew he'd either kill me or make me wish I were dead. I'd found his dart gun. He detailed what he did to Callie and how he'd left her with the foreigners to be raped. Then, he smiled and described what he planned for me. I was so scared. She didn't deserve it, none of it. Do you know exactly what that bastard did to her?" Words followed thought, jumbled but still flowing without censure or her ability to slow their passage.

"Yes. That prick deserved a lot worse than what happened."

Broken breaths between sobs kept her unstable while her tears dampened his shirt. All her hard work and planning to set another free would land her in jail. Fitting since she was a killer.

"I'm not a violent person, really. Before all this with Callie... I'd never hurt another living creature. But the things he intended to do to me... I just snapped. He rushed me and I shot him with the dart gun. He kept talking even after the tranquilizer slurred his speech. Said he'd track me down and have his fun, just like he'd done overseas to others."

Broken whimpers choked her, but she continued. "He had connections with some foreign spies. There's a parallel operation."

"Damn. This runs deeper than any of us figured. Listen, Sebastian can't hurt you now. No one will again. You've done what a special-ops man would've been ordered to do, with a slight twist." Calm and soothing, his murmured sincerity calmed the worst of her fears.

"But I... I killed him. Viciously." Hiccups interrupted her confession.

"Well, I have to say, I hope you never get that mad at me. You're a strong woman, loyal and talented."

"Talented?" The strangled word erupted like an epithet.

"I've seen the way you handle dogs in the veterinarian's office. They come in frightened or mean as snakes yet within minutes, they're calm and eating out of your palm, getting the help they need. Dr. Carari must love you. Do you remember this morning with Darius? He's never been x-rayed without sedation first, until he met you."

"Oh. Yeah. She's pretty great." Intermittent snivels continued to rack her body. He continued to absolve her worst sins and point out her better traits, the intensity of his gaze revealing compassion.

"You can tell a lot about a person by the way they treat animals. I've seen much, both through the military and in my private investigative work. I know you have a good soul."

"You wield sexuality like a weapon." Her accusation brought forth his smile.

"Would you have told me all this if I hadn't?"

"Well, no. I'd planned on acquiring a new identity and running. I should've been more alert and not let you scatter my thoughts with your sexiness."

That earned a deep and hearty laugh. "Sorry to be underhanded. Though, time is of the essence."

"But when I tried to turn the tables—"

"You would've succeeded before long. Trust me." Marc held out his hand, offering an olive branch. "Friends?"

Daniel accepted, then frowned. "Wait, so you're not attracted to me at all?"

Leaning forward, he nuzzled her hair then the sensitive skin on her neck. "If I wasn't, would I shudder with equal amount shivers and goose flesh?"

"This isn't fair, I couldn't divert your attention." Only when he leaned back could she pull a deep breath into her lungs.

"It's all about self-control. Doesn't mean I'm not equally affected. But right now, we have priorities."

"Keeping Callie safe is top. It's just all so unfair."

"Life rarely is. If we weren't neck deep in some weird shit, I'd prove to you just how much you *do* affect me."

She read the honest sincerity in his gaze.

With that, the world turned on its axis, and Marc switched gears. "Are you hungry? You need a break and some more food in your stomach. We can talk later."

As if in response, the gurgle-growl of her belly filled the quiet room. One sandwich hadn't made up for missing two meals yesterday and breakfast that morning. "Sure. But I hope you can cook, because I can't."

"Up you go. This will be your first cooking lesson." Again, his fingers lingered at her waist as if judging her fitness and need for calories.

"First?" Persistent heat in his gaze disrupted further thought.

"Yep."

"You mean, you still want me to stay here?" With the dawn of his intentions came a sudden weakness in her knees. Her knuckles turned white from clutching his shoulders.

"Dani, whether these are the same bastards trying to reacquire Callie through you, or you've got your very own psychotic stalker, clearly you can't go home. Therefore, you can either run and hope they don't kill whoever is nearby when they catch you, as they certainly will. Or you can stay here while we sort this out. The way I see it, I owe you one."

"If I stay here—"

"If you leave now, you'll die, plain and simple."

"If I stay, they'll kill *you*. What makes you think Hutson was after me and not you?"

"I'm not the one he asked out on a date." Marc's half smile preceded a subdued chuckle.

"But, how'd he know to show up at the trial?" Dani's thoughts would always play catch up when Marc was nearby. "Oh, he heard you say you'd pick me up at ten. He's into dogs, too, and knew about the trials."

"Yep."

The intensity of his gaze could start flash fires if the air hadn't been sucked from the room.

"You live here alone?"

"I do." His sexy grin amplified the dimple in his cheeks.

Marc, taking her hand and leading her to the kitchen, created more roiling sensations for her to savor at a time when she could once again think. For now, she was ill prepared to formulate a refusal.

"Here, you sit while I cook."

Pete's tail batted her leg while she contemplated her host's complexities, both confident and competent in any situation observed.

So sensitized to her surroundings now, she felt the cool air from the refrigerator puff over her skin when he opened the door. A narrowed gaze gave his expression an ominous quality. Whether he thought about what to eat or his next interrogation, she couldn't concentrate enough to discern.

"Let's set the basics for our working relationship. Rule number one, complete honesty."

This was a conversation she'd like to skip. "What are you making?" She admired his fluid movements in retrieving a cutting board and preparing vegetables.

"Stew. It can simmer while we talk." In short order, he added celery and garlic to the pile of carrots, onions, potatoes, and other vegetables once chopped.

Understanding her message, they discussed benign topics ranging from dog training to low-pressure weather systems generating big swells for surfing.

After cubing the meat and adding flour, he added onion, and garlic, and seasonings sautéed in a small skillet. Addition of beef broth and wine to the large pot made her mouth water. It came as no surprise to observe his agility with a knife and thick cut of beef.

When all was set to simmer, he leaned a hip against the counter and turned his full attention to her.

"Where're your thoughts going, Dani?"

"Sebastian."

"You see yourself as weak, per se."

"I could've called the cops. There had to be information on his computer."

Reflections of the kitchen knife induced flashbacks of Sebastian's threats and her ultimate response. All the blood, so much blood she'd vomited.

Sebastian had resembled another sadist from another time. She'd lost it and not realized she'd stabbed him until warm, crimson liquid stained her hands.

"You're not weak by any means, Dani. We all exist as more than the sum of our parts. Self-defense is a base instinct in us all. You protected yourself and someone you cared about. That took courage. I admire that."

"I can't believe we're having this conversation. I'd wanted to ask for help in acquiring a new identity so I can leave the east coast."

"Run? If Ray's thugs from the Think Tank are on your trail, you won't get far, but we'll discuss that later. For now, let's address some of your unasked questions."

How could she even consider this when she should be halfway across the country?

Chapter Eight

"It's great to cook for someone with a healthy appetite." Placing his hand on her lower back, Marc escorted her to the great room and noted the tremor flitting through her body.

From attraction, not revulsion.

He hated manipulating the beautiful spitfire, but if he didn't get a handle on her stalker, others were going to die.

The overstuffed sofa gave under his weight before Dani sat, swiveling to face him. Kicking her shoes off, she tucked her feet underneath her.

The now-familiar frown denoting intense focus slid into place. It'd become a familiar expression during their talks, but foreshadowed something more, something best avoided. Instinct dictated he needed to derail her concentration.

In a show of comradery, he took her hand and held it, smiling when she froze. "I know you're not afraid of me. I'm not going to touch you sexually, okay?"

"I know. It's just that I'm not your type." Rubbing her upper arm in a self-protective gesture, she let her gaze slide to the floor-to-ceiling windows and turbulent waves crashing against the beach.

"Smart, loyal, and strong-willed?" Getting to the heart of whatever abuse she'd suffered would open another door and help strengthen the base of their relationship.

"I'm... complicated. I can never shake the feeling of blood on my hands." Tears brimmed her eyes before she wiped them away.

"Tell me about what happened *before* Sebastian." The possibility of sexual abuse seemed slim, considering her uninhibited responses, but that wouldn't prevent a spillover from repeated verbal offenses. Slight shifting signaled her intent to get up.

His pre-emptive move with a hand on her shoulder barred her escape and froze her movements.

"Marc?"

"Dani, I need your trust in order to help you. I'm flying blind here."

Very slowly, he took her chin between thumb and forefinger, raising her gaze to meet his. Unadulterated fear radiated from the rich blue depths, but did it stem from divulging her secrets or remembering her past? How long could one mind tolerate such circumstances without fracturing?

She personified courage, intelligence, and loyalty yet lacked the confidence to believe in anyone because of some unnamed horror ingrained deep in her soul.

"You wouldn't like me if you knew everything." Pulling back, she tucked her chin down, hiding behind her thick fall of hair.

"You've spent years keeping people at bay. It's time to learn not everyone is the same."

"I haven't always been this way. I was adopted by a couple who loved me, in spite of my... weirdness."

"Tell me about them. I can't find you in any system."

She must have been with them for a while to develop such strong character.

"They were good people. They totally understood me. When puberty hit and everything changed, they helped me adapt. I knew I could always tell them anything. They made life bearable." Thinness of her voice betrayed pain.

"Where are they?" He kept his tone soothing, as if speaking to a cornered animal.

"Dead. Killed in a car accident. That's when I went into foster care and eventually ended up with the Tuckers. Both sons are brutal psychotics, just like the parents. They'll hunt me to the day I die. This is the closest they've come in a long time, if it's them. I just need a new ID. Please?"

"Did your adoptive parents leave some kind of trust? Offshore accounts?"

"No, the Fowlers were people I met later. They also arranged to have some of my records erased. I'm not sure how. Before they died, they'd set me up with the cottage."

"Ah, that explains a lot. So why are the Tuckers after you?" He needed to get to the core of the matter.

"Because of the things I know and have seen. It doesn't have anything to do with Callie. They want me."

"Because?" Once again, he felt as much as heard the hesitation to embroil him in her world, not realizing he stood in it hip deep.

"Marc..."

"Okay. Table that for later, too. For now, I have an idea. Something that might help you. You're wound so tight, I'm afraid you'll snap."

"I'm all right."

"Of course, you are, but this will help you relax." He'd given her little reason to trust him. In addition, he'd used her infatuation to extract information.

"What do you have in mind?"

"Come with me. I presume you have a scrunchie or hair band in your bag?"

"Yes..."

His little spitfire stood on the verge of a great chasm and didn't know which way to run. Instead of drilling her for details, he'd give her a break and let her thoughts catch up with recent events.

"Let's go. You need some down time."

He led her to the master bath where a claw-foot tub big enough for two stood in the corner.

"Marc?"

Shocked shitless wasn't a good look on her now.

Ignoring her hesitation, he continued inside and turned on the taps. "There's a robe on the back of the door. I'll set your bag on the bed. Help yourself to a long, hot soak. I'll be in the kitchen." He waited, watching the play of emotions cross her face.

"Dani?"

"Y-Yes. I-I don't know what to say." Trembling fingers reached to touch his upper arm before pulling back.

"Enjoy, and take your time."

"Oh, yes. This looks wonderful."

Indeed.

"Every woman should be pampered this way."

"No man's ever been this nice to me."

His finger pad caught the lone tear trailing down her cheek. "This doesn't belong here today." Tasting the salty moisture on his finger burned a path of molten heat through his chest.

"Consider this a token of friendship. A beginning."

Dani stared at the tub, then back at Marc. Her brows furrowed, eyes narrowed as she concentrated on his face. After a minute, she grinned, then smiled wide. "I've not had a friend for a very long time. I'd like that."

"This is part of a friend's duty. To help whenever and however needed."

"You see me as a duty?" Slumping shoulders and a wounded gaze reflected the hurt cutting deep.

If he didn't change the course of her thinking, he'd lose her. Leaning forward, he cupped the back of her head to draw her close.

"No, Dani. You are *not* a duty. But you are in a lot of trouble, and yes, I'd be honored to call you friend. I do believe, however, friends have a responsibility to help each other. This is a small token of my appreciation for you helping Callie and my brother Nate."

He leaned in until mere inches separated their faces. "That said, it doesn't protect me from a bone-gnawing infatuation. It doesn't mean I don't want to get to know you better. Much better. However, I *will* respect your boundaries."

Knowing intimacy and romance had just complicated her world necessitated treading a lighter path. "You all right, sweetheart?"

Without hesitation, she wrapped her hands around his waist and hugged him tight. "Thank you. It's hard to remember when someone was nice to me just for the sake of it."

The milestone she'd just passed would've taken some women weeks to embrace. Yet, he'd watched her reactions, step by step, and knew he hadn't moved too fast. Again, he wondered about her intelligence, secrets, and unusual situation.

His brother had boasted of Callie's incredible mind. What secrets did Dani hold?

An easy smile graced Dani's lips when she exited the short hall in corduroy slacks and turtleneck top to sit beside him. While she'd been soaking, his brother Conner, had dropped off some clothes, guessing at her size.

Marc had never seen her so relaxed. He nodded to the bag left for her, "My brother dropped those off for you."

Her ability to adapt amazed him. After all she'd been through, she accepted him. Not for the first time, he reviewed in his mind the nature of her advanced instincts and her brief interaction with Julien at the office.

To date, there'd been no sign of dishonesty, either voiced or nonverbal.

Since she'd been taught in the harshest way imaginable not to trust, how could she so easily accept him now?

A silk shirt lay on top of the bag. She stroked the sleeve's soft material with reverence. "This is the silkiest thing I've ever seen. Anyone wearing it should feel like royalty."

"Dani, tell me who first turned your world upside down. What did the Tuckers do?"

Her lips twisted into a grimace, but she didn't hide her face behind a cloud of silken waves.

"They're depraved, moral mutants. I wish I could end them all."

"So, *do* you have something in common with Callie?"

"What? No. I'm nothing like Callie. I—I really don't want to go there." The frightened and cornered look returned to her demeanor, infringing on the progress they'd made.

"All right for now, but tell me this. Is it because of what you can do, or what you've seen?"

Sometimes a roundabout avenue works better.

"Both." She squirmed on the sofa.

She'd just confirmed his suspicions, at least in part. "Give me their full names so we can pull their records. I need background on these shits if they're the ones coming after us." Marc mentally reviewed previous conversations and observations since meeting Dani. Either a dirtball from her past or Ray from the Think Tank hunted her. Countermeasure tactics would differ with each one.

"Us?"

"The bastard drew me in when he shot Darius." Marc needed to zero in on his targets but couldn't do it quickly without a bit of background. "What line of work were the Tuckers in?" Fitting puzzles together only occurred after collecting pertinent information.

Her curling lip and small shudder broadcast disgust with a side order of fear as she spoke each name and the jobs used for cover for criminal activity.

"I haven't seen them in years. I don't know what they're doing now or even where they live. They used to rent a house in Still Creek."

"Less than a hundred miles up the highway?"

And she remained close in spite of the danger?

"The father is a drunk, a mean one. Why his wife stays is a mystery to me. If someone beat me like that, I'd fight like hell."

"And their kids?"

"Two sons. They'd both adopted their dad's viewpoint of others, women in particular... Marc, I've stayed, hiding in plain sight for a reason. I don't go off the property except to work and the small grocery store down the street. The Tuckers hate animals, so working for a vet seemed like a perfect fit. I wanted to collect particulars on the missing prodigies before I left."

"By yourself? Sounds dangerous." Ways to convince her to stay sifted through his thoughts and like the flight of an arpeggio, couldn't stop on one specific arrangement.

"I hadn't found anyone else who seemed up for the job."

"Now that you have, isn't it time to combine our efforts? I have both the training and the resources."

"And your dog has already been shot. Callie's free—I think it's time I take off." Her second yawn mandated the conversation continue at a later time.

Run? Not freaking likely.

"Why don't you sit tight and I'll dip us up some stew? I'll call and see what my brothers have found out."

He grabbed his cell on his way to the kitchen. "Herbal tea?" He considered himself lucky when she didn't object or move to leave.

"Sure."

Conner answered on the first ring. They had a lot to discuss.

No way in hell was he going to set her up with a fake ID and watch her skip town. Her neck's disfigurement provided a physical reminder that the bastards played for keeps. Someone needed to take them off the board.

It was time to get his game face on.

Chapter Nine

Rumbling growls between deep-throated barking jarred Dani awake and brought her attention to the front bay window where Pete's stiffened posture alerted to an unknown threat. Darius hobbled out, voicing equal conviction.

"Intruder's bark. Stay put, Dani. I'll take Pete, Darius will remain with you. I'm gonna lock the door on my way out." Marc jerked the end table's drawer open without a glance in her direction.

A dull thud from the holster and gun's skid forward conveyed ominous intent prior to his plucking it out and tucking it in the back of his waistband. He'd rushed halfway through the great room before his objective blared an alarm in her mind.

The sound of the front door slamming swept the remainder of the cobwebs from her thoughts. Her imagination conjured the image of Marc yanking the slide back on his .45 Glock during a hunched race beside Pete to the thick line of trees fronting his house.

Unable to stay away, she padded to the side of the bay window and watched as her protector flashed into the edge of the woods. Darius whined and rubbed against her leg.

"Damn. I'm like this bad penny that brings disaster to whomever I touch. I have to run, Darius, before anyone else dies."

Indecision bound her feet to the floor like the majestic oak whose roots burrowed deep into the earth, allowing it to withstand nature's worst elements. Unlike the great oak, she had no roots, no support, and no way to weather the coming storm.

A gunshot rang out.

Terror born from horrific memories thrust her back and off balance to land on her hands and butt. "Marc? No! God, no. Not again. Darius, stay!"

She didn't remember opening the door, yet cool air brushed stray locks across her face to cripple her view in dashing across the front yard.

Something sharp dug through her sock and into her heel, but time couldn't be spared to dislodge the small stone or twig. She ran on the balls of her feet.

Uncontrollable shaking made her stumble at the edge of the woods while fear for Marc moved her forward over fallen trees and thick brush.

Briars tore at her clothes. Cold sweat cooled her body as her harsh breath burst in and out.

Four more shots blared in succession.

No. Please, God, don't let this happen again. I'll leave... I promise I'll leave.

Amid the leaf litter and fallen branches, her right foot slipped, sending her down shoulder and hip first. Pain shot up her leg. Only then did she notice the scratches and small lines of blood where briars had snagged her skin. She was up in a heartbeat and scrambling for purchase in her bid to help.

"Pete, platz! All the way down, boy," Marc yelled somewhere ahead, hidden by holly bushes and pine trees.

She paused. Should she go get his car in case he'd been shot? She couldn't carry him back to the house. She couldn't wait, had to know. Fear of the unknown and for Marc's safety drove her onward.

The roar of an engine to her right provided little relief amid the sound of tires grinding against loose gravel. Multiple plinks and pings of stones thrown against a vehicle's fender indicated the occupant's bid for escape.

Another shot, this time closer. Did Marc return fire?

Marc's cursing followed.

Branches slapped at her face at the same time briars cut her arms and prevented her from pulling loose. Blood roared in her ears to match her pulse, drowned by a whimpering originating from her own throat.

Please let him be all right.

The last time she'd ventured into the woods, she'd stood beside a man who'd wanted to help Callie. The thin whine of a rifle had split the night before blood spattered her face. Lots of blood. Franklin's friend was dead before he hit the ground.

Her knees had buckled, and in the next instant, flying tree bark from another shot cut her cheek. These shots reaffirmed her conviction anyone involved in her life became a target.

Marc? Please be okay.

The silent mantra played over and over in her head while images of Daryl's body, punched by the slug, jerked before crumpling to the ground. She should've been able to prevent his death. If only she'd paid better attention. Like now.

Marc's swearing confirmed proof of life, a life she'd filled with frustration and danger. Sharp rays of light filtered through the leafy branches as the sun dropped to eye level, eroding the scene ahead with its glaring beams.

"Marc? Pete?" Slapping the next bough of pine needles from her path granted a view of the wood's edge.

Marc kneeled beside a large oak checking Pete for injury. At the sound of her voice, his gaze whipped around, pinning her in place. "Dani? What the hell? I told you to stay in the house!"

Three strides and he grasped her by the shoulders to pull her in tight. "When I tell you to do something, it's not a request. Are you all right?"

"Just a few scratches. Is Pete okay?" Even as she asked, her hands roamed Marc's chest and back to search for injury. "Are you hurt?"

"We're fine. Let's get back to the house." After a hand signal to Pete, Marc swept her up in his arms while his gaze scanned the perimeter.

"Why are you mad?"

No words emerged, but his hard gaze and tight shoulders spoke volumes. The ground-eating pace jarred her thoughts in painful reminders of what happened to her acquaintances.

"Because I protect what's mine, and you're making that very difficult."

He's claiming me?

When they reached the clearing before the house, Marc stopped to give Pete a command in clipped words. "Pete is going to check the house since the door is standing half open."

"I'm sorry, I—"

"Not now. We'll talk inside." His jaw and arm muscles flexed rhythmically. The pulse in his neck jumped.

Jeez, he's totally pissed.

Minutes later, Pete returned and sat by his side.

"Okay, we can go." Long strides ate the distance in quick succession while he crouched over her body.

The door slammed shut from his kick using more force than necessary. A deep breath and slow exhale later, Marc's gaze roamed over her.

"Hell. You're a mess." Striding to the sofa, he hugged her tight before setting her down. There was nothing gentle about his expression.

"How is it that Darius didn't follow you?"

"I told him to stay." *That's just gonna raise more questions.*

The only way to stop her trembling hands was to clasp them in her lap.

"And he just obeyed? Guess that shouldn't surprise me."

Muddled grumbles between the click and slide of his cell from its case and his relating their situation in succinct terms increased her anxiety as he paced back and forth, running one hand through his hair.

Anger dissipated as he crossed the room and pulled her up and into his arms. Relief radiated in waves, proportionate with his hug. "You could've been killed. What if that asshole had worked with a partner?"

"Marc, I'm sorry. I couldn't let you go out there alone. Daryl was alone. I told Jake to be careful. I'd warned them both."

When he pulled back, shock vied with wrath for dominance in his gaze. "You couldn't *let* me? You know enough about my military background to realize what I do, things I've done. Do you understand?"

"Yes. I-I'm sorry."

"Why would you... oh, hell. Tell me one thing, and I want an *honest* answer." He held her at arm's length so his gaze bore into hers with the strength of a one inch cobalt drill bit.

"*Are* you like Callie? Do you have some type of special talent? Is that why you'd pull such a stupid stunt? Right now, nothing else makes sense."

"What? What do you mean? I've never met Callie." She could no longer meet his gaze, for fear he'd see the truth behind her oblique if evasive answer.

Again, he pulled her tight. "Lord help me, you are like her. I knew it."

"Id you get a ook at im?" Her muffled voice against his chest sounded unintelligible even to her own ears.

When he loosened his grip, she repeated her question.

In response, he sighed. "I didn't see his face. However, I did get his tag. Tall, a little over six feet, dark hair, jeans, denim shirt. Sound like anyone you know?"

"No, not any of the Tuckers. They're all short and red-headed."

So much emotion roiled in his gaze, she couldn't see how he'd contain its bulk. Some of it did seep through his hands in a tightened grip of her upper arms.

The inexplicable force pulling her closer, feeling his heat and determination, and the post adrenaline rush engulfing them both proved too much to resist.

He kissed her forehead, then her cheek.

A slight tug urged him into full body contact until she could taste him, opening to every nibble, lick, and bite, every degree of exploration, every thrust of his tongue—even the rumble in his chest that drove her wild.

The flash fire of emotions consuming everything in its path should've left her terrified. She should push and slow him down.

He pulled her tighter, razing her thoughts to the basest of animal responses until she clung to him for sustenance, accepting his breath, his urgency, his need. She'd suspected a controlled fierceness lay barely restrained behind the lazy smiles and flirting grins—until the savage beast broke free and decimated its target.

Aftermath of near-death experiences produced strong if varied results. She understood the phenomenon yet hadn't experienced anything like what now consumed her.

Damn.

It was hard to think with the overwhelming sensations filling her mind.

Marc groaned. "Follow orders. Please, Dani. I can't lose you."

He pulled back with a low growl she felt under her fingers drifting down his chest. His feral look declared the beast ravenous and wild before he stepped back.

"Ah... What are you doing to me?"

His withdrawal left her startled and shaken. When her legs gave way, he scooped her up and leveled a gaze holding a mixture of worry, regret, and promise.

"Time to cool off a bit, I'd say." The half grin promised everything even as her body shuddered with need.

"Why'd you stop?"

"Because I'm not looking for a one-night stand, and right now we have higher priorities."

"Do you think he'll come back? Shouldn't we leave?" She should've left by now. The yearning for something normal, something—more—kept her in place. She prayed Marc could keep them both alive.

"Not yet. I'm going to ask you some questions, and I want straight answers. We're going to figure this out and make a plan. My brothers will be outside and alert us if we have more intruders. We'll light out tomorrow when we're organized, have more information, and certain we're not followed."

Her lips felt swollen and bruised from his kisses and her body abused from a need withheld. "What do you want to know?" She couldn't think, couldn't fathom his thoughts with her tumultuous emotions scattered in the wind.

Without another word, he took her into the master bath and sat her beside the sink before retrieving a first aid kit from the medicine cabinet.

"Push up your sleeves and let's take a look." Marc pulled off her socks, then pushed the hem of her pants up. "Damn." His slow, careful examination delineated each scratch and small furrow on her legs incurred from her blind run. "I'm going to get these cleaned and disinfected before we finish our conversation."

A light probing defined each wound as he tended first to her feet and legs, then her arms. A soft wet cloth then antibiotic ointment was applied with a gentle touch while determination etched his features.

"Looks like you don't need any stitches. I don't expect of these to scar."

This time, back in the great room when he sat and pulled her into his lap, his gaze held a steadfast resolve advising his questions wouldn't be so easy to dodge. "I want to know everything about these goddamned Tuckers."

"They took me in, foster care, for a while after my adopted parents died. I stayed with them a little more than two years. They have two sons of their own, three and four years older than me."

"And?"

"They used me in their con games. I ran away, but they caught and punished me by hurting others."

"What kind of cons?"

"The first was a home invasion. He killed a couple in Templeton because I refused to hack their computer. I've no idea where he buried their bodies. Tucker said the police would put me in a cell for the rest of my life if I ever told anyone. I believed him."

Again, she couldn't look him in the eye for fear he'd recognize her half-truth and the avoidance of explaining the precise reason *why*

Tucker wanted her back as opposed to killing her. Those monsters were one of a select few who knew something of her darkest secret.

"They killed a couple when they first took you in to ensure compliance, which is why you never went to the police." Marc brushed his lips across the crown of her head before continuing. "The fact these assholes made it a family affair might make it harder to nail them."

"Two years later, I ran away—to a friend's family. I don't know how, but Tucker found me and killed Chelsie's parents. She got away and went to her aunt's house."

"Tucker killed your friend's parents for fear of what you might have revealed."

"The last con, after they got me back, they pretended to be rich investors. We met a *client* in his office late one evening and drew Mr. Fowler, the investor, out of the office for a tour. I got into his computer to gain account numbers while they were gone."

"And this Mr. Fowler didn't catch on?"

"Yeah, eventually. But Tucker didn't get much. The bulk of Fowler's money was in offshore accounts, and I fudged enough of the numbers to screw with the plan. I'd gotten Fowler's personal information and later went to him when I couldn't take living on the streets. I knew Tucker would still hunt me, so I've been very careful."

A quizzical glance exhibited his understanding stained with doubt. "The Fowlers took you in. Did they know anything about the Tucker family?"

"He didn't dig into the Tuckers' past. I begged them not to. Told him if he tried, I'd run away. They set up the cottage fore me before they died."

"All right then. We have a place to start. I wouldn't have pegged you for a computer prodigy... Interesting."

Her breath seized as he again scrutinized her face. She looked away to keep her secrets locked deep inside. If he challenged her outright and demanded proof on the keyboard, could she pull it off?

"I'm not a prodigy. I've just learned a few tricks here and there."

"Tell me about the first couple in Templeton. Would you recognize the house? Did you know their names?"

"No to both. That night, we'd been driving for a while, and I hadn't been paying attention. I was scared of Tucker, his wife, and sons. They made a game of it, invading the home, taking over, then making me retrieve account information.

"The man begged me not to do it, so I said I couldn't hack their system. I'd lied. Tucker shot them both. I puked. Then, Tucker's oldest son wrapped a wire around my neck and choked me until I passed out. I thought he was going to kill me.

"When I came to, I was back in the van lying between dead bodies wrapped in plastic. The boys laughed after stuffing a bloody rag in my mouth."

Marc shifted her upright as she dry heaved with the memories of a copper scent filling her mind and lifeless eyes staring through clear vinyl.

"That's the night you got the scar." Smoothing her hair back, he continued to comfort her with slow gentle strokes across her back.

"Yeah. From then on, I obeyed. Until I couldn't take it anymore."

When she'd regained control of her breathing, he rested his chin on top of her head. Soft, smooth brushes up and down her back anchored her while hushed, soothing noises rumbled in his chest. The vibrations against her face tucked against his warmth calmed the broken, guilty sobs.

"If I'd done as he'd ordered, the first couple would still be alive. If I hadn't run to a friend's house, Chelsie wouldn't be an orphan."

"*Shh*, I doubt that's true on both counts. You were young and naïve. They needed leverage to make you obedient. They probably picked the first couple and the area that was most convenient for their plan. By killing them, Tucker ensured compliance through fear."

"They succeeded, for a while."

"How did you get away?" Again, his penetrating gaze bore into her, delving deep to excavate dire truths from the darkest corners of her soul.

"I took a leap of faith."

His narrowed gaze demonstrated knowledge of her deception. "You feel guilty for the death of the first couple and your friend's parents. Because of that, you've been reluctant to form any type of relationship since." This time, the knowing twist of his lips nailed her.

"Yeah." She couldn't hold his gaze. In a few short hours, he'd burrowed into her mind, sifted through her subterfuge, and uncovered a trove of data that could end them all. She couldn't let him in further.

"I told you, Dani. Someday, you're gonna have to trust someone."

"I do. I trust you."

"We have a place to start. I know it's painful, but I need you to tell me everything you can about the first couple and their house. My brothers and I will look into each of the murders. Once we find the bodies, we can take the Tuckers off the board."

After unbraiding the satin of her hair, he spent the next hour culling the details she'd forgotten during those bloody, gruesome nights. He soothed her fears, held her through the sobbing, and comforted her with the warmth of his acceptance.

"You've certainly seen your share of slaughter, hon. I know that makes it hard to form and maintain relationships, but you'll learn."

"Franklin and his wife wanted to invite Callie into their home. He died at the institution during her escape." Her life existed as a magnet for destruction.

"You were there the night Jake died. Did he tell you anything?"

"No. We didn't get to meet, really. I wanted to warn him about the North Koreans targeting him. I was in the woods, just coming toward the pavilion. There was this muted, cracking noise. His body jerked and fell. I—" More retching twisted her stomach in knots.

Hours passed as they talked late into the night. Still, Dani managed to compartmentalize the threats against her and hide the greatest menace. Doing so might protect Marc. If they could neutralize the Tucker risk, she'd take her chances evading Ray.

Marc asked questions about her love of outdoor life and dogs, easing the tension and pacifying the internal demons wanting to sabotage her next sleep. When exhaustion took over and her yawns became more frequent, he stood in one lithe movement that belied his size.

"Time for bed. You can sleep in the spare room." Darius and Pete padded beside them down the hall. They both knew at least one of the dogs would sleep beside her, if not both of them.

Chapter Ten

"Well, you did it again. What is it with you and target practice with his dogs? And you missed at that." Frazier let the van's linear acceleration force him back against the driver's seat. Disgust at another miss along with little chance for another attempt formed a knot in his gut. Reporting to his superior entailed significant risk in and of itself.

"You saw we were too far away for accuracy. At least I distracted Crofton. He was too busy ducking for cover to get a good look at me." Dirk stared at the woods where increasing shadows would offer sanctuary. The chance of a large payday kept him on course.

"He's seen the van. We'll have to ditch it and steal another." Frazier complained as he took the curve a bit too fast, the rumble of tires on the shoulder's loose gravel making it difficult to steer.

"Yeah, the stolen one with no identifying marks. Listen, we know he's stashing the girl. We'll get another shot soon enough. Next time, I won't miss, and we'll have her. Let's pray this is the right one." Hope infused Dirk's tone.

"You sure he didn't get a look at your face?" The toothpick Frazier flipped side-to-side in his mouth snapped under the weight of his clenched jaw. Another botched kidnapping and his boss would replace them both, *permanently.*

"You're the only one Marc has seen. So, he doesn't know there're two of us." Dirk's smile revealed security in anonymity.

"Yeah, but the boss knows someone else is hunting her. If we don't get the right bitch before the psychopath nails her, *we* won't survive." Frazier needed hope, however small. "You really think this is the one?"

"Black hair, skinny, medium height, protected by a Crofton. What do you think? It's the first sign we've seen of any of those damn brothers with a black-haired broad we can't identify. Gotta be the right girl."

Silence drew out the minutes in excruciating detail as the day's events replayed on a continuous nightmarish reel of missteps and miscommunication.

How many ex-military friends does the bitch have?

For the next half hour, each new scenario of explaining the mission's failure ended with a bullet in both their brains. The boss detested excuses and would consider the lackeys unworthy to draw breath on the same planet.

Silence during the lengthy ride permitted them each to fashion their report and detail a plan for success.

The skid and slide of the van's halt next to the familiar block building heralded the end of deliberations. Perhaps their boss still rode the high of locating the bitch and could overlook today's blunder.

Probably not.

The warehouse quartered all the tools of a wet worker's dream setup. Every conceivable torture device and *toys of encouragement* held places of honor in a room designed for such purpose. A place waiting for the newest arrival. Only she wasn't here. Frazier, however, *was* available.

As they exited the vehicle, desperation and motivation expedited Frazier's thoughts. "*Aha,* inspiration in the eleventh hour. If we can't get Marc or the bitch just yet, let's take one of his brothers. They're so damn close, it'll work. I know it." Tension eased as his plan took shape.

As luck would have it, their employer stood in the front foyer with the backlighting through the full glass casting an eerie shadow across his face. In general, shifting weight from foot to foot spelled trouble.

Dirk shook his head. "You've seen their homes, security is tight as hell."

Ten steps to the front door.

Boss man scowled, fists clenched at his sides. Always in a suit, he contrasted the filthy surroundings.

Frazier murmured, trying to keep his lip movement from giving away his plan. "Yeah, but not so much at Ambrosia. Doesn't matter which one we take, either would do. They'd all trade their lives for each other, but I'd love to have Conner. Once we have a Crofton man, we'll have the girl. We'll need Marc *and* the girl alive anyway, considering the little bitch may have told him everything."

Smiling in the face of his boss' frown wasn't the smartest move, but at least a plan was solid in Frazier's mind as he continued. "I've gone to Ambrosia several times, and it's damned posh." Frazier masked his expression in favor of a somber, more appropriate demeanor for the situation.

"Okay. Let's go Monday night, there's a masque party, according to what I dug up online while you were running like a little girl. Everybody's required to wear a mask. Looks like you'll get your chance to shine." Dirk waited to let Frazier pass through the door first. A whisper of stale air tainted by a slight copper odor wiped the smile from his face.

"Where is she? I have her room prepared but I don't see her." Flaring nostrils and cracking knuckles contradicted the pleasant smile on his employer's face.

"Don't have her yet, boss. But we'll fix that Monday night." Frazier stepped forward with care, balanced and ready to flee. He'd already seen how fast his boss could move. Three feet between them would be nothing in the blink of an eye.

"See that you do. Meantime, you can explain your incompetence in my office." Shiny, corfam shoes scuffed the concrete with the abrupt turn. Their staccato click echoed off the dirty, cinderblock hallway leading to the back of the building.

Few areas in the structure were accessible to the men of peon status. When they headed away from the interrogation room, Frazier breathed a sigh of relief.

Three locked doors along the hallway contained unknown materials or devices he hoped never to feel firsthand. Status quo suited him just fine. Even a sadist like himself had sense enough to avoid pissing off the top dog.

A warm, cinnamon scent tinged the air of the private office. Though his legs ached from standing outside all morning, Frazier stood before the oak executive desk, thankful that no plastic wrap lined the floor.

"Well?"

"He's got the girl. Damn dogs were everywhere. He trains 'em for protection."

"Let me guess. You shudder at the thought of shooting Fido?" The executive chair creaked under the boss' weight.

"No problem there, sir. They just alerted him before we could get close enough." Frazier noted the fingers drumming a faster tempo on the desk.

"Sebastian's bomb-building *friends* have made contact. They want Callie *and* Dani alive—and soon."

"You gonna turn the girls over to those foreign shits?" Frazier had no problems indulging in a little wet work but wanted no part in reshaping the country.

"Not hardly. Once I have the girls tucked away safely, I'll let the military deal with the outlanders. Do not fail me again, Frazier. Understand?"

"Yes, sir. How'd they find out about Dani? If you think I've said *anything*..." Frazier took a half step back, his entire body tense and waiting.

"No." With a dismissive wave of his hand, the pundit smiled before standing, signifying the meeting concluded. "I don't know how they found out. Maybe Sebastian ratted her out before Nate or one of his brothers silenced him."

"Which means the foreigners might not know Nate has Callie," Frazier surmised.

"Exactly, so don't screw this up. They're a half step behind us at every turn. They may have followed Marc's friend, Jake, to the meeting spot where you missed Dani."

"What about all these murders of girls who look like her?" Frazier wondered how much information his boss would share. Pushing wasn't usually a healthy move.

"Not the foreigners' work. This is someone else. A true psychopath is hunting her. Find him and bring him to me. I want to question him personally. Perhaps the black-haired puss is just as special as Callie. Who knows? Two for one would be nice. Now that Marc has our girl, he'll be working on who's killing the look-alikes, also. Make sure you find the serial killer before that damn PI does, got it?"

"Yes, sir. I'll have Marc by the end of tomorrow."

Chapter Eleven

Pine scent from the candle curled through his thoughts as Marc sat at the kitchen table pondering Dani's reluctance in baring her secrets. Exposure would take careful handling and attention to detail.

Two close calls back-to-back had proven the stalking bastards were well-connected and fast. He needed to crack her shell and delve through the hidden skeletons, sorting the ones to illuminate and decipher, suspending the others for later.

"Dani?" It seemed she'd resigned herself into his care—for the time being. A small bonus.

"*Hmm*?" Her fingers curled against her thigh, as if waiting for the sting of betrayal.

"I've spoken to my brothers, and we've planned a meeting in Ambrosia. Until then, they've set up roving patrols."

"Why not meet here?"

"Because I want you to meet Colonel Kenson, a man who can help us. I also want a degree of anonymity in case we decide to keep your identity unknown. The colonel is adept at obtaining information. We'd already planned a masque party at Ambrosia tonight, so the timing is perfect."

"I've always been curious about what it's like to go to a night club." A slight tremor rolled through her fingers.

"Dani, I realize you have little experience in so many things."

"So, teach me."

"This isn't good timing. We both need to stay alert."

"I've learned to enjoy life while I can, since there's no guarantee of second chances."

"I agree with you to a point, but survival is top priority. We need complete trust between us."

"But I do trust you."

"On certain levels, yes. I'm talking about the type where there're *no* secrets between us."

She'd given so much of herself, but he hungered for it all—her taste, her knowledge, the very breath from her lungs.

The blush climbing her cheeks broadcast insecurity, but her gaze drifted down, holding something back.

The fact she'd avoided a bad sexual experience, along with her open-mindedness, provided a clearer path to his goal with less minefields to navigate. It also gave him more room to manipulate, distasteful as that tack was.

We'll have one hell of a deep connection, if she doesn't reject me in the end.

A frown accompanied the tilt of his head. "It seems you often know a lot about what I'm thinking. Is there something you'd like to tell me?"

She didn't fully trust him. Hell, she'd spent so much time looking over her shoulder she probably didn't trust her own instincts. To form the connection he envisioned meant attaining his goal in stages.

She was a strong, young woman who stood up for what she believed was right, regardless of the consequences. It was time she felt better about herself while acknowledging *all* the parts of her unique character.

"You're a good, kind-hearted person, Dani."

"No. I'm a murderer."

The scar around her neck attested to her instance of complete vulnerability, something she'd obviously feared since. Compelling her to expose her secrets would leave her vulnerable again. Did she trust him that far?

"I'm here for you, Dani."

"It scares me. When I ran away, I swore I'd live by my own rules. Rules I'd made. I wouldn't survive if I witnessed another murder."

"Yet it's your basic nature to help others, like Callie."

"I got Jake, Daryl, and Franklin killed."

In the back of his mind, he knew this all came too fast, too smooth. Considering what she'd survived, how could she sit so casually next to him?

"No, you just lacked the necessary support, which you now have."

"Jake was ex-military, just like Franklin and Daryl."

"True, but I'm talking about a wider base. Hell, if the wrong people discover your connection to Callie, they'll hunt you to the ends of the earth." His whispered concern filled the room.

"Which is why I wanted a new ID."

"That's not a path to survival. And, we *still* have things to discuss."

Stroking his thumb over the back of her hand as he held it came natural. The past several hours had changed his life's course, just as he knew he'd eventually break down her barriers. Is that how Nate had felt when Callie ensnared his heart?

"I'll answer your questions. What do you want to know?"

"Everything about you. How you want your life to be." He'd save the question burning brightest in his mind until she'd settled down.

"I want to be normal. I want to go back to school, go shopping, walk my dog down the beach without looking over my shoulder."

"Since whoever is stalking us already knows where we are, yeah, we can go out if we take backup." Breathing in her soft scent lent a calm he'd never known. A man could get used to it. "The sooner we neutralize this threat, the better."

"I always thought hiding in plain sight was my best option."

"Might've been at that time, but now we're on a new path. With new players."

"Speaking of paths, I've no idea what to do next. I've saved some money and thought about getting my GED, going to college and vet school if I could get scholarships. But after all that's happened, I'd just love a simpler life."

"You can do anything you want, sweetheart. First, we need to sort out these other issues." Marc inhaled a slow breath before continuing.

"I need to call Dr. Carari and tell her I need some time off from work."

"She's a reasonable person. I don't see that as a problem. I'm curious... I couldn't find any records of your birth, although children's records are more difficult to obtain. I wasn't sure if your DMV records were accurate. Lots of fake driver's licenses out there, and I've never seen yours."

"You do background checks on all the girls you meet?"

"You're the first. You've intrigued me on so many levels. You're curious yet always aloof. I've been trying to crack your shell for months. I'm surprised you didn't avoid me altogether after what you've survived. You're amazing."

"I'm good at reading people, but it's hard to pick out someone's intentions when I'm nervous."

Odd turn of phrase. "Hmm, okay. Tell me about your life after the accident."

"When my folks died, I learned they'd adopted me, but I couldn't locate any records. Still can't find my biological parents. It's as if I just materialized out of thin air one day. No one wanted to claim me."

In spite of many painful experiences, she'd opened up, to some extent. It was a start. *Does she have siblings?*

Perhaps the thought was too painful to contemplate. For now, he wouldn't push it.

"Consider yourself claimed, sweetheart. And we *will* dig into this as soon as it's safe to do so." Despite their uncertain future, he wanted to be part of her life.

"I know you have more questions about my past."

"I won't pressure you now. We need to see you safe, but eventually we'll have no secrets between us. Understand?"

"I do."

The look in her eyes said otherwise.

Chapter Twelve

"I thought I'd have to wear, like, something slinky or low cut. Thanks for finding something with a high collar. I'll pay you back when it's safe to access my accounts."

Damn thongs look better than they feel.

"Consider your debt paid by helping Nate and Callie."

High heels tapped the walkway leading to Ambrosia as heat from Marc's fingers scorched her waist. She couldn't remember feeling so nervous.

The way he'd manipulated her to tear down her mental barriers, then taking control of her fear and reluctance was no accident. It wasn't even a demonstration of superiority. It was simply—Marc's way of solving problems.

"I love seeing you in a skirt. Don't get me wrong, you look fantastic in jeans, but you have great legs. Might as well show 'em off."

"Thank you." An elegant mask covered most of her face and indulged an alter ego she hadn't realized existed. Though nervous, she felt secure in his presence.

"The other items will arrive in a few days."

"Other items?" She swallowed hard. The relative safety of high-collared turtlenecks and baggy jeans sounded like a thing of the past.

His wolfish grin boded ill. "Yeah, I ordered a few things. I wouldn't be a proper host if I didn't see to my special guest's needs."

"Special guest?"

A parrot displays more sense.

"As I said, you have great legs, a great figure."

Oh, hell.

"*Hmm*. About three dozen vehicles present, bigger party than I expected. I thought Conner was being more selective with tonight's participants."

She gulped when he held the front door open.

The point of no return.

Stepping out of her old life and into this new and exciting adventure required all her courage despite who stood beside her. She checked her mask's placement one more time.

"You look fine. Everything's covered, sweetheart, especially that luscious hair. Interesting way of wrapping the braid."

Something niggled at the back of her thoughts like a catastrophe waiting to happen. Stopping just inside the door, she turned to Marc and pulled him close to whisper in his ear, "I can't think straight."

His light touch on her cheek just under the mask's edge sent tingling sensations down her neck while his breath in her ear raised goose bumps across her back.

"Don't worry. We've got this covered." He closed the distance until separated by mere heartbeats.

Damn, he did it again.

"So, what's Kenson like? Am I gonna want to kick his ass within minutes of meeting him?"

Marc smiled but shook his head. "Possibly. He's a no-nonsense kind of guy, but he's smart and crafty. Not one to be underestimated. Follow my lead, okay?"

She nodded.

Exposure to the public was one thing, but she'd not drop her defenses around the colonel. At least she could get a read on him and learn the extent of his knowledge concerning Callie without losing her anonymity.

"He's talking with Conner now. I'll meet with him in the office while you look around. Julien will introduce you to some folks. Then, I'll come and get you, and we'll all meet in my office. Afterward, Kenson will leave, and we're free to enjoy the evening."

If not for prior snooping, she wouldn't be prepared. There hadn't been so much change in her life since the *dark years.* Dozens of tables dotted the main hall's center space, surrounded by comfortable seating lining the walls.

Months ago, when she'd first met Marc and learned of his work, she never dreamed she'd end up in her current situation, however temporary.

Mingling with strangers wearing masks had never made her to-do list, despite her unusual ability. Knowing Marc and his brothers intended to keep an eye on her helped take the edge off her anxiety. Anonymity had its advantages as she again hid in plain sight.

"Hey, bro. Good to see you in one piece. Wanna fill me in on what the hell is going on?" Dark eyes matched the tone of Julien's voice. Though his words were for Marc, the narrowed gaze never left her mask, as if trying to discern some deep and dark mystery.

"Thanks for helping." Mutual forearm gripping marked their typical style of greeting.

"No problem. Wouldn't miss this meet and greet for the world. Been waiting for it." Though only his eyes were visible through Julien's mask, anyone could see the resemblance to his brother.

"Hello, Dani. Good disguise." His smile was knowing. Answering her unasked question, he continued, "Who else could retain my older brother's undivided attention?"

"Hi, it's nice to see you under better circumstances." With her nerves so taut and mouth so dry, she could manage nothing else.

Looking back at Marc, Julien nodded before continuing, "Colonel was here the moment we opened the doors, and chompin' at the bit at that." Nodding toward the offices, he said, "He's been prodding Conner at every turn."

Fisting her hands brought Marc's attention back to her. Expecting the extended hug, she leaned into his strength and wrapped her arms around his waist.

"Hey, sweetheart, you're fine here." Whispered words for her ears only.

"I know. I'm just nervous. I'm okay."

"I won't be more than a half hour. Julien will stay with you. Feel free to wander around, okay?"

"Thanks."

Her smile seemed to reassure him. After brushing his lips across the top of her head, Marc turned to Julien, his warning clear, "Not one hair, got it? Not. One. Hair."

"Man, ease up and take a laxative." Julien chuckled then turned to her. "Shall we make the rounds?"

Marc grumbled something about retribution as he pivoted and headed for the main offices toward the front of the building. As much as she wanted to call him back, she saw no justification.

Julien snorted before adding, "He's always been a bit overprotective."

Marc's diligence in ensuring her safety came at a time when the earth constantly shifted under her feet. She wouldn't complain about his proximity.

"First time in a club, Dani?" Julien respected her personal space and radiated confidence but also a curiosity which overloaded her senses.

"Kinda. I'm excited to be here."

"Let's circle the room and you can ask some of the questions I see swimming in your gaze."

"Marc said he doesn't keep secrets from his brothers, but I'm worried about dragging you all into this mess."

"Don't worry about it. We're family. Simple as that."

As Marc began to fill a void in her life she hadn't known existed, running became less of an option. She remembered family, and the near indestructible bond possible.

"So, how'd you meet Marc?" Julien kept his tone casual.

"Um, vet's office where I work." With every few steps, patrons stopped and spoke with Julien.

"My brother can frustrate the hell out of you at times. Tight-lipped as hell but a good man just the same."

"I'm worried about bringing more danger to you and your brothers," she reiterated. None of them understood the true nature of their enemy.

"Don't think twice about it. This is what we do. Besides, no one here knows who you are. It's why everyone's wearing a mask. Don't be nervous."

Dani shifted her weight. "How'd you know what I'm feeling?"

I like it better when the shoe is on the other foot.

"Body language tells a lot. Care for something to eat? There's a table loaded with all kinds of food and drink in the back." Part smirk, part sympathy, his expression didn't help her predicament.

"Yes. Actually, I'm gonna freshen up first, then grab a plate. Where's the restroom?"

I need a damn break.

"It's just inside the hallway leading to the back exit. I'll wait here for you. Okay?" Julien's lip biting and poorly suppressed smile would earn retribution on another day.

Heeled shoes tapped an even rhythm with each step toward the relative safety of the hallway. Regardless of the idea's merit, hiding until Marc was free equaled cowardice.

Another patron entered the rest room before her, holding the door.

Removing her mask and splashing cold water on her face gave Dani time to rein in the tension controlling her body's responses to the public setting.

Stone countertops supported her weight as her reflection in the wall-to-wall mirror depicted anxiety above excitement. Tonight was a golden opportunity, a chance to explore Kenson's thoughts while remaining hidden.

Around the time she hit puberty, psychic sensitivity announced its presence in the company of teenage boys with their raging hormones. Now, reversed circumstances meant she needed control over *her* body's responses.

After checking her lipstick in the mirror and replacing her mask, the other guest smiled and nodded before leaving.

Minutes passed. One deep breath followed another to relax her mind until she sensed others' thoughts from the main hall then turned them down a notch in her head.

An entire range of emotions—from excitement, jealousy, insecurity, and lust—devastated her equanimity.

"No wonder they have tons of food."

People need something to do with their mouths.

Well-oiled hinges refused the smallest squeak when she opened the door to the hallway. In the next instant, an intent so malicious and strong assaulted her senses as her steps froze. How'd she miss that viciousness earlier?

Because he's a newcomer.

It was a man, close by, with a gun.

He wanted to kill.

A deep breath. Dani briefly closed her eyes, denying one sense to improve the others. The invisible trail she followed led to the main hall. Picking up the elusive threads of his target required more effort. She stood still and concentrated.

He waited just outside the arched entrance by the food-laden table, watching and scheming.

"Death or capture, death is always preferred."

His feeling of security came from more than the mask worn. Confidence in his ability to assassinate without sound wrapped his mind in soothing psychotic comfort.

Ribbons of lust intertwined his thirst for bloodshed to form a twisted vision of debauchery and brutality involving a woman nearby. Natural inclinations weakened the restraints of his willpower, dividing his attention between brutally raping the young woman and blowing a hole in Marc's forehead.

Images of Marc and his brothers took shape in his thoughts. They were in uniform and clean-shaven, then older pictures taken after military discharge.

Height would make the brothers stand out regardless of concealed faces. The dirtball's extreme rage directed at Marc induced a shudder she couldn't suppress.

The bastard's compulsion to kill originated from more than duty. He shared a past with Marc, difficult to untangle. Something about a court martial concerning insubordination and assault charges ending with a dishonorable discharge.

Recognition of Julien formed a knot of disgust in his thoughts. To capture the youngest brother would be a pain in the ass. He wanted—no, *needed*—to kill Marc. That motivation kept him frozen like a wild jaguar waiting to strike. His gaze roamed the room for his objective.

Within minutes, two things would happen. Marc would come out of the office, and Julien would wonder why she was detained. Both would search for her.

Franklin died in his bid to free Callie in a poorly formulated plan. Daryl was murdered before her eyes during a clandestine meeting. Jake died soon after.

No one else need lose their life because of her. If she could distract the beast and create a scene, he'd forfeit the relative cloak of invisibility despite his mask. Every action had a consequence, but she'd pay it herself rather than see Marc die.

In contradiction to her trembling limbs, her resolve strengthened with each step toward the refreshment table despite the razor's edge of fear sliding through her chest.

Keeping her gaze on her target, Dani swallowed the fear, refusing to feed it or allow stark terror and panic to dictate a coward's retreat. A small perverse pleasure filled her with the knowledge of his impending shock and frustrated goal, something to sustain her.

Red wine would suit just fine. Crimson liquid swirled around the glass's rim when she snatched it from the table. Its chilling effect welcome as the fruity aroma curled around her nares. A small sip to give her courage and a final, deep breath calmed her raging nerves as she strode toward her mark. The alcohol would provide a nice contrast to his white shirt.

"Hey, I know you."

"Get lost, puss. I don't have time now, not even for a tasty morsel like you." His leer dismissed her, returning to scanning the room for Marc.

"You're the creep who dated my friend Cindy—and left her with bruises." Honing in on his thoughts while standing two feet away was easier than not spilling the contents of her glass over its shaking rim.

"Beat it. Now. Or I'll do the same to you." His voice remained low and controlled, unlike the images forming in his mind. He'd found his target.

Raising her voice, she continued, "No, damn it. You don't belong here. You're a bully and a creep." Several nearby guests turned their attention to them.

Good.

"She has a scar across her cheek after you hit her, prick."

Shock and rage warred for supremacy in his eyes when she splashed his mask and face with the contents of her glass. Red liquid dribbled down his pressed shirt and onto his black jeans.

"Bitch! You'll pay for that. This leather jacket is brand new." The growled threat stopped surrounding conversation.

Faster than she could react, he grabbed her wrist and squeezed to the point she feared broken bones. His words and her glass shattering on the floor secured the full attention of watching spectators.

Low murmurs got louder.

Her target swiveled his head, his ponytail flinging over his shoulder.

At least she'd diverted his attention. Thoughts of how she'd pay the price doubled the heartbeat pounding in her ears. She couldn't stop the cry escaping her mouth even as she tried to pull away from the crushing pain.

"Let go of me, dirtball." Dani tried to stomp his instep with her heel, but sturdy boots resisted her effort.

"Not hardly. Let's take this outside."

When she looked down, he held a knife to her belly.

"Smile pretty and ask me to go for a walk—or die where you stand."

Tears filled Dani's eyes as she managed a tremulous, "Let's step out back for a moment to discuss this. Shall we?"

Ponytail backed her up through the hallway and to the door. As she reached behind her to steady herself against the door's push bar, a voice cut through her panic.

"Hey. What's going on here? Dani? Where are you going?" Julien's puzzlement over her obvious, if not confusing behavior didn't preclude him from protecting her.

"This bitch comes up and throws her wine in my face. I don't even know who she is or who she's talking about. But she's agreed to discuss it calmly. Outside." The searing, icy blue of his gaze remolded to a coldness that defied human expression, as if they were no longer human but replaced by the mechanics of an otherworldly robot.

Leaning down, Ponytail whispered in her ear, "Come with me or watch me gut a Crofton."

The smile conveyed every bit of malice contained in his gaze.

"I-I'll be right back, Julien. We're just going to have a chat where it's a little quieter." She hadn't heard Julien's approach but felt his presence. If she didn't get Ponytail out fast enough, another death would suffocate her conscience.

"I think not." Menace vibrated in Julien's tone.

Subsequent events prevented her from defining the sequence.

Julien reached to grip Ponytail's shoulder and spin him around at the same time her assailant released his grip on her wrist and spun.

Dani sidestepped to attack from behind, but the prick's backswing knocked her against the wall. Her head thudded hard and knocked the breath from her lungs.

Darkness closed in from the periphery as she slid to the floor.

Pain roared from the back of her head down her spine, the throbbing in her wrist a small token of surfing back to consciousness.

Vague awareness of a stranger scooping her up and holding her close offered proof of life. She didn't care who he was or what he said. Low words of encouragement and praise combined with his enveloping arms insulated her in an environment of safety, one apart from psychopathic stalkers and deceitful lunatics. Shudders wrenched her frame from her near brush with death.

"Why won't anybody love me?" Her head dropped to his shoulder.

"Don't worry, young'un. I believe my little brother already might. I sure as hell have never seen him react like this." Warm breath on her forehead matched the comfort of the voice, both seeping in through the pores of her body, cocooning her in a world of safety.

"W-where are you taking me?"

Her foggy mind comprehended the jostling movement but couldn't discern more than dark hair as he skirted the edges of the main room. Hushed murmurs from guests couldn't be forced into meaning.

"You did well, Dani. Marc's proud of you. I'm gonna take you to his office where you can sit with him. By now, he's probably tearing the place apart."

"What?" Convulsive whimpers prevented her from saying more.

"He's already given Julien a shiner and tried to take the security team apart when they blocked him from going after the thug you encountered. I hope holding you will calm him down."

When her gaze finally focused on his eyes, compassion and confusion filled her mind. "Conner?" Wearing no mask, the eldest sibling resembled Marc in countenance and coloring, his features sharpening as her senses cleared.

"Dani, when I take you to him, he's going to ask you questions, like why you provoked a man twice your size." A long sigh born of struggling patience in dealing with younger siblings seemed to be a habit. "I'll try and buy you some time, but he's pretty worked up."

"I had to do it. That pervert came here to either kill Marc or kidnap one of his brothers. If I hadn't drawn attention to him, he would have shot Marc, regardless of others present or the consequences. He mumbled something about a court martial and dishonorable discharge."

Conner's step faltered. "What?" With a muttered curse, he hurried through a short hallway then turned to fit through an open door. Except for a large desk and sofa, most of the room passed in a blur. Two men stood on either side of Marc, releasing him when Conner entered.

Julien, standing near the door, let out a deep breath before mumbling, "Finally."

"You took off your masks." She could think of nothing else to say as another sob broke free.

Hushed voices had fallen silent with their approach. Marc's strained features smoothed as he took her from Conner and held her close. "I've got you now, Dani. We're gonna sit here on the sofa for a while and rest. Okay? Close your eyes. I assume you checked her for a concussion?"

"Yes," Conner replied. "But you'll need to make intermittent checks tonight."

"Marc—" Dani didn't know where to begin.

"No. Listen to me. Close your eyes." Whispered words brushed minty breath across her forehead. Softening his tone, he praised her for being strong and brave.

"Marc, she had good reason for creating the ruckus. She overheard that asshole's intentions to either kill you or kidnap one of us. You were his primary target."

"And I let the bastard get away? Shit." Julien slammed his chair against the wall.

Tension expanded and pressed against her mind. Conner's voice drifted through her thoughts as Marc enveloped her in a domain safe and sound. She couldn't deny the overwhelming tug into a dark and solemn oblivion devoid of fear and entangled alliances despite the sudden fast shuffling of large bodies leaving in haste.

"Damn, she saved a life tonight." Marc's soft voice declared awe and reverence. "What an independent spitfire. You do follow your own rules, don't you, sweetheart?"

Chapter Thirteen

Countless minutes passed before Marc checked her pupils again. "Appears normal." In reality, he knew her to be extraordinary.

"You expected otherwise?" She huffed her frustration, sitting beside Marc on the couch in his office. Low lighting battled with shadows on the opposite wall shading most of the room.

Marc reached out to stop her when she lifted the mask. He'd wrapped her in a blanket but remained close.

"Hey. Sorry, we should leave it on till after we've talked to Kenson. How are you feeling?" Guilt ate at each thought parading through his mind.

"Damn that prick. I'm all right, but would love to return the headache."

"I've got some aspirin for you. Here." He'd let her out of his sight for a few minutes and an asswipe had gotten to her.

"Tell me what you know about the bastard. Was it Hutson from the vet's office?"

"Marc, she said the guy mumbled something about a court martial. This could stem from your military days."

"What? That was years ago. Why wait until now to settle an old score? This is fucking strange," Marc grumbled.

"It wasn't Hutson. This guy was creepy, demented." Dani squirmed a little to get a better position.

"Hon, the only reason someone would come after me now is to get to you."

How in the hell did they know to come here, tonight? Marc struggled to make sense of it all. Nobody had tailed him to the club, and the prior connection between Callie and the foreigners had ended weeks prior.

"The bastard got away, but we'll track him. Security cameras should get his tag," Conner confirmed. "Though I'd bet my best bottle of scotch he came in a stolen vehicle."

"I've never heard that voice before. I was nervous and couldn't pick out much of his mumbled words. Sorry."

"It's all right, Dani. You did well, real well. I'm proud of you."

Seeing her rest allowed Marc to take a deep breath and release some of the tension building within his head.

Since first meeting her at Dr. Carari's office he'd endeavored to convince her to spend an evening out for dinner, dancing, anything, only to realize his ultimate goal of escorting her to his club. Then, this crap sidelined it all.

Someone wanted her more, for different reasons, and the body count didn't matter to the group intent on finding her.

Priorities.

Guilt from incompetence rode him hard, sinking claws into the recesses of his memories and excavating old wounds. He'd failed someone once before, as a teenager. Those disastrous consequences still haunted his nights.

"Hey, bro, mind if we come in?" Julien's tentative voice outside the door whispered through his consciousness.

"Yeah, yeah. I know. Come on in, might as well bring the colonel with you."

"Hey, we're all concerned. The bastard wanted you in his crosshairs. The idea of having to clean out your house would motivate anyone to keep you breathing." Conner's voice contained no fragment of Julien's hesitation.

The growing flood of light poured over the opposite wall as the door swung wide. Julien and Colonel Kenson followed the oldest Crofton in, each claiming a wingback chair while Conner leaned against his desk.

"Sorry, bro. Didn't see this coming. Either of you tell *anyone* your plans tonight?" Conner jumped right to the point in a low controlled voice.

"Not hardly."

Dani opened her eyes to meet each man's intent gaze. No doubt, she'd follow his lead in the conversation, but the thought of her slipping and the colonel ferreting out the secret he suspected she hid wasn't a chance he'd take.

"Look at me, sweetheart." Taking her chin between thumb and forefinger, he raised her face to meet his gaze head on and prayed her pain-filled mind would understand his words. "Did you tell anyone you were coming here tonight?"

I don't want the colonel knowing who you are yet.

Maintaining a firm pressure on her chin denied her the ability to nod or shake her head.

The corners of her mouth lifted slightly. "I haven't talked to anyone but you and your brothers since Sunday morning."

Marc nodded his approval.

"Hello, Dani. I'm Colonel Kenson. Sorry you've had such a rough night. I have an extra soda here if you'd like one." Kenson stood and ambled over to hand her a drink.

A rugged-looking man with suspicious deep-set eyes, he appeared to take in everything around him while cutting through any lie or deception.

Before she could move, Marc accepted the can and set it on the coffee table beside him and nodded his thanks.

"Hello, Colonel. Thank you, but I have a bit of a headache. I think I'll wait a bit."

As Kenson walked back to his chair, Marc flashed Conner and Julien a hand signal.

"No DNA, no handwriting samples either, Colonel." Protective irritation harshened Marc's voice more than he'd intended.

"No harm, no foul. Even if she is who I believe her to be, she's done this country a tremendous favor. I'd thank her for her service, not arrest her." Kenson rested his right ankle on his left knee, a practiced nonchalance.

"What makes you so trustworthy," Dani challenged.

"Experience and history." Kenson accepted the question in stride. "Ask any of these men here. They've all worked for me."

"Which doesn't answer the question of why you'd trust *me.*"

Kenson leaned forward to meet her stare with one of his own. "Young lady, *if* you're a friend to Callie, you're certainly a friend of mine and worth protecting. Do you think this guy tonight was after Nate's girl?" The colonel frowned before murmuring. "I should double Callie's detail while assigning one to you, too, Marc."

Redirection to their current problem would facilitate the conversation and get the colonel out of their hair sooner. Dani's challenging his ex-boss didn't faze him in the least. "Callie's fine, Colonel. And if the dirtball was after her tonight, he wouldn't have talked about nailing me."

Please don't say anything else, Dani. Just nod when appropriate and don't offer any information not requested.

Marc stroked the sides of her face, willing her to stay calm.

"Marc, think this through," Julien spoke in the colonel's direction. "They've been after Callie and know Nate has her stashed somewhere. What better way to draw her out than to go after his brothers?"

"All right, all right." Kenson stood once again. Pinched lips and an index finger tapping the seam of his jeans portrayed his frustration. "You boys have always stood united, not letting anyone inside your inner circle." Looking again at Dani, he added, "Dani, hear this. You are one lucky girl. If there is *ever* anything you'd like to discuss with me, anything at all, at any hour, I'm all yours. And unless you're some kind of mass murderer who builds atomic bombs, I will never lock you away for your own protection. I'm not like those Think Tank bastards."

Conner snorted. "Good luck with that, sir. So, you're going to assign a detail to Marc?"

"Yeah, even though I realize you all aren't giving me the whole picture. I'm a little confused as to why they'd want Marc dead instead of Nate as a hostage."

"Maybe it has nothing to do with Dani or Callie. Maybe this stems from one of our PI cases or Marc's time in the military." Julien shrugged a shoulder, his blatant attempt at misdirection not affecting the colonel's scowl.

"Yeah, and I'm riding a purple elephant home. They'll use any of you to get to Nate and Callie. You'd do well to remember that." Kenson sighed. "I'll have three men here within the hour, Marc. They'll look after you two until we figure this out. Any threat remotely connected to Nate's girl, I take seriously." Looking at Conner, Kenson continued, "Son, you worked with Lightning before you left the unit."

"Yes, sir. I did. Lightning, Byte, and Wire. Triple threat to all the ladies," Conner replied.

Marc ground his teeth. "Sir—" With his older brother's subtle warning referencing Dani, Marc had no intention of letting three unknowns into their lives.

"Forget it, Marc. I'm not taking chances. And I'm not as clueless as you believe." Colonel Kenson frowned at Dani.

"Sir, I've never thought of you as clueless. Ever. Moreover, you've always been one to hold your secrets close. If history is repeating itself, there's a lot *you're* not telling *us*."

"Ditto, Marc. Just keep our girl safe. If she's half as special as Callie, there'll be lots of people *asking* her to work for them. At any cost."

"Understood. Thanks for the backup, Colonel," Marc said as he pushed to his feet.

"Yeah, call me when you feel like sharing secrets." Colonel Kenson picked an imaginary piece of lint from his jeans, a stalling tactic.

When the colonel reached for Dani's hand, Marc just shook his head.

"Fine, but I want a detailed report when this is over, guys. Gonna have a nice shiner, Julien." The colonel's grumble spoke volumes as he walked out the door.

Marc sighed at the thought of dodging another bullet. "That went well."

"Hey, Marc, tell us how Darius' trial went. Sorry we missed it." Conner flashed another hand signal as he and Julien inspected the seat vacated by the colonel.

"Well, he *was* doing great till he took off after that bastard who shot him." Marc held his finger to his lips as a silent message for Dani to remain quiet.

They're looking for bugs the colonel has no doubt, placed.

Dani glanced at him, the question in her eyes clear. He'd explain how the colonel generally worked when they got home.

A quiet snap and Conner's low chuckle let them know their ex-boss hadn't changed. "Hey, Dani, how about some of that soda?"

After popping the top and holding the can for her to take a sip, Marc handed the drink to his oldest brother. Conner sauntered over to display the small disc pulled from the cushion's underside. Acid from the soda assured its destruction with the liquid filling its electrical compartment.

"Guess that's that. Now, down to business. Lightning and his team will be here soon. How did that asshole track Dani from the vet to the trial, then here, yet not know *who* she was tonight? Unless we have different players?" Conner reached for Dani's mask, then hesitated.

"I got it." Dani removed her cover and set it on the table beside her. "I'm not helpless."

"You've proven that in spades." Looking at Dani, Conner continued, "Welcome to the family."

"Thanks." Dani pursed her lips before thinking aloud. "Ray works for an organization. He was recruited in Maryland and sent to Minnesota."

"Name of the organization?" Conner stilled, waiting.

"Don't know. He brought his dog into the vet's office, making calls and acting weird. I found out about Callie, then dug up what I could."

"Name of the asshole in charge?" Conner asked.

"Holland Freeman."

"And the depth of your snooping?" Julien sat beside them, zeroing in on her face.

"I, uh, got into his house once, but was too afraid to go back after he almost caught me. All I got was some information on Ray, Callie, Franklin, and the institution."

"Seems spotty. That's when you contacted Franklin?" Conner crossed his arms over his chest, evaluating her honesty.

"It's all I could remember. I lost my phone somewhere on his property."

"All right. At least we have a place to start," Conner sat at the desk and ripped a post-it note off to take notes.

"No! He's added all kinds of security since then. He must've known someone was in his house."

"*Shhh*, Dani. You're okay." Marc scowled at his brothers. "Enough for now."

"No, Marc. We need to get a handle on this." Speaking again to Dani, Conner asked, "How long ago? Maybe he already had outdoor security cameras. Maybe he's the one searching for you."

"It was right before I contacted Daryl, and Callie escaped. As for the other, no. There were no cameras outside when I first went there."

"This can wait." Marc reaffirmed. "Dani, when the team gets here, they'll ask all kinds of questions. Follow our lead, okay? Obviously, the colonel is going to stress your safety since he knows you're a part of this whole puzzle, even if he hasn't fit the pieces together."

The directness of her gaze lacked recriminations concerning her earlier near-abduction. She was a rare young woman with strength of conviction and determination.

"Okay, Conner, Julien, this bastard obviously wants Dani pretty bad and me dead. Since this started at her work, how about we divide and conquer, search the vet's office and her cottage."

Conner continued Marc's line of thinking as only close-knit brothers could do. "I'll take the office, Julien, you take the house. I'll call Nate and give him a sitrep since we need everybody on the same page. I assume you'll be taking her out of town."

"Yes. But not till tomorrow. We need more information so we don't lead the worthless pieces of shit to our destination." Marc looked to Julien.

"Got it. I'll fetch her a bag after making sure her house isn't bugged." Julien smiled in the face of Dani's glare.

"Julien, don't antagonize. She's dealing with enough." Marc's groan elicited a chuckle from his siblings before continuing, "She doesn't want a stranger snooping among her private things."

"Hey, if the place is bugged, you want me to take care of them, right? Gotta search to find 'em." Julien's smile bared his delight in the covert needling.

Marc grumbled in the face of his brother's smug certainty. He'd like nothing more than to beat the shit out of someone. Anyone would do in a pinch.

"I'll bet you guys fought like cats and dogs when you were kids but united to stand against any outsider." Her tone held a longing difficult to ignore.

"You don't have siblings?" Compassion filled Julien's tone.

"Actually, I don't know. I have no information on my past." She couldn't hold Julien's gaze. "If I do, they may be in hiding, like me."

"We'll add that to our list of things to find out." Marc considered her situation. A realization sparked to life. If her siblings were as exceptional as he was certain Dani was, they would also be hunted.

"Um, when my parents died and I found out I was adopted, they'd left papers saying I would learn everything when I *came of age.*" This time, she met Marc's gaze to show the truth in her own. "I don't know where or how the disconnect occurred, but I've never learned anymore."

"What else did you hear that bastard say earlier?" Julien asked, all business once again.

"He wanted a piece of my hair with the root."

"How'd you know that, Dani? Kind of an odd souvenir." Conner's speculative look prompted her squirm.

"Um, well he reached for my hair and said he wanted a sample." Dani looked away from Conner's silent probing.

"Anything else, Dani?" Marc found his position behind the eight ball tiring. One day, things would add up, until then, he'd gather facts for assimilation.

"I think he works for Ray."

"What? Way to bury the lead. What makes you say that?" All kinds of mental alarms sent Marc's mind racing and his hands fisted at his sides. Any connection to Ray spelled more trouble if the traitor again contacted his foreign counterparts.

Her deceptive smile was not encouraging. "He said something about Ray and money, but I didn't catch it all."

"Have you seen him before tonight?" Marc asked.

"I think he's Ray's driver, bodyguard, or whatever. Obviously, Ray hasn't identified me if he's still searching and going after one of you." Her words elicited grumbles from each man present.

Conner's whistle mirrored Marc's frustration.

"Okay, sweetheart, I'd say it's time to bring my brothers in on the rest. They can help us with the Tuckers. This is too much of a tangled mess to separate."

She remained mute while her gaze slid to each of his brothers as if gauging their trustworthiness. A quick nod signaled her obvious acceptance and eased tensions. The following discussion detailed events back to Tucker's murders, exchanging and examining information and opinions.

A light knock on the closed door ended their exchange.

Dani breathed in a sharp inhale as her gaze swung in that direction.

"What is it, Dani?" Marc started to reach for his pistol in his ankle holster. "Damn, three assaults in two days. What's next?"

Julien stood and edged toward the door while Conner reached inside Marc's desk and retrieved the Glock stored in the upper, right drawer.

"We got your back and trust your girl's instincts," Julien murmured as he stepped to the side before opening the door, giving Conner a clear shot if needed.

A split-second of silence. No one moved.

"Hey, Conner. Ease up on the caffeine. It's just me," Hutson's voice held more amusement than alarm.

Springs protested as Marc leapt to his feet. Three strides brought him face-to-face with the dirtball. "Fucker, you shot my dog." Marc's chokehold was broken from behind when Conner yanked him back.

"Hey, man. Darius saved my life." Hutson stepped back and adjusted his shirt.

"Marc, he's on our side. Ease up." Conner's gun remaining trained on the intruder belied his words.

"Marc. I. Didn't. Shoot. Darius." Hutson drew his monotone out, annunciating each word.

"Then, who did?" Marc's hands fisted, the need to choke the bastard strong until Dani's cry penetrated his angry haze.

"Please don't hurt him, Marc." Her frown in Hutson's direction spoke of concentration before transforming into a shy smile.

"What? What in hell's going on?" Once again, Marc stood in the dark.

"Um, well, I was just thinking. If he—"

"No, Dani. Don't say anything. I know your instincts are good, but I don't trust this clown." Moving to stand in front of Dani, Marc used his body to block Hutson's view of her.

"Now, that's our girl. She knows who to trust. I'll bet she's every bit as special as—" Hutson's next words failed to emerge with Marc's solid punch to his jaw.

Chapter Fourteen

"She's not *our* girl, asshole. Ask her out again, and I'll take your head off."

"Marc! No. This is Lightning. He worked with my unit under the colonel." Conner struggled to pull Marc back again. "I thought you'd fingered him for a traitor, not competition."

Turning to Lightning, Conner added. "Sorry, man, we're more careful after the colonel's second in command tried to bushwhack us not long ago."

"So I heard. However, you know *I'm* not like that." Lightning's rumbled answer resembled a threat.

"Dani?" Marc turned to see her standing, studying the newcomer.

"You take direction from a wisp of a girl?" Lightning's gaze turned to Dani with a new respect in his eyes. "You really are special like Callie, aren't you? Damn though if anyone will give us the full scoop on Nate's girl."

"Never mind that, dipshit. It's above your pay grade." Unable to offer an apology, Marc crossed his arms over his chest.

"Just like your brothers." Lightning's chortle declared he enjoyed how much his statement rankled.

"You're pushing it, dickweed." The audible grinding of Marc's teeth preceded Dani's palm reaching to cup his face.

"It's all right, Marc. He's not here to hurt me." Dani's voice, so cautious at times, radiated confidence.

"We'll talk when we get home, Dani." Marc didn't want her inadvertently giving away the secrets she'd held tight.

"Damn. Second time I've been a day late and dollar short. Didn't mean to step on your toes. Conner once said you're a possessive bastard. I think he underestimated you." Lightning rubbed his jaw as he worked it side-to-side.

"Now that introductions are out of the way..." Julien's attempt at placating stemmed from years of practice. "As we all understand the score, I'm sure we can get along for the common goal of everyone's well-being."

"He'll have to explain how and why he was at her workplace coming onto her before I believe he's not guilty of colluding with the enemy." Marc's point elicited curious frowns from his brothers.

"Listen, the colonel told me to keep an eye on her. Women matching her description have been disappearing around the area for the past couple months. That's all I know." Lightning held his hands up in a silent gesture of surrender.

"Damn Colonel Kenson, always holding out. How many other girls is he watching, and why is the military involved anyway?"

"Dunno. Something about a crime scene is all he'd say."

Looking at his brothers, Conner motioned them to sit. "Let's catch *Lightning* up to speed."

"If you're not guilty, why'd you run from me at the trial?"

"You didn't see the suit watching you? He was standing in front and slightly to the side of me." Lightning ran his fingers through his close-cropped blond hair.

"When your dog started the ruckus, the guy bolted. I was *chasing* him, not running *from* you. When he got to the parking lot and pulled a gun, I was in the open and dropped. Darius continued and almost had him, but the creep was too fast and got off a shot. I wasn't sure at first whether he'd shoot the dog or me, but Darius was closing fast. Afterward, the bastard got away."

"So, why's the colonel concerning himself with a civilian serial killer?" Marc still didn't like the newest member, which had everything to do with the way he'd talked to and eyed Dani as a Christmas present ready to be unwrapped.

"Hey, lighten up. I'm just here to serve and protect. You'll have to take that up with the colonel."

Information exchange among similarly trained men followed in abbreviated jargon common to all. Details of Lightning's team and experiences echoed in his mind as he recalled drills and missions that left a black void, begging for a human connection to fill them. Which was why he eyed Dani like a sweet confection.

"Marc, can we go home now?" Dani rubbed her brow and turned toward the door.

"Sure, sweetheart, in just a minute."

The many facets of her personality enthralled him, from the image of a small waif cocooned in a blanket, lost and alone, to the determined young woman who'd face a deranged killer to protect a friend. Little would the others suspect her strength and endurance.

"Marc, I'll get straight with Lightning, Byte, and Wire on patrols." Nodding toward Dani, Conner added, "Looks like she's had enough. Get her home, and we'll shore up our plan tomorrow. Or, if you'd rather—"

"No. I don't want to involve anyone else's home, and I don't want to go to the cabin until I know we're clear."

Conner and Lightning checked the vehicles for trackers before Marc escorted his tenacious bundle out to the SUV. She may well have saved his life, again.

The story of her hearing her assailant talking to himself didn't wash. The guy was smart enough to get in undetected and get out unscathed. Psychopath or not, he'd maintained his composure, not the mark of carelessness, either here or at a vet's office.

Before starting the engine, Marc tucked the blanket under her chin. "We'll be home soon."

"Thanks."

"No heavy conversations. Tonight is about getting you comfortable. Okay?"

"I owe you. A lot."

Not even close, Dani.

Soon it wouldn't matter. He'd make sure she never felt the need to keep score.

Winding his way along the lonely highway, he thought about the evening's events. Gauging the lights in his rearview, Lightning kept an even distance behind them while Byte's SUV paced them from the front.

"You don't know the team that's helping us now?"

"No, Conner worked with and vouches for them all. I trust his judgment until given a reason otherwise."

Except the deviled look in Lightning's eyes.

The driveway was wide enough to accommodate two vehicles side by side. Next to his parked truck, Byte stood while another man waited at his front door. Grinding his teeth, Marc reminded himself of the informal invasion's necessity and that Conner had verified their legitimacy.

Inside, both dogs' intruder's bark continued, threatening anyone to enter their domain.

"You like your privacy, just like me." The soft reassurance of Dani's fingers wrapping around his clenched fist brought him back to the present.

Turning his wrist, he held her small hand in his, the disparity in their sizes disproportionate to their commitment of protecting each other.

"Yeah, I guess I do. Let's get you inside." Pocketing his keys, he decided a few words to the team would go a long way. "Dani, I'm gonna get you settled before I have a talk with the guys."

She cringed with the overhead light when he opened his door. Again, he cursed the thug in Ambrosia for hurting her and interfering with the progress they'd made. Time would tell the extent of the damage. "Dani, that bastard in Ambrosia—"

"I know. He wasn't normal. He wasn't like you."

"How could you tell when you know so little about me?"

"Because I *do* know you."

Maybe they had a chance, after all. Cool air brushed his cheeks and swept away doubt. He'd always had a knack for figuring out a person's situation and moods based on verbal and nonverbal cues.

Still, Dani continued to defy the logical progression of healing in some ways, jumping forward by leaps and bounds as if by innate understanding. Always one step ahead of him, not in the way of a genius, just the fact she seemed to know his moves before he made them.

However, she hadn't asked to use his computer, odd for someone reported to be so adept. He decided to avoid confrontation and let time reveal her secrets.

So small and fragile, she rivaled a castaway with enormous courage.

Byte and Wire stood on the porch waiting while Lightning climbed the steps behind him.

"Hey, Marc. Conner told me to secure your house before you got home. Hearing about you and your dogs, I figured I'd wait out here. Hell, if anyone got in there, they wouldn't be alive by now." Respectful and calm, Wire's gaze roamed the perimeter before settling once again on Dani. "Hi. Nice to meet you. You can call me Wire." A thick mustache covered the upper lip of a handsome face with cool gray eyes.

Dani nodded and accepted the hand held out in greeting.

"Conner's told me a bit about you all. I appreciate the help." Marc respected Wire's polite if formal tone.

"No problem. The colonel said this might turn into an offer of a long-term gig." He eyed Dani with curiosity, his gaze lacking the hunger emanating from Lightning.

"Give me a minute and we'll discuss ground rules. Fridge is stocked, so help yourself. I'll join you shortly."

Marc unlocked the door after giving both shepherds clipped commands. Each fell silent but watched the three new visitors enter. The men threw wary glances in the canines' direction.

Pete padded beside Marc as he guided Dani through the hallway.

"Dani—"

"I feel like I should be a part of further discussions, as a courtesy."

"It can wait till tomorrow. They'll understand."

She smiled as he pushed the spare bedroom door open. Sad that the expression didn't reach her eyes, as if doubt suddenly assaulted her.

Pete continued to pad along beside them, nudging her thigh.

"Take some time to rest. I'll check on you in a few minutes."

Pete hopped on the bed, no doubt he'd sleep with his head on her stomach with his tail thumping her legs.

Marc's thoughts revolved around the enigma of Dani as he strode back toward the kitchen. All three men had taken him at his word. Containers of leftovers covered the table. Shopping would be on someone's to-do list tomorrow.

"Thanks for your help tonight, guys. I assume you've already discussed the details Kenson gave you?" He joined the others at the large kitchen table.

"Yeah. Two out, one in. Since Byte has a tender hide, we figured he'd be your inside man tonight. 'Sides, he can start digging for digital information." Lightning's assumption and no-nonsense demeanor expedited the assignment.

"Okay, sounds good. Let me fill you in on what I suspect so far. There's a couple from the past who might've caught up with us. Collin Tucker has a wife and two sons, all killers, extortionists, and semi-local as of a few years ago. Also, there's the Think Tank administrator, Ray McMillin, who might be wanting to use me or mine to get to Callie."

"I'd already started digging into Ray per the colonel's request." Byte's disgust translated into tight expressions in Wire and Lightning. "In the corporation's business accounts, there's a farm outside Hensington, about twenty miles from here. We were planning on checking it out tonight, but the colonel put a nix on it, doesn't want us crossing waters. He's sending another team and keeping us tight with you and Dani."

"Damn, he moves fast." Marc approved of the older man's diligence if not his methods. Further details put everyone on the same page.

"I've never seen Kenson so uptight about anything." Methodical twisting of copper strands between Wire's fingers appeared more of a habit than distraction. His curious gaze drifted around the room before returning to Byte, who swiveled his screen to show an aerial view of farmland.

"All right. I'm going to check on Dani." The ease and expediency in which they'd covered the details promised a good start.

"Cool. But, Marc, just so you know, I don't wear ear plugs when I'm working... just saying." Byte covered his cough as tiny crinkles around his eyes coincided with his laughter.

"Right. Thanks for the tip, and not necessary. I doubt the scumbag from earlier will be back tonight, but stay alert." Turning to his dog, he continued, "Darius, *bravy*. Good dog. You keep watch tonight." With a final pat on the shepherd's head, Marc turned his thoughts to the biggest puzzle of his life.

Dani's circumstances had him wrapped in equal amounts of awe, respect, confusion, and infatuation. When he'd first seen the quiet, unassuming beauty in the vet's office months ago, intrigue gnawed at his mind and gut, urging him to expose more of her layers.

Now that he'd learned of her connection with Callie and put some pieces together, he suspected what vital secret she still held tight.

We all keep secrets.

Hers, however, could result in the capture or death of others.

It was time to arrange another distraction and exercise in trust.

Pete perked his ears when he inched the door open, the dim hall light spilling over her bed. She must've gotten up since the bathroom light was on, but now lay quiet and still under the covers.

"Hey, everything all right out there?"

A thin, elongated beam of light fell across the middle of the mattress. The steady rise and fall of her quiet respirations indicated a relaxed state, the only movement her hand stroking Pete's head.

"Yep. Glad you're still awake."

"Just thinking about tonight." A slight tremor infused her voice.

Holding up several items he'd brought, he softened his tone. "If you'd like, I'll rub the knots out of your back. No strings attached. I brought a bottle of water and some aspirin for you."

"That would be wonderful."

The bed dipped as she curled up to take the pills. Once rolled onto her stomach, she kept her head faced his way.

He retrieved a bottle of scented lotion from the nightstand drawer. "Before you ask, this came with a house-warming gift basket. Never been opened." Marc popped the seal and waited for her nod of approval.

Her back remained tight for the first five minutes, until he used his strength to probe and release each knot, adjusting his touch to caress the surface. "How's the shoulder?"

"Fine."

"I'm sorry, Dani. There's no excuse for this happening to you."

Roll a little to your right side so I have better access to your neck.

Dani turned to face him.

"Why'd you move?"

She hesitated before speaking. "Um, you stopped. I figured you were done."

"Almost."

It took twenty minutes longer before she relaxed to a boneless mass, pliable and calm. A few little moans escaped as he'd worked each muscle group. Her eyes drifted closed.

Why'd you do it, Dani? Why risk your life for us?

His thoughts kept circling that mystery, like a wound that festered. He couldn't let it go.

"I care about you and what happens to your brothers, plus I need to protect Callie. She's special and deserves to be free."

Marc froze at the very specific answer to the question he'd just considered asking. It was more than intuition, but confrontation would shut her down.

"I care about you, too."

"Maybe you care so much because we share a connection?"

A sudden coughing fit tightened every muscle along her spine as she curled on her side, away from him. When she'd caught her breath, he gently repositioned her and found steel in place of muscles.

Thirty minutes later, she remained just as tense. He continued to praise her courage and strength, yet failed to loosen her up.

"It's all right, Dani. You're safe here, regardless of anything else." Realizing he could do no more tonight, Marc turned off the light and stood.

"Want to talk for a while?" Her tone was steady if contemplative.

"Sure." This time he sat in the chair beside her bed, letting her pick the topic to see where her thoughts wandered. Not surprising, she talked about family, her quest involving both Marc and his brothers, then recollections of her childhood and dreams of a family of her own.

After all she'd survived, she held precious memories of her adoptive parents, loving and loved in return. It was two hours later before her soft breaths evened out in sleep.

The puzzle of Dani kept him awake much longer.

Chapter Fifteen

Pre-dawn light gave form and life to misty fog and shadows lingering beyond the ferns and young saplings to set a macabre scene worthy of the best horror movie. Being called out to a secluded area usually didn't end well.

Marc had expected to hear from the colonel, just not so soon, and not summoned to a murder scene deep in the forest. The fact that local PD and military were both on site boded ill since the colonel had never fancied inter-agency cooperation.

Two uniformed officers stood by their cruisers parked on the grass shoulder with red and blue lights flashing on the low-profile bars. "Hey, Marc, ma'am, head straight in. Captain's waiting for you. Thanks for coming and bringing Pete."

Marc shook the officer's hand, trying to remember the new recruit's name and came up empty. "No problem. It's good to help."

A glance down the dirt road bisecting the thick wooded land rolling gently into the adjacent mountains signaled it a perfect place to dump a body. The narrow ditch separating rutted grass shoulder from forest held water from the previous night's rain. Gravity willed it toward the natural reservoir farther south.

Marc hopped over the narrow ditch then offered his hand to Dani.

Just inside the shadowed forest, she halted. "Marc, I'm gonna take my jacket back to the SUV. It's warm enough I don't need it."

"Hold on, let's leave it with the guys there and snag it on our way back." Marc backtracked and handed the jacket to the sergeant. "Hey, John. You mind holding onto this till we get back?"

"No problem. How's Darius?" Metal pins ground against their hinges as the older officer opened the door and placed the jacket on the cruiser's front seat.

"Healing, he'll be all right in a few weeks. Can't wait to catch the piece of shit who shot him."

Once again, Marc questioned his sanity for bringing Dani to a crime scene, even if it was the lesser of two evils. Since last night's fiasco, he didn't trust her safety to anyone else.

Forensic techs had already processed the murder scene, the girl's body removed before he and his brothers were called to consult.

Maybe Dani would rather stay here with Officer Collins.

Though he'd offer for her comfort, he didn't want her out of his sight.

"I recognize that look, but I'm coming with you." Once again, Dani's determination took a front seat.

The prior night's scene flashed through Marc's mind with her answering his unspoken thoughts. The strong likelihood of her hiding such an extraordinary ability turned over in his mind once again.

He'd test his theory at every turn to see where and how many times she slipped. Where did intuition give way to psychic ability? The word psychic fell short in description. Hell, he couldn't even categorize what he suspected.

Dani's stumble over thick weeds necessitated several quick steps to escape her toppling onto dead leaves and low budding briars. A blush climbed her cheeks. "Sorry, I'm a bit of a klutz."

"Uh-huh. Be careful, hon."

Together, they picked their path over fallen logs, around tangled briars, and broken limbs on the deer path to the edge of a moderate-sized meadow where Captain Fuller conferred with two detectives.

Each nodded with their passing.

Fuller's double take of Dani caught his detectives' notice. His conversation ceased with the dropping of his jaw.

Colonel Kenson's conversation also stopped as Marc neared the middle of the clearing. The shrewd mind, always at work, went into higher gear judging by his narrowed eyes and smile that didn't reach his eyes.

Pete whined and perked his ears, sidling closer to Dani and accepting her hand on his head with a big doggy grin.

Marc's oldest brother, Conner, frowned as he strode to greet them.

"You didn't tell me the colonel was here." Marc hesitated, glancing at Dani in hopes she remained calm enough to understand his nonverbal.

Frowning, he tilted his head fractionally toward Colonel Kenson then with a slight shake of his head, mouthed the words, *Stay away from him.*

Marc had never doubted his ex-commander's sincerity or loyalty, but Dani's hesitation gave him pause. She had enough to deal with, sans anxiety over Kenson's probing questions. And question her he would, any chance he got.

Her near imperceptible nod allowed him a tense, slow breath. After talking into the wee hours last night, it felt like they'd stayed on the same page and in a state of constant sync. Despite that, her fear of all things military moderated his step, his first priority being her security, physical and psychological. Losing Dani by any means was not an option.

"I like to help out when I can." Kenson drew near and offered Dani a warm smile along with a handshake.

Her chin lifted and eyes narrowed. Kenson would recognize the firming of her resolve.

With Kenon's back to Conner, he wouldn't see the flashed hand signal referencing caution. Conner stepped closer and greeted his younger brother. "About time you got your lazy ass out of bed, kiddo." Anything less than a soft admonishment wouldn't have been a true greeting.

Kenson winked at Dani. "Damn, Marc. You sure know how to court a woman. Bring her to a crime scene after a night of hell. Can't wait to see what's next."

Scrubbing a hand over his jaw garbled Marc's retort.

Pete's sudden attention interrupted the tense exchange. Captain Fuller and one of the detectives closed the distance.

"Marc, thanks for lending us a hand. Our newest dog is doing well but not finished training, and this case is too big to take chances." Fuller's quiet, authoritative voice curbed other conversations in lieu of hearing what he had to say. Tall and broad, his years of city homicide experience were just what the town needed. Like his stride, his gaze held purpose.

"No problem, Pete's ready to work." Training canines pulled Marc together years ago after his world had fallen apart. Déjà vu struck him between the eyes when events of the past aligned with current circumstances.

Though too young and untrained at the time, Marc had offered his protection to a girl running from her father—and failed. Inexperience and lack of knowledge concerning various legal systems defeated his courage and honor. He hadn't understood the treacherous ways deviants could devise to hurt others.

Special Forces training then entering private investigations prepared him for a variety of circumstances. Yet today, he felt out of his element.

Psychos always find new and depraved methods to surprise you.

He prayed they caught the degenerate killer before another woman was murdered and left like garbage.

Did this one look like Dani, too?

Marc kept his gaze on the colonel while the captain shook first Conner's hand, then his own. Like Kenson, the lead detective studied Dani, his narrowed gaze warned of a mind that could spin infinite threads of a web to snare the unwary.

"Dani. It's nice to see you. I'm sorry you got dragged all the way out here, if you'd like to wait in my car where it's more comfortable, one of my men can escort you." The colonel's small chuckle with Marc's immediate refusal held a familiar if mischievous note.

Dani raised her chin. "Thanks, but I'm fine, Colonel. I'm a lot sturdier than you think."

"What do you have as far as a scenting object? And why is the military involved?" In his mind's eye, Marc saw his ex-boss transforming liquid silk into solid form. Anchor threads attaching to solid points bridged fibers between himself and Conner, with Dani caught fast in the spiral.

The corner of Fuller's mouth twitched as he contemplated his military counterpart. "I have a piece of cloth we think belongs to the perp. Hell, the colonel got here before us. Said we could tap into his resources if we'd cooperate. Isn't that a first?"

Shaking his head, Fuller led them to the small area where something had recently lain. Dried crimson spatters dotted the dead leaves and broken weedy grass. "This is where they dumped her body."

"Who found her?" Marc studied Fuller's expression and body language.

"Couple of hikers," the captain replied.

Colonel Kenson had kept pace, studying Dani with intent.

"Conner, do you mind—" Marc began.

A glimmer of stubbornness rose in Dani's expression before disappearing behind her fall of hair when she turned to Conner. Taking his hand, she let Marc's older brother draw her away from the cluster of investigators who'd searched the area for evidence.

Damn. She did it again.

Dani stumbled but righted herself with Conner's assistance. She didn't look back.

"You okay?" Conner took Dani's elbow. "Let's hang out over here and out of the way," Conner murmured over his shoulder. "Bro, give us a bark when Pete's finished. If he finds a trail to follow, I'll take her to the cabin." As the oldest brother and the one who'd worked longest with the colonel, Conner understood the military man's way of scheming.

"No, call me first. I'd rather take her myself and make sure we're not followed. But, thanks anyway." Marc smiled as Captain Fuller's narrowed gaze followed his girl.

"Dani followed? Marc, what's she involved in, young man?" Captain Fuller's mock frown wouldn't fool anyone. He was every bit as sharp as his military complement, Colonel Kenson.

"Looking in the wrong direction, Captain. Dani's not involved." Every tidbit of information blurted equaled details he couldn't retract.

The colonel's lips twitched as his gaze flicked again toward Dani and Conner's retreating backs. "Was it something I said?"

"Yeah, as if you didn't know I'd come when you requested canine help. And no, Dani doesn't need to hear gory details."

"Yet you bring her to a crime scene? You know I'm more than happy to see to her protection while you're busy. Where's Lightning and his team?"

"Perimeter."

Like you didn't already know.

The police captain's gaze marked Dani's retreat before suggesting, "Protection? Considering her likeness to the murder victims, if there's something you'd like to share, now would be a good time."

Years of knowing both men and wanting to catch the bastard responsible for the murders meant having to divulge information to keep their cooperation. Marc opened his mouth to speak, then paused when Kenson cleared his throat.

"Sorry, Captain." The colonel shook his head. "But that gets us into a classified area. Let's just leave it at this. Someone's looking for a dark-haired girl matching Dani's description. I don't even know if she's the one they're searching for, and *that* knowledge would probably be above *my* pay grade."

After hesitating a minute to let the significance of his words sink in, he continued, "Which is why you don't see me banging out a ton of questions at Marc." The colonel's intense gaze conveyed everything he'd say—in public. Once those circumstances changed, so would the colonel's tact.

The captain grunted. "Figures. All right, then. Let's catch this piece of shit."

"Make that plural. I'm thinking more than one is behind this." Kenson gestured to Pete. "How about you get to work. I want to poke around this area a bit more. Maybe we'll get lucky and find something." Before he turned away, Kenson added, "Oh, since we didn't get to finish our conversation yesterday, how about we meet this afternoon, at your place?"

Intelligent hazel eyes bored deep as Marc contemplated his ex-boss's thinly veiled attempt to gather information. "Let's just see how today goes. I think she needs a little time to adjust to her new circumstances. But I would like to talk to you after Pete's finished."

"And what circumstances might that be?" Again, the colonel's gaze flicked to where Conner and Dani had disappeared into the woods.

"Why, life with me, of course."

"Then God help her," Kenson added with a chuckle.

"Huh, very funny, Marc retorted. "Pete. Let's see what we can find. *Voran.*"

Furry ears perked up as the shepherd sniffed the offered cloth before looking around, his nose twitching. Not all tracking dogs could do so by air scenting.

With his nose in the air, Darius established his target direction, a deer trail leading deeper into the woods.

An hour trekking through briars, small streams, and steep inclines yielded the usual scratches, ticks, and mud-splattered clothes. Pete's trail ended when trees gave way to a small, dirt road. Focusing on his dog and the trail, Marc hadn't realized how close the colonel kept pace until the older man snapped a branch behind him.

"Okay, so the prick got into a vehicle here. Damn shame the rain washed away discernable tracks. But kudos to your boy for following what has to be a weak scent."

Running his fingers through his hair delayed Marc's next bit of conversation with Kenson. "Guess you want your pound of flesh now. And why didn't you use one of your own dogs?"

"We both know your boys have the best noses around." Kenson grinned wide before adding, "Hey, I'm thinking it's in everybody's best interest to protect your girl even if I don't know what makes her special... yet."

"What makes you think she's special? While we're at it, tell me why you sent Lightning to sweet talk her at the vet's office and how you knew where to find her?"

"First of all, tell me I'm wrong. Tell me that's *not* Callie's friend and the DNA sample I got from Sebastian's murder scene won't be a match."

"You said there wasn't any DNA found."

"I said the *police* didn't find any."

"Sneaky bastard," Marc mumbled as Pete whined, demanding attention. Scratching behind the dog's ears afforded Marc a breather. "Sebastian was a traitor, we proved that. If he'd survived and his plan to sell Callie to the North Koreans had worked, we'd be staring down the results of undetectable bombs right now."

"Hey, I'm not saying his death is a bad thing. Hell, if she hadn't ended him, we wouldn't have found him in time to protect Callie."

"So, you should be thanking her." As soon as the words left his mouth, Marc realized he'd been outmaneuvered.

"Excellent idea. Why don't we go and do just that, nice and proper. Hell, if she's *anythin*g like Callie, I'd have no trouble finding a team wanting a permanent protection assignment."

"Damn. You probably don't even have a hair from Sebastian's apartment to compare, do you?" His ex-boss' tenaciousness would result in eventual confirmation, but Marc had no intention of giving the colonel access to Dani yet.

"Actually, I do, plus a bit of vomit. And you know I'll confirm her identity at some point, along with what makes her extraordinary."

"How'd you find her at the vet's office?"

"Resources, Marc, lots and lots of vast resources. This has been in the wind for years. Nevertheless, Ray is not the only one who's looking. The foreign bastards are narrowing their search. The fact we have another Dani look-alike victim means nobody knows where or exactly who she is, but it's only a matter of time before they do. In addition, somebody has Dani's scent even if they're not sure she's the right one. Dead is dead, regardless."

I need Kenson's help.

"Yeah, they want Dani and Callie."

"Besides her link to Callie, why do they want Dani? Is she another super genius?"

Ahh, the heart of the matter. No fucking way do you get that information.

"Let's just leave it as she's a link to Callie."

"Jesus Christ. What can she do?" Mental salivation evidenced in the icy, piercing gaze transformed the colonel's expression into jaw-dropping awe. Marc could see the wheels turning in the colonel's mind, scheming and plotting to snare either woman into an uninhibited conversation.

Shit!

"She's a conduit, colonel. That's it." One glance declared Marc's words falling on deaf ears.

The path back to the clearing was long and riddled with detailed questions. Dogging his every step, Kenson was one of the most skilled men at friendly interrogation ever encountered. Marc kept his mouth shut except for a few inconclusive nods until he met with Conner and Dani again.

"Marc, where the hell did the bastard go?" Conner's tone held none of the colonel's patience.

"Path led south to a dirt road where he hopped in a vehicle. Pete has the scent. We'll find him."

Colonel Kenson rolled out the fatherly charm as he stepped closer to Dani. "You look like you're feeling better, young lady. And despite what the brothers may think, I'm not an evil mastermind."

Pete growled with the colonel's approach.

"I know exactly who and what you are, Colonel. And even if you detain me, I'll answer none of your questions."

"Whoa, we're not heading down that road. Ever. I don't know what these boys have told you, but let's set the record straight right off the bat. As I said before, unless you plan on mass murder or selling secrets to our enemies, you have nothing to fear from me." Kenson ran a hand across his jaw then nodded as if confirming something to himself. "How about I have you all over for dinner tonight? Think of it as an early spring celebration. You boys could each bring your girls, and we could have a nice relaxing evening."

Dani's jaw firmed, the belligerence in her face apparent.

"Sorry, Colonel. We're busy tonight." Marc looked to Conner, who always took the lead when asked, verbally or otherwise.

"I don't have a girl, but I'd welcome a nice evening and a chat, Colonel." Conner chuckled at the older man's frustrated sigh.

"All right, then. How about six? You know where I live." Defeat edged the older man's voice.

"Cold beer and hot dogs?" Conner asked.

"Yeah, but it won't matter since that's probably your normal diet, and your damaged taste buds have succumbed to years of the same." Kenson fished his keys from the front pocket of his jeans. If he thought dressing down made him more like *one of the guys*, Dani shot that impression down from the start.

"Let's go, Dani," Marc thought but held stock still, waiting.

Dani turned toward the path leading out of the hellish visual reminder of death and the danger chasing her.

"Hold on." Circling her waist and tucking her under his shoulder allowed their steps to fall in sync. "You're gonna be okay, Dani."

"No, Marc. These girls are being tortured and killed because they look like me. This is not okay by any means."

He'd like to tell her it was random, and the psychopath happened to like black-haired girls about her age—but wouldn't lie.

After leading her off the worn path, he pulled her to his chest, her shivering frame dwarfed by his arms holding her tight. Minutes passed as she breathed deep and snuggled close.

"That doesn't make their deaths your fault." *It makes them unfortunate.*

"If not for me, they'd still be alive."

"You're not the one wielding the knife, Dani. We *will* catch him."

He escorted her back in silence. Pete chuffed several times in his bid for attention all the while focused on Dani and paying no mind to scampering squirrels nearby.

Since he believed her shiver derived more from their developing situation and not the stiff breeze kicked up from the coming storm, he needed to make her understand.

"Listen to me, Dani. We're going to catch these bastards. It's not the first time we've dealt with them." Per her description, none of the Tuckers sounded like the brightest bulbs in a pack. It shouldn't take long to pin them down, as long as they didn't have foreign backup.

Along the path again, she appeared to find her inner strength. He'd do anything to maintain it. "Let's grab your jacket and have an early brunch, shall we?"

Dani yawned after hopping over the gully beside the road. "And a nap?"

"Hey, John, I'll take Dani's jacket back." Marc scanned the front seat. "You put it in the back?" The loud squeak ceased as he froze with the back door half open.

The seat was empty.

Damn, Kenson did it again.

"No, one of the colonel's men came and got it. Said she looked chilly. Didn't you see him?"

"No, we must've just missed him. We'll get it later." *Shit. Now he's got her DNA and a scenting cloth. That calculating devious shit.*

Dani's low growl echoed his feelings.

Chapter Sixteen

Lightning leaned over Byte, who sat at the kitchen table, the keyboard's constant clack and clatter the only sound. Several half-eaten pastries and coffee mugs detailed the team's rushed breakfast.

Dani insisted on gathering the dirty plates and mugs, taking them to the sink and rinsing them. She seemed to prefer distance to anything without four paws and fur.

"So, what did you find out about Tucker?" Pulling out a chair, Marc twisted it around, straddled it to sit, and studied the laptop's screen.

"Hasn't filed taxes in like, forever. No criminal charges that stuck. Been picked up for questioning several times. Damn thing is, it's never gone further because the witness in every case has disappeared, never seen again." Byte continued to tap on his keyboard.

"We talked to the colonel. Tucker doesn't know it yet, but he's gonna have some midnight visitors tonight. I'd love to be a fly on the wall in that house." Lightning smiled at Dani as she circled the table to collect his dishes. "Here you go, hon."

Marc grumbled.

"Hey, just being helpful. Ease up." Lightning's *innocent* look didn't quite make the grade considering the slight quirk of his lips and arched brow.

"Where's Wire?" Marc righted his chair and toed another out for Dani when she'd finished.

"Rim checks." Byte laughed as he shut his computer. "You don't stand a chance, Lightning. Give it up."

"I realize that. I just like poking Marc. I'm going out to help Wire." Lightning's booted retreat echoed on the tile floor as he winked at Dani, glared at Byte, and grinned at Marc. "I'd give my right nut for someone like that."

Marc's deep rumbled warning earned silent chuckles.

"Don't promise something you don't have," Byte countered. "Stay alert, Lightning, but I'm sure if anything comes up, you'll have it well in hand." He grinned before finishing the age-old joke. "And hold it till its conclusion."

"Jesus, I'm surrounded by minutemen," Lightning retorted.

The door closing allowed Marc a deep breath. "Byte, what did Kenson give you on Ray, the institution, and the other holdings?" Marc asked.

"Basic outline, but they haven't finished scouting all the locations. Ray's security measures include non-American based systems, which is interesting to say the least. Dani, how is it *you* know about Ray?" Wire's intense focus switched to her, his curious frown creating small furrows in his brow.

"I've heard Marc talk about him."

"Wire, can you connect Ray specifically to any of the properties other than his parent's farm?" Beside him, Dani shuddered.

"No. Not yet. Either he's not directly responsible for them, or he's one clever prick." Byte's curious gaze remained on Dani but lacked the sexual interest prominent in Lightning's eyes. "I'll let you know as soon as we find more information. Dani, you catching a cold?" Rapid, asymmetric clicking ensued as Byte tapped on his keyboard again. "I've got another angle to try."

"I'm fine." Dani rubbed her arms, then settled her hands in her lap.

"Hon, let's sit in the living room for a bit."

Country music drifting from Byte's laptop in the kitchen provided a bit of privacy as they sat together on the sofa.

The incomplete picture they'd formed equated a funhouse experience with distortions and missing pieces. He, the blind man, sorted and felt his way to find the correct fit.

She sighed and tucked her feet underneath her, curling into herself. "What did you want to talk about?"

"First of all, how are you feeling?" Soft caresses of her hair filtered the silken weight through his fingers. He continued the strokes while contemplating the view framed by the bay window. In counterpoint, the crash and slide of breaking waves on the water's shoreline were constant and soothing.

"Better. Just a bit of soreness in my shoulder."

"About last night—"

As if wanting to avoid discussing her ordeal, she took a deep breath before blurting out, "I liked going to your club, despite what happened."

It was her method of putting distance between them, counterproductive to solving their murder riddle. He needed her secrets, but needed her trust to gain them, which gave him an idea.

"How about we go in the office?"

"What about your brothers?"

"There're not coming over until later. We have a few hours." He'd thought about and prepared for this exercise earlier in hopes of breaking down the final barriers between them.

Years of discipline in the military honed his self-control allowing him to keep his thoughts blank. If his suspicions were correct, the talent she wielded could rewrite the future.

Her fluid movements hesitated in standing.

"Anything wrong, Dani?"

"No. I'm good."

Each step down the hall occurred a little slower than the last as she fingered the scar at her neck. A deep breath and slow exhale indicated her struggle for composure before padding through the doorway. Her startle response with the click of the lock made him grin. Her throat visibly worked to swallow.

The weight of his thoughts tipped the corners of his mouth down. He'd been right all along, but must tread with care.

She stood by his desk but let her gaze wander to the sofa and table near the window. He pulled the shade to ensure privacy for what he deemed a crucial stepping stone in their relationship.

Nudging her back against the edge of his desk boxed her in when he took her chin between thumb and forefinger. "Dani, the people after you are dangerous and persistent. To figure this out, we need transparency within the team. That takes time, consistency, and patience."

She nodded in agreement.

"Time we can't control. The rest *is* up to us. Everything we do is based on trust. Though trust is earned, it's a two-way street, built on the backs of communication and honesty. If one fails, the road fails, and the working relationship is doomed before it starts."

"I understand that. I don't want anyone else hurt or killed."

"You up for a little exercise?"

"Sure." Her gaze flitted from him to the desk, then to the shaded window.

"Okay. Since you're wearing a tank top under your shirt, take the shirt off."

She tilted her head to the side, but complied. Biting her lips detailed nervous anticipation.

"Good. I want you to sit on the desktop, Indian-style." From the drawer, he removed a square piece of felt eighteen inches wide and placed it on the edge next to her, noting her hesitation.

"Dani?"

"I'm fine, not made of glass."

It was times like this, when she revealed a backbone of steel that doubled his admiration and curiosity. Marc guided her to sit on the felt square.

She frowned, studying his face with a concentrated effort he hadn't witnessed earlier. It was all he could do to keep his mind blank.

"You okay?"

"I'm fine. Just curious."

"I need to get some things. I'll be right back." She needed to understand he'd read her cues, both voiced and nonverbal, whichever side of the spectrum her signals fell on, then follow through in an appropriate manner. When he returned with a bag containing specific items, she sat quietly, watching his every move.

"Now. How do you feel about a blindfold?"

"As long as you're in the room, I don't mind. I wouldn't want to be left alone wearing one. This is an exercise in trust..."

He invaded her personal space so she could gauge the sincerity in his voice and in his eyes. "Yes. I won't leave you unattended and blindfolded."

Will you trust me?

She smiled and took a slow, deep breath as he slid a silken mask over her head.

"Now, I'm going to spin you around so you're facing away from me with your back to my chest and sitting on the edge. But don't worry, I've got you."

Lip nibbling accompanied her slight hand tremor when he slid her back. When she pulled her legs up a bit, he maintained contact, her back to his chest, stroking her arms then shoulders.

"We okay?" His reassuring touch glided across the rounded edge of her collarbone before returning to the sensitive area behind her ear and down her neck.

"Um, yes."

"Good. We'll take that for the moment. You're very strong and self-sufficient, sweetheart. Your beauty lies as much in your mind as in your body. Do you object to me being close? Our clothes will stay buttoned and zipped." Nuzzling her neck, he inhaled deeply, a combination of vanilla and her own unique scent filled his mind with images of his body deep within her heat.

"My mind is ugly." The uncensored revelation wasn't unexpected.

"Your mind is as beautiful as your body. You'll see this someday. I promise you." Leaning forward, he wound his arms around her waist to hold her small hands in his.

Maintaining contact between his chest and her back, he reached into his bag and pulled out his first item. "This, Dani, is a test of sensations. The blindfold will help you focus. Tell me what you feel." He guided the soft feather down her cheek and neck before sliding it down her arms. She hummed low in her throat.

"A feather."

Several minutes passed while he grazed the backs of her arms and inner elbows with the lightest of touches. He smiled each time she shivered.

Removing the feather but maintaining contact, he reveled in her uninhibited responses, his own muscles hardening, pulsing.

So damn beautiful.

With her body relaxed and chin to chest, her breathing evened and pulse slowed. She leaned into him as a spineless mass.

"That feels wonderful."

He didn't give her much time to contemplate the future before adding, "There's something else we need to work on. I'm going to take a step back."

"What? O-okay." Frustration edged her tone as her muscles tightened to pull her upright.

He snatched a blanket from the side table after setting the feather aside, then kneeled beside the desk.

This is the test, Dani. Do you trust me?

"Dani, I want you to roll backward off the desk. I want you to trust that I'll catch you and not let you hurt yourself with your arms folded over your chest and your legs crossed. If it's too much or too fast, say so." He kept his thoughts blank.

Her head swiveled, eyes covered by the mask but furrows marked her brow in a look of fierce concentration.

Hesitation.

A thin mewl escaped her lips.

In the next second, she tucked her head to chest, leaned back, and rolled off the desk with a drawn-out whine.

As soon as her bottom lost contact with the desktop, he caught her tight to his chest and whispered against her hair.

"Good girl, sweetheart. I've got you." He nuzzled her neck, inhaling the scent that calmed his mind.

"Now, I'm going to sit with you on the couch while we talk."

She started shaking before the first sob left her throat.

He expected as much. The strongest tree could only bend so much before breaking. She'd held in so much for so long, it was a miracle she could function at all.

Gently lifting her mask off, he caught the first tears brimming her eyelashes. "I'm proud of you. You've managed to do in a couple days what it would take weeks or even months for others to accomplish."

Tears dampened his skin as he sat on the sofa and whispered words of encouragement to soften her turbulent emotions. The soft puffs of her breath against the crook of his neck did nothing to cool his raging libido.

"I-I swore I'd never trust anyone again, not completely. I'm so tired of... being hunted." Her whole body shook.

"*Shh*, it's going to work out. We'll keep you safe. Your courage is phenomenal."

Chapter Seventeen

Dani's hands fluttered against his chest before clenching in her lap in palpable frustration. Snuggling her close, he covered them in hopes of imparting a sense of tranquility he himself strived to obtain.

His heart perceived that, in a few short days, she'd captured that vital organ, holding it within her mental grasp as sure as she held the secrets he would soon expose.

The soft snap of cap breaking seal brought her attention to the water bottle he held. "Here, have a little." Holding it to her lips, he let her sip before setting it aside.

"It's all right. Quiet your mind to take it all in. We're not going anywhere. I'm just going to hold you close." From the end table drawer, he pulled out a candy bar. "How about a bit of chocolate?"

A few minutes passed until her tears dried, and her breathing evened out. "I'm feeling better now. Thank you."

"You're welcome. And thank *you*."

The question in her gaze demanded an answer.

"For trusting me."

"All this to prove I trust you?" She wiggled under his steady gaze.

"I know you want to meet Callie. It's mutual. Nate's having a time holding her back."

"Then, why wait?"

"Because—for us all to be together, we need open communication. My brothers and I don't keep secrets, nor will either team."

"But I've told you everything I've done."

"Ah, but not everything you *can* do."

A low growl preceded an indelicate snort.

"Tell me your secret, Dani."

"Marc, please."

"Tell me, Dani. Now!"

"Ah… I-I'm a psy-psychic s-sensitive!" Her words came out on a shrill cry echoing in the room.

Marc held her tight and brushed his lips across her forehead.

"Y-you did that on purpose? Just to learn my secret?"

"Sweetheart, I *do* need to know in order to keep you safe. You don't have to tell the others, but that will prevent you from meeting Callie. We'll talk about that later."

"Okay, but—"

Her gaze searched his, betraying a depth of connection and trust he'd never imagined. In that split-second of time, dawning came in her slow smile and lip nibble. They were joined, irrevocably and eternally, regardless of which way fate blew them.

"I just, well, except for my parents, I've never talked to anyone about this before."

"Hon, you can say anything to me without fear of judgment. Your courage and strength rivals any I've ever seen."

Thoughts of how she'd shunned the world after being forced into a self-induced solitude for her own protection explained much of her behavior. To think she'd been reading him all along, learning to open up, be vulnerable and trust him, granted a satisfaction nothing else could ever top.

So, what was her relation to Callie? Did one even exist? Callie's telekinesis, the uncanny ability to move things with her mind, still freaked him out. Leaning his head back to rest allowed his thoughts free rein to swirl with the possibilities of her potential and what people like Ray would do to possess such a formidable weapon.

In another man's hands, she'd be exactly that.

When his brother Nate took Callie under his wing, he was lucky to have his old team now on permanent assignment to protect her. On the flip side, Marc didn't know Byte, Wire, or Lightning. Could they be trusted with a secret of this magnitude without running to the colonel? Conner could help answer that question. He wouldn't put that burden on Dani.

"I'm gonna need to make a quick call." It was time for a Q and A session with big brother. One that didn't involve breaking Dani's trust.

"Wait, Marc, there're still things I need to tell you."

"I suspect there are."

"Do you want to tell the others and Colonel Kenson?"

"That's up to you. By now, the colonel already knows you're associated with Callie in some way since he took your jacket this morning. That DNA will trace back to Sebastian's apartment. The discovery was inevitable."

"He's curious about me but doesn't know what I can do."

"You were picking out his thoughts this morning the same as you've been doing with me all along, yes?" He smiled at his little enigma, encouraged by her capable and self-reliant nature.

"Well, yes." She looked away from his probing gaze, a blush stealing up her neck and spreading across her cheeks.

"It's your decision to share what you know or not. Only you can decide who you trust and who you think can protect you."

"But I already have. I trust you. You can ask me anything."

"Thank you, Dani." He couldn't resist when she reached up to place a kiss on his lips, soft, feather light, and hesitant.

Though he wouldn't take it further yet, he couldn't resist a taste. Taking his time, he explored the sweetness of her mouth, twining their tongues, wishing they were both naked and in bed. She moaned when he pulled back.

"Conner says Lightning's flirting with you is normal. He did with Callie, too, but he's solid and upstanding."

"I sense Byte and Wire are also. But I don't know whether they'd tell the colonel about me or not."

"Then, until you're sure, we say nothing. I'll ask them questions that let you navigate their intentions. If we both agree it's okay, then you tell them. Sound good?"

"Sounds like a plan. Except you need to know that when I'm anxious or upset, I can't hear anything but my own thoughts."

"Like in Ambrosia?"

"Yeah. All I got from that sadist was a need to hurt and kill. Most everything else got shut out. I was so scared he'd hurt you."

"Jesus. We *will* keep you safe."

"How's the headache now?"

A wide smile led her answer. "Gone, I'm fine."

"Uh-huh." He kissed the tip of her nose when she smiled her acceptance and confidence. "In a few hours, Conner and Julien are coming over to help formulate a plan. We can't continue to stay here, but we can't go to the cabin until we're sure this trouble won't follow us."

"I understand." She twirled her fingers in the light furring of his chest hair above his collar.

"Tell me something, does Tucker know you can read minds?" With more pieces present, he began to fit them together to form a coherent picture.

"No, he thinks I talk to ghosts and get information from them."

"Clever girl." Marc hesitated, then frowned. "Can you?"

"Um, not that I know of. Sometimes random thoughts pop in my head, but I can't tell where they originate."

"Huh, interesting. Can you implant thoughts into others?"

"Uh, I've never tried."

"Save that for later."

"My adopted parents understood me. They were teaching me how to hide my ability. We were a real family... well, I didn't know they'd adopted me or the circumstances."

"You've lost two sets of parents."

"Only one that I was aware of."

The history of her childhood after her parents' accident was relayed with pain that clenched his heart. Though he shared a similar initial tragedy, he'd been fortunate. The Crofton brothers had remained together, solidifying their sense of family. No one should feel abandoned.

Thank God her extraordinary abilities allowed her to overcome self-imposed solitude and reservations concerning trust. With the help of his brothers, they'd put the current trouble behind them and open a new chapter in her life. One that included freedom of choice without looking over her shoulder.

Chapter Eighteen

Meal preparation previously existed as part of Dani's robotic life, for what little she cooked. How many others muddled through the same rut of work, eat, sleep, and repeat? Now, her world opened to myriad possibilities, opportunities dreamed about long ago.

Funny anecdotes of prior missions brought out the relaxed side of each of the team's personalities even as they described the enhanced security systems in place.

"Been wondering if I'd ever get to feel anything but these dogs' teeth." Lightning accepted Pete's offered paw then rubbed his chest.

"Long as you behave yourself. Otherwise, he gets extra meat in his diet." A low irritated grunt followed Marc's warning.

"Hey, baiting you helps pass the time. Nothing meant by it." Lightning's comment earned chuckles around the table.

As she helped Byte clear the dishes, Dani heard a slight hum from each man's cell indicating an incoming message. The immediate change resembled a pride of jaguars tensing in the face of a potential threat.

"What now?" Anger negated her ability to pick out anyone's thoughts.

"It's just Conner. You can silence the alarm, Byte." Marc gestured her to sit. "Hope he got something useful from his dinner with the colonel."

Tires slid on the crushed-gravel driveway, audible evidence of their visitor's impatience. The clinking of stone on metal indicated his stop near the mailbox.

"And he does *that* to irritate me." Marc shook his head in disgust.

The eldest Crofton bustled in, nodding to his old team.

"Well, did he give anything up?" Marc toed a chair from under the kitchen table prior to giving it a gentle shove.

A weary set to Conner's shoulders rivaled his answer. "Ugh, he's a cagey bugger. But he did offer some info in hopes of getting something in return." His gaze slid from Marc to Dani.

Dani squirmed in her seat. At present, her life pivoted on current events and the men present. Each wanted to keep her safe. Ability to pick out current thoughts didn't equate to knowing future reactions.

Evening shadows lengthened and caressed the smooth oak table, crawling forward but falling short of the centerpiece, a large three-wick candle burning bright in its center.

"Dani, help yourself to any and all thoughts."

"Kind of sloppy, letting the colonel get hold of her jacket, Marc. He got her DNA from a strand of hair. You sure you're up for this?" Conner drummed his fingers on the table in a rapid-fire beat.

A slight throat clearing swung her gaze to Marc.

"It's his form of distraction. He's trying to ferret out what makes you different."

"Stuff it, Conner." Marc glared as only a younger sibling could. "He would've found out eventually, and you know it. You think he didn't have a dog at the scene where Dani met Jake or in the woods this morning before anyone else arrived?"

"Yeah, damn his tenacious hide anyway. So, he'll soon figure out Dani helped Callie escape from the Think Tank." Conner's quizzical expression turned to her once again.

"What Kenson doesn't know, hon, is why some psychopath is killing innocent women to get you. The killer isn't savvy enough to avoid leaving a trail of bodies, counterproductive in a covert operation. No military-based unit would do that. That combined with the colonel's involvement makes it obvious there are two different sources searching for you."

"Whoa there. Wait a second." Lightning's piercing gaze zeroed in on Dani. "You? You're *the* Penny?" Shock and disbelief warred for dominance in his tone.

"Yes, guys. Meet Dani, aka Penny. Catch up and move on." Marc's grin softened his words.

"Holy shit. Does the colonel know? What else does he know?" Wire's excitement mirrored Byte and Lightning's expressions.

"Kenson suspects but hasn't verified. Keep in mind, we want it to remain that way. Any problem there, guys?" Marc stared hard at each of the team until a chorus of denials assured their clear-cut loyalty to her.

"Thank you. I know keeping my secrets will prove dicey at times." Dani nodded to each man in turn.

"No problem. We've got your back. We're tasked as a protection detail, not spies." Wire's verbal assurance matched the intentions of them all.

"Conner, we think today's mess stems from someone else in Dani's past. Asshats by the name of Tucker." Byte opened his laptop and started tapping on the keyboard between flicking glances at Dani.

"Why do the Tuckers want you?" Again, Conner's gaze bore into her in an attempt to discern what made her extraordinary.

"She witnessed several murders," Marc spoke up while gently rubbing her forearm.

"Oh." Conner looked disappointed before understanding the significance of his brother's statement. "Oh, shit. Sorry, hon. How long ago? What happened?"

After relating a brief synopsis of her history with the Tuckers, she looked to Marc for direction.

"I know this is difficult, Dani, but can you tell us about the night you met Jake? It was three days after Callie escaped the Think Tank. You might remember something else, something that might help us now." Conner's tone softened at the end.

Marc took up the conversation and relayed the facts, starting with Daryl and censoring her earlier account so she could take the time to study each man at the table.

They had all worked with Jake. Conner, Byte, and Wire were close, but Lightning considered Jake a brother after having grown up together. The combined weight of their feelings compelled her to swallow hard with repeated blinks.

One more emotional blow would see her shattered in thousands of shards. Marc finished the story of how Ray's minions killed Jake.

"So, why does Ray want you now? It was late at night that took place. He wouldn't think you could identify anyone. Does he think you can lead him to Callie?" Lightning kept pushing in a need to make sense of his friend's death and ascertain that she was indeed worth his life.

The team surrounding Callie was tight-lipped as hell, which meant they held back extraordinary knowledge. Each man present wondered if Dani did, too.

"And exactly who wants to know, Lightning? You or the colonel?" Marc attempted to give her an inside view of Lightning's thoughts.

"Hey, as long as she's not a mass murderer who wants us all dead or threatens the country's security, her secrets are safe with me." Lightning's declaration spurred like statements from Byte and Wire.

"I'm not the one who still wants Weapons of Mass Destruction built. That would be Ray. He's the one who imprisoned Callie for most of her life." Her voice carried the conviction of her need to protect.

"Shit. He's a dirty bastard. I knew Ray was holding back. We only met him once. But, how did *you* find out, Dani?" This time Wire's curiosity got the better of him. Like the other three, his motives were sincere, however.

"Ray was hired by a man named Holland Freeman. He's a political power mogul and CEO of a very discreet organization."

"Figures politics would come into this," Conner crossed his arms over his chest and studied her. "How do you know this Freeman character?"

"You're not the only one who can investigate. I can tell you where he lives, but he has security you won't penetrate."

"We'll table that for another day," Marc advised. "Since the current murders involve Dani look-alikes and bodies left for discovery, it's not the work of pros. We need to handle the Tuckers first, then go after Ray and Freeman. Agreed?"

Assenting nods around the room confirmed the unanimous vote.

"Are you a computer genius like Callie?" Byte's smile divulged his eagerness to commune with another nerd. "Maybe you can help me search Lightning's records. I've always wondered how he managed to get through college."

"That's like asking Wonder Woman to open a jar of fruit," Marc retorted.

"Well, all right then. I'll adopt you." Lightning slapped the table. "Screw the colonel's desire for intel. I have a bad memory anyway. But understand there are lines I won't cross. As I said, protecting mass murderers and evil scientists are at the top of my list."

The entire room breathed a sigh of relief, tension blew out while a certain cohesiveness formed, a bond she hoped would outlast the terror stalking them. Still, what would they think of her darkest secret? There was only one way to find out.

Conner took up the conversation before she could confess.

"Okay then. For now, we found listening devices in the vet's office around the receptionist's desk. Dani, have you ever communicated anything to anyone that indicated a connection with Callie, either verbally or electronically while there?" Like Marc, Conner's analytical mind worked overtime.

"No. Just that I intended to watch the Schutzhund trials on Sunday. But that shouldn't have been unusual since I work for a veterinarian."

"Actually, it gave Ray the opportunity to connect you to Marc." Conner frowned, connecting dots while still wondering what special skills she withheld.

"We don't know who planted the bugs. If I could have a look..." Byte mentally reviewed all the devices he'd used in various scenarios in the past.

"Colonel said they weren't his. He sent Lightning in for first contact this past Saturday, but he wouldn't say how he came by the lead." Conner arched a brow in Lightning's direction.

The team leader held up his hands, palms out. "Hey, I don't know how he caught on. He just told me to do a meet-and-greet, see if she'd go out with me." Gazing at Dani, he continued, "Sorry, darlin'. Even if he hadn't suggested it, I would've asked anyway."

Marc growled, his amber eyes studying a rival with a calculating nonverbal as cold as the nethermost crevices of the ocean, formidable and restrained.

Dani tapped his forearm for attention. The clash of their gazes confirmed the connection which bound them together. "He was just doing his job."

Had she been standing at the time, a sudden wobble in her legs would've dropped her on her ass. Raw, stark hunger poured through his thoughts and into her mind and left her hands shaking. His thoughts couldn't be missed.

"Sorry, sweetheart, I'll trust your judgment. Do you want to tell them?"

She smiled. She had the perfect way to do just that. "This has been a really stressful day, guys. How about we all relax and play some cards or something."

Each man's expression equaled a frame-worthy addition to her memories.

A deep, rolling laugh reverberated in Marc's chest and echoed through her body. "Good idea. While we're at it, we can discuss how we'll get to the cabin undetected."

Marc smiled to cover his thoughts straying to the wealth of practical jokes he'd like to play on the others. "We've got a bit of time yet with

Julien and his dog, Nika, making rounds."

"All right." Conner sighed, frustrated. "We wouldn't leave till morning light, anyway. Let me give the colonel a brief version of this talk. I don't mind keeping him in the dark about personal things—everybody needs privacy in their lives—but not concerning Ray's intentions and this Holland Freeman. The colonel's got several teams trying to check out the institution's properties, but they haven't finished and haven't found anything of significance. Yet."

Gathering utensils, plates, and cake allowed Dani to form a plan, amazed at how her fortune had reversed.

Further conversation appeared to be an everyday occurrence while Marc sliced the cake. To the men, the easy conversation and backslapping amid ribald jokes occurred as a normal course of nature. It equaled a portion of heaven she'd never thought to experience again, sweet and satisfying.

When the dishes were cleared and cleaned, Marc produced a deck of cards after she placed another bottle of soda on the table. Time slipped into an easy camaraderie as each hand of cards produced more conversation, understanding, and acceptance. The relaxed atmosphere allowed her further time to study them. When satisfied, she smiled and squeezed Marc's hand.

"I can't tell you guys how much I appreciate your dedication to keeping me safe."

"You sure you don't wanna play, Dani? After all, blackjack was *your* idea." Byte added a few chips to the pile on the kitchen table. "This pot looks like a pretty good-sized haul."

Wire and Conner folded in turn.

"No thanks, I just thought it would be nice for you guys." As if she needed further distraction while sitting so close to Marc.

A moth fluttering near the candle's flame flirted with disaster even as it flew closer to the light. Its reckless flight mimicked her path with Marc, except she also endangered the others dedicated to keeping her alive. Was the driving need to be with Marc worth the risk? Absorbing the warmth of his thoughts, she knew she couldn't change her course.

"Well, sweetheart? Do we fold or play?"

Several taps of her fingers on his thigh indicated he was a go for the pot. With only two players left angling for it, Lightning's determination provided a deep sense of amusement.

"Let's sweeten this deal, shall we?" Marc called then tossed two more chips on the pile. "Let's see what you've got there, Lightning." Tossing his cards face up, Marc reached for the pot before the team leader's cards revealed a losing hand.

"Hold on a sec. That's the third pot you've grabbed without seeing your opponent's cards. Yet, you didn't try to claim any that you didn't eventually win. Plus the fact you upped the ante on the hands you *did* win." Narrowed eyes in Dani's direction, combined with pursed lips and a silent chuckle led to a full-bodied laugh.

Marc wasn't ready to reveal her secret. "Hey, Conner, about tomorrow, can we use your house for meeting with Julien and Nate? It's better located, central, and all that."

Like the others, Conner studied Dani as he answered his younger brother. "Sure, why not? Long as you understand the kitchen is pretty much bare."

"Never mind, then. We'll meet at Julien's instead. He's a great cook," Marc said amid snorts and guffaws.

Brushing her locks aside, Marc created a wave of heat that sent her thoughts to other games she'd prefer to play. "Sweetheart, you haven't met Nate. He's a lot like Julien, only more serious." He folded early in the next hand, giving her a few minutes to relax before starting a new tact.

"Conner, remember the action figure I loved when I was a kid? You said the neighbor's brat broke it." Marc stilled his hand on Dani's back and gave her a moment to study Conner.

"Yeah... what about it?" The way his older brother narrowed his eyes and tilted his head signaled a gauge for extreme focus.

"You never told me which one." Marc smiled, his gaze assuming a devious quality.

"And you'd want to know that now because...?"

"Just curious." Marc didn't look in Dani's direction.

"The youngest one, uh, Jonathan." Conner looked away as he spoke.

"Anyway, don't know why that came to mind. I've been thinking of doing a bit of construction here, adding a dojo. We're always going to Julien's house. This would give him a break. What do you think? With the help of my three brothers and under my skilled leadership, we could have it up and running by summer." Marc's expression lacked the guile present in his thoughts.

"Sure, I don't mind the work. It'll keep the rest of you out of trouble."

Dani covered her mouth while coughing to hide her smile and disguise the overwhelming flood of emotions inundating her mind.

Marc's empathy emerged with his next thoughts. *"Okay, pass on Conner, moving on,"* allowed her to catch her breath.

"You all right, Dani?" Lightning's suspicious countenance echoed in the other men's faces. "You look a bit flushed."

"I'm fine. Just need a bit of water."

"Dani. One more question. This one is for your safety." Marc set the glass on the table then focused on Lightning, Wire, and Byte, one at a time.

"I appreciate you guys helping us out. I know babysitting jobs rank low on the fun-things-to-do list, so this means a lot. Since we both seem to be targets, it's great that we have such solid backup for when these bastards make their next play."

With nerves bundling and twining in her stomach, Dani reached for her bottle of water. Closing her eyes helped concentration. One after another, they held sincere thoughts to protect her. When she touched on Lightning's thoughts, she found not just the replicated dedication to her safety but visions of them naked, sweating, and—

Her eyes flew open as water spewed in her choking and sputtering fit. A wave of heat overtook her entire body as she continued to cough.

"Dani? What's up?" Marc gripped her upper arm, waiting.

"Ha! I knew it! I damn well knew it." Lightning's chair legs landed with a thump when he leaned forward and banged his fist on the table. "Each time you ask a question, she's patting your leg. I can see her shirt move just a bit."

"Knew what? What the hell's going on?" Wire looked first to Dani, then to Marc. His confusion deepened as he glared at Lightning.

"Marc, if there's something you wanna tell us, we're listening." Byte frowned at Dani then turned to Lightning for insight. "What's wrong with them?"

"Nothing you'd describe without dolls in a shrink's office." Lightning's deadpan delivery belied shaking shoulders.

"She's reading our thoughts. Took you clowns long enough to figure it out." Conner's chair grated against the tile as he stood. A pointed stare at Dani reinforced the seriousness of his statement. "Dani, be careful with the weapon you wield. It's quite formidable, and many would kill to control it."

Glancing at his younger brother, Conner continued to address Dani, "As for the rest, I'll save you from being put in the middle. Marc, I broke your action figure when I put it in the model rocket Julien and I set off one night in the park. Moreover, yeah, I'll help you build a dojo, but *I'll* draw the plans to whatever specs you want. Your drawings suck."

"Thanks, Conner. But you can see why we've vetted these three before revealing her secret." Marc took her chin between his thumb and forefinger, bringing her gaze to meet the deep golden warmth of his concern amid the hoots and hollers of the team.

"Thank you, hon, I know you don't like invading others' thoughts, but your protection will always come first. I'm assuming Lightning checked out despite his personal desires?"

"Um, yes." The grumbled words re-established the images Lightning conjured. She had no intention of entering into *that* type of relationship with him.

"Lightning. I'll tell you this one more time, then we're gonna have it out." Marc's other fist clenched and relaxed only to clench again. "Dani is off limits."

"Hey, man. I realize that. I just needed to provoke a reaction to substantiate my theory. The card thing gave you guys away pretty quick. Can I ask Conner a few questions, Dani?" Lightning's shoulders shook as Conner punched him in the bicep.

"Just keep your thoughts clean," Marc warned.

Doubt, excitement, insecurity, and curiosity crossed their visages as each man debated his circumstances and the possibilities of their predicament. In the end, the assigned duty of protection came to the forefront, yet each retained a sense of wariness. Could she win them over as Callie had with her team?

"What a terrible burden that must be at times, Dani." Conner frowned as concern and puzzlement warred within his gaze. "Especially with people like Lightning in the world."

"Hey, I resemble that remark," Lightning confirmed. "Though, it does pose the question. Why didn't you pick up my thoughts in the vet's office? Why did you think I was your stalker?"

"I've spent years learning how to tune people out. Now that I need to read them, well, it's difficult, and I'm a little rusty. When I'm flustered or distracted, everything kinda shuts down or gets jumbled. I honestly couldn't read you when you came into Dr. Carari's office. I got flashes of you in fights, now I see they were in the line of duty."

"So, Marc distracted you. Um, sounds like we should provide more distractions to fine tune your talent." Nods and mumbles of assent greeted Conner's voiced assumption.

Marc sighed.

"We know you want to protect her, but think about this with your big head, dude. You'll see the logic," Conner retorted.

Marc nodded. "Now that you know Dani's secret, I ask two things. One, don't let it slip to the colonel. Two, since Julien and Nate aren't aware yet, don't blow it for us. I have questions for my *other* brothers."

"Ya know, there are some things I'd love to know about the colonel. Why don't you invite him, too?" Wire's question, while innocent enough, drew a mixture of frowns and agreements around the table.

Though they each eyed her as a little odd, their eagerness kept their inquisitive minds and thirst for knowledge searching for new ways to test and analyze her ability. Absent was the condemnation she'd seen from people like the Tuckers who saw her as a freak.

"No. Absolutely not. Dani will not be used in that manner," Marc declared.

"I'm not talking national security stuff, just like, what're the chances of making this a permanent assignment?" Wire's curiosity mirrored the other reflective and introspective demeanors.

"You want to be her guardian angel?" Lightning's dubious laughter echoed in the others.

"Why not?" Wire's innocent expression still contained a little wariness.

"Jeez, man, you become more like a case of herpes every day—" Byte's retort halted with Conner shaking his head.

"Don't finish that thought. STDs are only funny when you don't have 'em."

Lightning gave Conner a thumbs up.

"Well, there is one thing we need to consider. What if the colonel or any of his men are working both sides of the coin, like his lieutenant did with Callie?" Conner's point struck a nerve in everyone.

Each man sobered, no doubt recounting the traitor's actions, an incident which almost ended in Nate's death.

"We'll check out the colonel, but we're treading a fine line here. It's a damn slippery slope. I want to confirm his intentions are what's best for Dani." Marc's brows pulled in as he tapped his index finger against his chin, concern twined with cunning consideration in his features.

Chapter Nineteen

"'Bout time you got here." Julien opened the back door and ushered Marc and Dani inside. "Any later and you'd have missed out on most of the food. Where's your team?"

"Perimeter checks. They'll be in shortly," Marc answered, sweeping by to grab a plate.

"Hi. Thank you for inviting us." Kneeling brought Dani eye-to-eye with a black shepherd, whining since she'd entered. She'd waited for this moment to meet Callie for so long. Now that it'd arrived, she couldn't think straight for the excitement strangling her equanimity.

"Hey there, Nika." Soft fur under her fingers lent warmth which, when combined with the rasp of a warm, wet canine tongue, elicited a giggle.

"How'd you know her name?" Julien paused in closing the door."

Dani froze mid-giggle, but before she could answer, Marc spoke up.

"I told her all about your sorry ass, and the food is why we came." Marc's gaze roamed over the kitchen island covered with an assortment of mouth-watering dishes.

"And here I thought you missed me." Gently tapping his fingers on the counter, Julien continued, "What is it about Crofton women and dogs? Nika never takes to anyone. Then, along comes Callie and Dani..."

"Where's Callie's team?" Marc glanced through the wide arched doorway into the great room beyond.

"Seems Blade has a soft spot for dogs. They've got Callie's pup out for a walk."

Dani grinned at the thought of the hardened ex-soldiers existing as a giant chew toy.

"Come on, Dani. Let's get some breakfast before you meet the rest of the crew. Julien's a good cook, and breakfast is the most important meal, yada, yada."

"From what wall of graffiti did you learn that piece of wisdom?" Julien's brow furrowed, still studying Dani.

Just as in Marc's kitchen, a gourmet cook would feel at home. Glass-fronted cabinetry highlighted stemware and colorfully designed plates while recessed and pendant lighting reflected off gleaming, granite countertops.

An assortment of copper and stainless steel pans hung from a uniquely-shaped, black iron rack, ready for a culinary artist to transform the ordinary into extraordinary.

Julien's six-feet-four-inch frame towered over her as he gestured toward the mounds of food. "I can hear you rolling your eyes, Marc. That's just rude."

"Julien, aren't you due for a vacation soon?" Marc asked.

"Yeah, but with the office being so busy, I can't justify taking time off, what with Nate and your lazy asses not pulling the weight. Why?" Pursed lips verified Julien's acknowledgment of the distraction.

"I hear Antarctica is nice this time of year," Marc quipped.

Dani appreciated Marc's attempt to draw attention away from her as he filled his plate with muffin frittatas, bacon, fruit, and other things she couldn't identify but smelled wonderful.

"We're eating in the great room to keep things informal. Grab a seat and dig in. Coffee's fresh, or if you'd rather have a latte..." Julien gestured to the other counter at an elaborate if not diabolical contraption which looked capable of piloting the next spacecraft to Mars.

"Thanks. This is quite a spread." Dani spooned small bits of breakfast casserole and fruit on her plate before pouring some juice from the nearby pitcher.

"Thank you. The others are quite anxious to meet you, Dani. Callie's team, Virus, Whisper, Blade, Nerd, and Spirit will join us after a bit. This might seem like a lot of food, but I guarantee by the time those guys eat, along with Byte, Wire, and Lightning, there won't be a crumb left. Trust me."

"I understand the colonel's coming later?" Julien looked to Marc for confirmation.

"Yes. But I wanted time for us to talk first." Marc poured a cup of coffee then added a dollop of whipped cream and a sprinkle of cinnamon. "Come on, sweetheart, this is gonna be great."

Dani needed no further encouragement. She'd waited so long for this moment. A certain breathlessness accompanied the adrenaline rush while the orange juice in her glass suffered the effects of a mini earthquake, swilling side-to-side from shaking fingers.

On any other day, the view of the ocean would've stolen her attention after rounding the corner into such a large, elegant yet cozy room. But she hadn't been in such a social situation for a long time. Overwhelming curiosity from everyone present swamped her.

Too much too soon?

"Hi, guys. Glad you could meet with us today." Ever the gentleman, Marc set his plate and cup on a low coffee table before taking hers to place beside them. "Okay, Dani, let's run the gauntlet." His massaging caress slid warmth up and down her back in gentle, slow swirls of encouragement.

On the other side of the room, a couple rose from the opposite couch. Previous descriptions of Callie's grace and refinement failed to do her justice. Blonde, waist-length hair and blue eyes lent an ethereal air to her delicate features.

Resemblance between the brothers defined Nate, Marc's younger sibling. She sensed his equally overprotective nature in continuing the family trait.

Nika brushed her leg, the comfort firming her opinion that regardless of the myriad horrors and terrors of the world, fate procured sublime moments. Each could shed the quiet anxiety routed in darkness harbored by all souls. She couldn't resist a moment to scratch behind the dog's ears.

"Hi, Dani, Marc. I have so many questions, but first, thank you so much for helping me escape from the institution. I will always be grateful. I don't know how you gained knowledge of the passwords..." Elegance and kindness etched Callie's expression as she stepped forward for a hug. "This is Nate, as I'm sure you're already aware."

Years of rejection and humiliation combined with the overwhelming presence forced Dani a half step back until Marc's rigid arm brought her under his shoulder. Stinging along the backs of her eyelids provided further humiliation. Both Nate and Callie's gentle smile displayed an innate understanding of her situation.

"Good to see you again." Stepping to the front, Marc reached forward to shake Callie's hand. After nodding to his younger brother, Marc nudged her back toward their seats. "Let's eat, Dani. I'm starved."

"Dani. I am forever in your debt. Thank you." Tiny crinkles formed at the corners of Nate's eyes to accompany a sympathetic and sincere smile.

“You're welcome.” Dani smiled. “It looks like you've adapted to life outside the institution very well, Callie.”

“I have. I never dreamed the world could be so full of... well, just everything.”

“Dig into breakfast, guys.” Julien sat in a deep-tufted easy chair before adding, “We have a lot to talk about.”

“About that. Let's save the question-and-answer period for later, okay? We need a bit of a break.” Marc's arched brow and pointed stare toward each of his brothers conveyed the warning.

“We just wanna enjoy a good meal and great company.” Conner's refereeing became a suggestive throat clearing. “That's why we're eating in here and not the kitchen. Figured everybody'd relax a bit.”

“Coming from the guy who used to freeze my bowl of cereal before breakfast.” Marc took a deep breath, clearly preparing for an inquisition.

“Yeah, but I seem to remember you put a halved peach on a layer of yogurt and pretended it was an egg. With the early morning light through the kitchen window, I bit into quite a surprise,” Conner retorted.

“Don't be shocked when I fix a party-popper to your bedroom door in the near future.” Marc smiled at his oldest brother with the instant camaraderie Dani had only dreamed of experiencing.

After Conner, Nate, and Callie took their seats, Dani took a deep breath. Expectant air carried the same comradery as around her team.

Relaxed conversation flowed for the next few minutes with fond memories and brotherly shenanigans. The warmhearted companionship of the brothers eased the needles of tension while providing an insight she'd never expected to find.

To picture this gathering on a regular basis brought moisture to her eyes. She blinked several times before anyone noticed.

Marc's reassuring caress down her back gained her attention. Letting her mind relax, she concentrated on his thoughts.

“All right, how about a little exercise?” His wide grin spoke of devious pranks among brothers.

She smiled.

“Conner, Julien said you made cookies for later. I'd love some as long as Nate didn't help. Which reminds me, when we were kids...” Marc smiled at Julien, one full of sly calculation. "I remember getting punished for replacing the cream in cookies with toothpaste. I know it wasn't Conner, so it had to be either Nate or you."

"Why would I do that to my older brother?" Nate's innocent face never made it to the realm of sincerity.

Julien's expression wasn't much better.

Glancing at Nate then Julien, Dani sucked her lips between her teeth to keep from laughing. She couldn't look at Marc as the mental flashes of an innocent boy sent to his room for a prank he hadn't committed came to mind. Still, she picked up Marc's thoughts.

"Was it Nate? If so, nod once."

Dani gave a slight nod, feeling Marc's need for revenge.

"And, you know, I've always wondered who put the air horn under my office chair before our meeting with the CEO of Jackson Chemicals." Turning to Dani, he said, "Some half-wit waited until we had a very important consultation with an influential, corporate type in our conference room. I believe the guy thought us professional until I sat down and nearly ruptured his eardrums." Spearing each brother with a thoughtful frown, Marc held her hand snug.

When he glanced in Julien's direction, she squeezed.

"Seconds, anybody?" Marc pressed his lips together, a slight twitch at one corner the only evidence of a vengeful mind at work.

"Julien, your cooking is too good to turn down." Nate slipped his hand from Callie's, preparing to push to his feet. "Unlike the urinal cakes Marc conjures up in his kitchen."

"Hold on, Nate. Dani and I were just going in for more. We'll get you some. Anyone else?" When the others declined, Marc stood and pulled Dani to her feet before grabbing his brother's plate. "Anything specific, or a little of everything?"

"Um, just a bit of eggs and scrapple, thanks." Nate cast an uncertain glance between Julien and Marc. The hesitancy in his smile joined forces with the slight marring of his brow indicating knowledge of impending disaster without knowing how or when.

Whistling a small ditty, Marc led Dani to the kitchen where a dozen food platters waited, innocent but dangerous in the wrong digestive system.

"Hm, let's see. Nate sometimes has a bit of difficulty digesting certain foods. So, let's give him some quesadillas with broccoli along with eggs and scrapple. Oh, and some of this with beans…" Marc chuckled as he heaped extra-large helpings on the plate. "Ready to expose your secret?"

"Yeah, just a little nervous. Don't forget to add some wheat bread." Dani smiled before adding, "If we're going to nail him, might as well do it good and proper."

"I love the way you think. Welcome to the family. Nate's next gut action will signal the beginning of Armageddon, like the pitter-patter of small meteorites landing in a lake." Marc snagged several pieces of wheat toast then spread a thick layer of pear jam on top. "Yep, this should shoot him into orbit within a few hours. Tonight, we should apologize to Callie for suffering his sphincter-based expressions."

"I'll fix you a small plate." Listening to his thoughts, Dani spooned seconds for Marc. "With all the trouble he has with beans, roughage, and wheat, I'm surprised he's not lactose intolerant, too."

"Yeah, but this'll produce the same results. Thanks, sweetheart. Now, let's go make a big deal over Julien's cooking, shall we?" His grin had never looked so wide or so evil. "Ready for some more eavesdropping?"

Back in the great room, the brothers had continued the small talk and reminiscing, yet thunderclouds appeared more inviting than Nate's expression after receiving his plate full of biologic calamities in the making.

"Dude, not cool. Not cool at all." Nate's comment accompanied his glare delivering a dire warning and the devilment of a man plotting revenge.

Dani read his turmoil between not accepting his brother's challenge and the dire consequences of consuming the food. With the large gathering, he'd at least eat some of it despite the ribbing received. A slight grimace accompanied his first few bites.

"What's wrong, Nate?" Marc winked at Callie before adding, "Sorry, Callie." His smile brightened as he gestured to the outdoors. "Great day for opening up the house, don't you think, guys?"

"Not so soon. We've some time yet," Julien said, his shoulders shaking.

Across the room, Nate narrowed his eyes at Marc before leaning over to Callie and whispering in her ear. Her smile of acknowledgment hovered between sympathy and amusement.

"Since it's just us, how about a demonstration. Callie, why don't you help Marc with his coffee? Careful, though, it's bound to be hot, still." Nate grinned wide. "Nothing like having a telekinetic girlfriend."

Marc's smile faltered. He hadn't considered retaliation from the innocent prank.

Of all the books portraying psychic talents, Dani had always wondered what telekinesis in action would *look* like. From the coffee table, Marc's cup floated up several inches above the glass top. In slow motion, it drifted, carried by unseen forces to hover before his face. He grabbed it with a gentleness belying his speed.

"Why, thank you. You're very sweet." Marc nodded but remained alert.

"Wow, that is so cool. I envy you." Dani watched as Marc eyed Nate and Callie with wariness. Julien waited with lips nipped between teeth while Conner tapped his toe with impatience.

Callie's stare bore into Dani as if trying to discern her deepest thoughts. In counterpoint, her smile held a shade of Nate's deviousness. "You know, I've always wondered how you managed to help me. Was it a case of being in the right place at the right time kind of thing? Not to mention, how did you stay one step ahead of the Think Tank geniuses trying to recapture and nail anyone associated with me?"

Dani swallowed hard, not quite ready to divulge her secrets. Sticking with the cover story bought her some time. Looking around the room, those same curious but penetrating stares radiated from Nate and Julien.

"Well, um, I worked in a vet's office. Ray used to bring his dog in. He'd talk and text while there, but never thought to turn off his Bluetooth." Concentrating hard, Dani picked up the remnants of Callie's intentions.

A heartbeat later, Marc's quesadilla flew off his plate toward his chest—and straight into Dani's waiting hand. The warm bread oozed scrambled eggs and topping between her fingers and into Marc's lap before he could move his plate.

"Hey, what's that for?" Marc looked at Callie, laughter in both their gazes.

"Ha. I knew it. She's reading our thoughts! She's been anticipating your moves and helping you ferret out our secrets since the moment you arrived. Catching that quesadilla? Nobody's reflexes are that fast. When you first got here, even though her back was turned, she took the plate you offered without fumbling. How? And until now, you never knew it was me who scraped out the cream and replaced it with toothpaste when we were kids, or which one of us played the other pranks." Nate glanced at Julien and Conner for confirmation.

"We've known your mind was special all along. We just didn't know the particulars." Nate chuckled as he set his plate aside.

Her secret was out, no going back, no rescinding. A wave of panic swept from head-to-toe vanquishing the warmth derived from Marc's proximity.

Chapter Twenty

"Hey, Dani. It's all right. It's just Callie and my brothers." Marc gave a pointed stare at Nate. "Cool it. It's only the third time she's told anyone." Marc set aside his plate and wrapped his arm around her shoulders.

"Technically, she hasn't said or verified, except she's turned white as a snowdrift." Conner grabbed a blanket by his chair and tossed it to Marc.

"Dani, I know how you feel." Callie looked to Nate. "When I first told him about my telekinesis, I was so scared. On the other hand, if I hadn't trusted him, I'd have ended up in the hands of those foreign dipshits who continue to search for me."

"And now, they're looking for me, too."

"I suspect from the recent serial killings of women matching your description, it's not the same. Neither Ray nor the foreigners would leave such a bloody trail." Callie stood and walked over and sat beside Dani.

Compassion and kindness shone from her gaze as she reached for Dani's hand then hesitated before folding her hands in her lap. "If it weren't for you, I wouldn't be here. I might not have survived. I'll help you in any way I can. Okay?" Tears graced Callie's lashes.

"I couldn't stand the thought of you trapped in that institution. I know they'll do the same to me if they find out what I can do. Or, what I can do most of the time."

"Most of the time? Let me guess, when you get nervous it doesn't work out so well?" Callie smiled as she offered her hand in a show of support.

Dani took it. The encouragement and friendship in the light squeeze meant more than she could express. "Yeah. When I'm anxious, I kinda shut down or forget to monitor my speech and actions, something Marc picked up on pretty quick."

Nika's excited bark and tail thumping compelled their gazes to follow her energetic scurry toward the door, the tiled surface precipitating a slide into the kitchen island. Rumbling car engines outside announced visitors in various stages of impatience with the drum of tires skidding on dirt. Each man tensed and stood.

Julien snagged his cell, pulling up his security system. "It's Nate's team."

Three brief knocks accompanied the loud commotion at the back door as Julien left to greet their guests in the kitchen.

"Nika, sitz," Julien commanded. The canine's excited whine accompanied soft chuffing noises. Doggy groans and grumbles further marked the shepherd's vocal reception.

Five gruff voices in all, each distinct and filled with confidence, mingled with the clinking of plates distributed and food scooped from bowls and platters. Feeding the men would be a full-time endeavor.

"Honey, I'm home." The lack of hesitancy in the newcomer's tone suggested a familiarity born of long-standing relationships. Each man articulated his compliments to the chef as the sound of good-natured shoving ensued.

"Hey, Whisper, guys, come on in." Nate stood to welcome the men striding into the room. "Dani, these bruisers are Callie's protection detail."

The first in line placed a shepherd pup in Callie's waiting arms.

Three of the five took up equal mass as they dwarfed the wingback chairs. Two others sat cross-legged on the floor with their backs to the large stone fireplace.

"Wouldn't miss this for the world." Turning to Dani, the speaker's intelligent, dark gaze exhibited eager anticipation. "I'm Virus, the brains of the team, electronics specialist."

"I'm Spirit. This is Blade, and Nerd. Blade is our weapons expert, and Nerd is our gator-hunter-turned keyboard expert." Spoken in a quiet and curious manner, the Native American's words echoed the question in his mind.

Deciding to go all in, Dani jumped in with, "Hi. I'm Dani, or, better known by you all as Penny."

Utter silence ensued, except for puppy yips as Faith rough-housed with Nika. Each man stared in fascination.

"It's mighty nice to finally meet you." The tall Native American stood to offer a hand shake.

With introductions out of the way, each blurted out questions until Marc held up his hand. "Enough, for now. Let's finish eating."

Picking up the conversation before her revelation, Spirit continued, "Whisper can fly or drive anything mechanical."

"We want to thank you, Dani, for helping Callie and Nate. We wouldn't have ended up here unscathed without your assistance. You probably saved our lives, just as Callie has done." Nerd, one of the electronics' specialists, gestured between his teammates and Callie.

"We've been looking all over for you. You're good at hiding—and you've been right under our noses." Nerd tilted his head to the side. "I've been hacking records from here to China. Couldn't find any trace of you. Not that we had much to go on except the name *Penny*. Perhaps you could help us with something."

"She's not a fashion consultant. Sorry, Nerd, you'll have to stick with croc boots and snakeskin belts." Julien's comment earned a round of guffaws.

"I've had years of practice, Spirit." Dani smiled as heat swept up her neck. Keeping up with the friendly zingers flying would soon give her a headache. Marc's hand twined in her curls then rubbed her back.

"Tone it down, guys, or I'll ask Callie to pour your drinks over your heads." Marc eyed them with firm determination, receiving sighs and muttered threats in return.

Putting thought to action, Callie smiled as each of Nate's team straightened when their drinks rose in midair.

"Okay. Okay. We give." Virus' mouth twisted in a wry grin as he grabbed his cup.

"The colonel's not coming?" Whisper asked. "I thought we were going to pool our resources and tap into his."

"We are, and he is. Later. I wanted Dani to meet you barbarians first, get acquainted and comfortable before he shows up. We have about an hour or so." By directing attention back to himself, Nate accorded her time to take a deep breath.

"We've looked forward to this meeting. I have a couple questions." Virus looked uncertainly at Dani.

"Not so fast. She's not a new form of bug," Marc spoke up before anyone else could.

Their furtive glances bounced between Callie and Dani, one they knew, the other, a complete enigma. They each suspected a link—after a fashion.

"Considering how long we'd worked together and how special Callie is, we saw no reason to break up the squad now." Spirit's puzzled frown morphed into a wide grin. "If my guess is correct," he tapped his forefinger on his belt buckle as he crossed his stretched-out legs at the ankle, "You, Dani, are every bit as special as Callie. We just have to discern the particulars..."

Marc growled his admonition.

Spirit's smile widened on throaty laughter as his cup of coffee elevated out of his grasp in warning. "Message delivered." His glance to Callie bore no trace of contrition.

Marc lightly squeezed her knee. *"Take a turn at each one of Callie's detail. Squeeze my hand if they're all on the level, sweetheart."*

Conversation flowed with easy banter between old friends and family, becoming white noise in the background. Each member relived experiences accompanied by bawdy wisecracks, absurd proposals, and indecent suggestions.

Soon it drifted to their common goals—protection of the girls and the search for information. Similar character threads wove throughout the four brothers and Nate's team in their discussion of how to find the serial killer and end Ray's threat.

All were dedicated to their job, their goal of protecting Callie foremost in their minds. Their initial and begrudging acceptance of a woman as part of their group melted away after she'd saved each from a bullet in their brain.

They were more than a team. They were a family, forged through interdependence under fire, honor, integrity, and compassion. Nothing short of death would separate them.

"Hey, Virus." Nate smirked at the computer expert. "Was it you or Blade who changed the language on my cell phone last week?"

"Naw, man. That wasn't me." Virus bit his lower lip and looked out the window.

Each brother looked to Dani, who smiled with an almost imperceptible nod in the computer tech's direction.

"Spirit, I know you denied it. I can't help but believe you coated Nerd's cigarettes with the anesthetic ointment to numb his lips before reporting to the colonel last week." Callie beamed while delivering the challenge, daring him to deny it.

"Nah, not me. I wouldn't have used lidocaine," Spirit replied. He frowned when everyone looked at Dani again.

Dani nibbled on her lower lip, unable to meet Spirit's gaze, but nodded once.

"Nerd, seems to me, either you or Virus glued all the eggs to the carton last week, setting Callie in a fit while trying to make *you* breakfast." Nate's statement earned chuckles from around the room even as he glared at the younger man.

"Hey, why would I sabotage my own meal? That's ridiculous." Nerd's attempt at an innocent smile never made it to his eyes.

Dani coughed behind her hand, nodding ever so slightly in Nerd's direction.

Conversation continued with friendly accusations, finger pointing, and dubious threats. Each person equal in the others' eyes, part of a whole.

Would Lightning and his team ever feel the same way about her, or would they garner protection of their thoughts? She'd always viewed the world as an outsider, never sharing the camaraderie enjoyed by present company. The dull ache in her chest morphed into a sharp burn.

"Hey, sweetheart? What's the matter?" Marc murmured in her ear. Tension in his frame spread concentrically outward until his brothers waited for her answer.

"Everything's fine." Dani squeezed Marc's hand. "I'm just a little jealous, I guess."

"Why did you turn to Dani for an answer after each question?" Blade looked to each Crofton for clarification.

Spirit's smile widened as his gaze swung from Callie to Dani. "So, the girls may not be sisters, but they do have at least one thing in common. Isn't that right, Dani? I'll bet if I—" His reach toward the side table halted midair.

"Don't even think about it," Marc warned. "Whatever you're thinking of doing—don't." With more than a little determination in his gaze, Marc started to rise.

"No, he wasn't reaching for the book. He was gonna toss the coaster to see if I stopped it." Dani cringed with her slip.

"And how would you know that?" Virus' whispered words echoed the confusion in his thoughts.

Dani sighed with frustration.

"Ha! I'm right." Spirit jumped to his feet.

Bared teeth and flared nostrils revealed Marc's frustration. "Damn it, Spirit."

"He's fine, Marc." Dani's voice filled the deep stillness plagued with menace vibrating between the two men.

"Oh. She's telepathic?" Virus, sitting cross-legged on the floor, rubbed his hands together. "Holy shit! How cool. I'd love to take you all home to a big family dinner next month. How 'bout it?"

In retrospect, apprehension need not have occupied so much of her thoughts, considering the like-minded men. They'd already adjusted to Callie's telekinesis.

Dani's ability wasn't that spectacular on the heels of witnessing Callie's extraordinary talent. Once their minds were open to possibility of exceptional abilities, understanding, belief, and acceptance came with demonstration.

"How about a little moral clarity, buddy?" Conner's no-nonsense assertion didn't ease the men's overwhelming excitement. Each held ideas of utilization ranging from practical jokes to rooting out traitors.

"Yeah, I know. But think of the fun we'd have." Virus' wide grin was infectious.

"Guys, the colonel's gonna be here before long. We still have things to discuss before he arrives." Marc's enlightenment sobered each man, leaving them grousing as if a treasured prize slipped through his fingers.

Despite the threat they faced, each stole furtive glances at Dani between offering information about Colonel Kenson.

"So, what does he know about Dani?" Nerd asked as he pulled his laptop from its case and booted it up. His look of near adoration preceded Marc grinding his teeth.

"Since he got a piece of her hair, hence her DNA, he knows by now she's the girl we've been searching for. Also, there's a serial killer whose victims all bear a strong resemblance to her. Each victim was tortured before they were murdered," Marc offered the information without further explanation.

"Is Ray involved, or is it more of the foreigners?" Blade balanced a knife over the back of his third knuckle, swaying his hand back and forth as if it helped calm and sort his thoughts.

"The colonel has checked out a few of the institution's more obscure properties around the country, but to date, hasn't gotten inside any of them. We'll know more when he gets here," Marc said.

While spared the verbal details of the recent killings, Dani couldn't scour the images gleaned from Marc's thoughts in her mind. Shudder followed shudder, wracking her body. A sympathetic smile acknowledged his understanding before he considered a new tact. Still, she respected the way his mind worked, able to see and fit odd pieces together regardless of the threat.

"The colonel's gonna hound us all until he learns the girls' secrets, Marc." Nerd's click-clacking on his computer keyboard echoed in the quiet.

"I wish him luck with that. For the meantime, since my house isn't set up for tight security, Dani and I will stay at the cabin for now," Marc replied.

"So, you'll be near Nate and Callie." Julien, mostly quiet until now, appeared to study the situation from different angles, concerned about their safety. "Which means not only will your protection detail be close, Dani, but Whisper and these guys will also be near should anyone track either of you down. Two teams, very good."

As sunlight chased the shadows from the room's corners, Nika announced the next visitor with a deep rumbling growl. Anticipation of Kenson's presence formed a sour knot in Dani's stomach.

He could yet decide to imprison or quarantine her in protective custody without her consent and without legal consequences. Not even the warmth of Marc's caress could reverse the cold dread inside.

His stride through the room revealed the confidence she'd associated with him.

"Hello again, Dani." Faded jeans and a flannel shirt seemed out of place on the middle-aged soldier. "Nice to see you, too, Callie. Men." His casual attire didn't help him fit into the group the way he thought it did.

Each man nodded in turn with the wariness of a nearby shark in bloody water. Their collective protectiveness united them in a way known only to a close pack. Nate wrapped his arm around Callie's shoulders just as Marc shielded Dani.

"Hi." A light sheen of moisture cooled Dani's brow.

"Colonel Kenson, would you like some breakfast and coffee? There should be plenty of food, despite the army-sized appetites here today." Julien leaned forward, stopped by Kenson's next words.

"Thanks, I've already eaten. But you know I wouldn't miss this meeting for the world." The colonel's intense gaze studied Dani before sweeping over to Callie. "Looks like you guys have already closed ranks. Wanna fill me in?"

"Right to the point, as always." The humor in Marc's voice replicated in the smiles on each man's face. "Okay, let's start with the serial killer. Any news or connection to Ray?"

Dani concentrated on the colonel when his gaze focused on Callie. *He doesn't know she's telekinetic.* She felt the tightly controlled frustration in the older man who desperately wanted to know the extent of her talents.

"Yes. I was thinking we'd swap information." Kenson's calculating stare swung between Marc and Dani before a grin kicked up one corner of his mouth. "How about telling me how you got involved in all this, Penny?"

Intense scrutiny shut Dani's thoughts down with the tidal wave of *Oh, shit* flowing through her body. "I, um—"

"*Dani*, as you know, worked in a vet's office where Ray brought his dog for care. His own technology gave him away, seeing how she's tech savvy. She relayed information about Callie to Franklin, through an intermediary, Daryl. Then, as you know, Jake was killed." Marc's narration held no hesitation.

"Well, you've certainly done this country a service. It seems now Ray wants you both. Maybe thinking of Dani as a conduit to Callie." After a second's hesitation, the colonel went on, "Or perhaps he wants you both for different reasons." Firming his lips in obvious frustration, the older man frowned.

"The former scenario makes sense," Conner said.

"Well, since we know the bastard's still after Callie, and anyone associated with her, we'll keep Dani under wraps, too." The colonel's speculative look again swung between his two objectives. "You two don't look like sisters, except for your eyes. I wonder..."

"Ah, so you haven't obtained Callie's DNA." Conner chuckled in light of the colonel's half-stifled groan.

"Colonel, how'd they find Dani in the first place? Hell, we found a key logger and voice recorders along with other devices at Dani's work. And they don't look like anything you've ever used." Conner's stepping in again broke the colonel's line of thought.

"Not mine, guys. I only suspected her identity the end of last week. That's when I sent Lightning in for a meet-and-greet."

"Which doesn't explain *how* you found her." Marc persisted in following this trail as far as allowed, which had the added benefit of directing the colonel's thoughts in that direction.

"Sorry, guys. Above your pay grade. There are several other women I've had under surveillance sharing the same look. I wasn't sure, but I'll maintain those other details in hopes of snagging one of the bastards after *you*." Kenson's intense gaze zeroed in on Dani.

"Anything to do with Holland Freeman?" Marc asked.

Kenson sucked in a quick breath and studied Marc. "How'd you come by that name?"

"He runs an organization. Clandestine shit." Marc didn't flinch under the colonel's glare.

"It isn't something *I* should know about. I'm making discreet inquiries but have to tread lightly." His gaze swung to Callie. "I could use some help there, if you wouldn't mind."

Callie met his gaze with an up-tilt of her chin. "Be glad to, as soon as Dani is secure. Since Ray's duties are in Minnesota, why is he in Maryland?"

"And why am I not surprised you know that?" Kenson shook his head, mumbling about keyboard prodigies. "He had a meeting with Freeman. I'm guessing they're pooling resources to regain Callie and snag Dani in the process."

"Where's the closest institution? We know there's at least one more." Nate directed his question to the colonel.

"I know you all are looking into this, but you need to stop. If they trace back to you—" Kenson began.

"They can't trace my hacking, Colonel," Callie confirmed with a nod. "But they keep few sensitive digital records where there's online access, probably because they know I can cut through their firewalls."

Despite the older man's unnerving scrutiny, Dani concentrated on delving into secrets not meant for public consumption.

"We'll table sifting through Freeman's life for now. The bottom line is Ray's men got a description of a woman matching Dani the night they killed Jake. He must realize if he gets Dani, he gets Callie, and the ultimate bomb he wants built." Marc's summation brought agreements around the room.

"Now that Ray knows we're onto him, do you think he'll run?" Callie's uncertainty echoed in Dani's mind.

"No. He's determined and well-insulated," Dani said.

"And how would you know that, young lady?" Colonel Kenson smiled warmly, hiding the predator's rapacious appetite as his mind latched onto a trail like a dog after meat scraps.

"Just the way he kept texting all the time."

"Tech savvy. Remember?" Nate spoke up.

Marc patted her back, lending strength and encouragement as he addressed Kenson. "Any news on the institution's employees?"

"Not yet, and I haven't found Franklin's body. We did pull DNA and prints for Ray and several others from his institution. Unfortunately, Ray's in the wind, so we don't know if he's working in collusion with anyone else."

"He's got a farm not far from here. It belonged to his family, but under a different name," Dani supplied in hopes of gaining the colonel's resources and not endangering either protective team.

"And aren't you a wealth of information?" Kenson tilted his head to the side in speculation.

"I'll send you the details," Marc added.

Colonel Kenson nodded, his tight grimace implying a warning of some distasteful consideration. "Men, there's another reason I wanted to be here without Lightning, Byte, and Wire. I've come across *other* information. I believe it concerns a member of your team, Marc."

"Hey. I don't believe that for a second. Who—" Conner didn't get a chance to finish.

"Lightning. And no, I don't believe any of them would turn traitor either. Then again, I didn't believe my own lieutenant would sell us out, but he did. If Ray has a hook in someone on the squad, we could backtrack that information to find him." Kenson canted his head and pursed his lips, waiting for Conner to fill in the dots.

"You're saying you want to use Dani and Callie as bait?" Conner finished everyone's thought.

"No," Marc and Nate barked simultaneously.

"They wouldn't move in until they saw the girls, which would put them at too much risk." Marc shook his head with vehemence.

"If we don't, we may never end the threat to both girls." Conner seemed the only one on board with the colonel's plan. "And we may never get an opportunity to trap Ray like this again. Besides, we don't want to push him deeper into the foreigner's pockets, do we?"

Dani studied each man in turn, determining the likelihood of a member of Lightning's team turning traitor. The thought balanced in everyone's mind followed by the memories of prior interactions. No one considered it possible.

"I trust Lightning and his squad." Proud of losing the waver in her voice, Dani met the colonel's gaze with equal determination.

Each man rallied with assent, drawing the Colonel's attention around the room. "Interesting. Your word seems to carry a lot of weight. How is that, considering these men just met you?"

"She's the one taking the greatest risk, isn't she? After all, the serial killer's victims all look like her." Callie's logic didn't appear to faze the commander.

"Okay, let's take a bit to think about this. I'll add a third detachment for the time being." Kenson sighed. "Are you guys ever going to let me in? I know there's more to Callie than her IQ."

Directing his narrowed gaze at Dani, he continued, "The same goes for you, young lady." A certain caginess mixed with frustration edged the older man's tone as he blew out a defeated breath. "So, the question remains, where will you go from here? I realize you've been staying at Marc's house but—"

"Already settled. I'll take Dani to my cabin. Might be a little tight for space with the guys, but we'll work it out." Marc's decision was final. No one argued.

"You sure about the entire team? You've just met them. A few months ago, I wouldn't have doubted them, but recent events has changed my way of thinking." Kenson cleared his throat. His mind sought answers to the long-standing puzzle of how any man could betray his country.

"Yes, absolutely. Now, for trapping Ray and any cohorts dumb enough to follow his misbegotten path. We'll meet again and finalize a plan." Conner nudged the meeting toward its conclusion. "When you leave, Marc, you'll probably be tracked, if only by satellite."

"Yeah, we'll go via the woods. It'll give you guys time to set up around my cabin. Dani and I will head to the beach house first to pick up Darius and Pete."

"All right." Colonel Kenson pushed to his feet. "You want Lightning and the rest inside with you, Marc?" A muscle jumped in his jaw.

"Yes," Marc replied.

Dani smiled at the rest of his thought. *"Where you and I can keep an eye on him and his thoughts."*

Chapter Twenty-One

"Colonel Kenson made it sound like catching Ray would be simple." Dani slipped her hands in her jacket pockets as she glanced out the passenger side window of Marc's SUV. "He's finding it hard to be patient. He wants our trust, our secrets."

"You having second thoughts about this plan?" Despite having a vehicle in front and behind him, Marc felt exposed and vulnerable among the scant mid-week traffic. In the coming months, the coastal highway would bear many vehicles carrying the hopes of sun worshipers and beachcombers alike. For now, they had the road almost to themselves.

"No, not at all. It's just Ray, he's the most paranoid man I've ever met. I wish there was more I could do."

"We're having a difficult time tracking him down, but we'll get him. Listen, hon. I wanted to discuss something before I talk with the guys. We need to test your talent to know your limits, maybe help you work under more trying circumstances. It could give us an edge."

"Distraction?" The uncertainty in her voice alerted him to her tuning into his idea of the best diversions. He let his mind conjure specific details as he watched a light crimson engulf her face.

"It didn't take long for the guys this morning to pick up on your ability. They're very intuitive and expected you to be special in some way, so we need to teach you how to disguise it among those who may scrutinize harder."

After several minutes, he cleared the images of her hair spread out on his bed sheets before continuing, "Every security system has flaws, regardless of its sophistication. However, if you could pick up an intruder's presence regardless of what you were doing at the time, it would increase our chances of capturing Ray alive. Then, we could nail down his co-conspirators."

"I don't know what my range is. I've never tested or tried to enhance it."

"Okay. Let's see what your scope is and what we can do to increase the distance while dealing with complications." Marc checked his rearview again when his sixth sense warned of something being off.

"Back in the house, did you get a sense the colonel was hiding anything?"

"Just that he knows there's something special about me but can't figure out what it is. It's driving him crazy since he also knows that Lightning and the team won't divulge my secrets."

"He's already tried?"

"Yeah, when he talked with Byte this morning."

"Well, it's good to know who we can trust."

"Marc, what if I'm wrong... about Lightning? What if I'm not reading people accurately? There's been a lot of upheaval, and I'm afraid I'm not as precise as I need to be."

"Conner vouches for every member of this team. He knows and trusts them. And I trust him."

Her sudden intake of breath brought attention to his little bundle of nerves.

"What is it?" Checking front and back, nothing appeared out of place as they passed through a T-intersection.

"I've felt him before."

"What?"

"Hate. Same thing I picked up at your club. I think it's the same guy. It was just a flash."

"Where?"

"I don't know. I'm guessing in the pickup at the intersection we just passed. Marc... what are you doing?"

Marc rolled down his window. "Hand signal to Lightning behind me. These bastards are picking us up so damned quick. We need to stay off the cells. Some of Ray's projects are tied to the military, so I don't know what type of equipment he can access." From the passenger side view mirror, Marc watched the pickup with tinted windows at the intersection roll out onto the highway, following from three vehicles behind.

"What are we going to do? Where're Colonel Kenson's other men?" Fear furrowed her brow and shivered through her voice.

"We'll be at the house in just a minute. Lightning is gonna move ahead and check the perimeter while Wire follows us. If the jackass gets close enough to capture, we'll end this, but I doubt he will. Otherwise, we go in, get our stuff, leave, lose him, and switch vehicles under cover so they can't track us by satellite. Kenson already sent the others to the cabin. He can backtrack to get this prick."

Lightning's black SUV zooming past them rocked Marc against the driver's door. He didn't doubt the man's loyalty, only his promise to keep his distance from Dani.

The operation required critical timing and abject focus. He'd hoped to catch a break like this and have one of the dipshits show themselves. "This means Ray has no clue what you can do."

"Still thinks of me as a conduit to Callie."

"If he understood your abilities, I'm sure he'd throw a lot more at us." Marc grinned in anticipation of ending their nightmare. On one of the road's long bends, he caught a glimpse in his side view mirror of darkened windows concealing the driver.

"So, you were expecting this?" Dani's voice gained volume as she squared her shoulders.

"In one form or another, yes." To sense her uncertainty sharpened his determination to strengthen her emotional boundaries.

Children learned life could be scary, holding its own horrors, dark and strange. Some also learned people were meant to be free to enjoy the wondrous sights and adventures encountered. Dani had lived both but needed reminding of the latter, those parts that remained in her memories to bolster spirits during the darkest hours.

"We're gonna get through this just fine."

She merely nodded.

With each mile traveled, the pickup kept an equal distance from behind. "I can't tell how many people are in the truck." Damn, he hated not controlling a situation.

"I can't either."

"Hey. Don't sweat it. We're okay." Turning off the highway, Marc followed the lane to a less-traveled road, then to the quarter-mile winding gravel driveway bisecting the woods shielding his home. A low hum preceded him snagging his cell. "Ah, coded text. Lightning says all clear and the colonel is en route. Good. Never thought I'd say that. We'll be getting new cells today since these are likely compromised."

He didn't need to raise the possibility of Ray's men in the woods surrounding his home. The tension in her thin frame combined with a look of pure concentration told him she was working hard.

"Anything unusual?"

"Yes, but I can't get a bead on it. I'm too anxious."

"Remember when you soaked in the tub? Remember how relaxing it felt?" Marc couldn't afford to lose the opportunity to end her nightmare.

"Yes, but I'm nervous, now."

Rounding the final bend of his driveway, Marc watched the house come into view. Lightning's black SUV sat in front with no sign of disturbance or intruders.

"Where's Lightning? Shouldn't he be out front?" Dani asked. "I can't feel his presence."

"Yeah. He sent an all-clear signal just a second ago. He's probably circling." Marc's gut growled its own foreboding. He stopped the vehicle twenty-five yards from the porch, facing out in case of a necessary fast retreat. "Stay in the car. Byte is in the vehicle behind us. He'll stay with you while Wire and I check things out."

"Where is Wire now?"

"He waited at the end of the lane, concealed until we arrived. He'll be moving up now." Marc reached over and squeezed her hand. "You'll be okay."

From the center console, he removed two collar mics and ear buds before handing a set to Dani. "Watch me and put these on. You can tell me if you pick anything up. But remember, only talk if you need to tell us something. Don't break the others' concentration unless it's important." He watched as she settled the electronics into place.

"Marc, both dogs are in the backyard. Something's wrong with them. I think they're sick. I can't communicate with animals the same way. It's like I feel their presence, their moods."

"Do you sense Lightning anywhere yet?" Marc slipped his gun from his ankle holster.

"No. No, I don't." She startled when Byte tapped on the window.

"It's okay. Just sit tight. I'll be back in a few minutes." Marc studied his house and grounds. Despite the absolute certainty that something was wrong, he saw no telltale disturbance in the landscaping or window curtains slipping to the side.

"Byte, call the colonel. Tell him we have a problem with Lightning," Marc whispered before turning into the stiff offshore wind, Glock in hand.

Byte surveyed the perimeter. "You wanna wait for the colonel before advancing?"

"No. Lightning might not have the time."

Lightning's empty vehicle displayed no signs of struggle. No scuff marks in the dirt or other indication of a fight.

Where the hell is he?

The fact Marc hadn't worked with him and his team previously shouldn't matter. Conner's teammates shared the same signals and methods of operation even if they lacked direct experience together. Equally worrisome, neither of his dogs sent up an alarm.

Wire rounded the front of the SUV. "The asshat that followed you parked a half mile back on the main road but stayed with his truck. Colonel knows to look for him and the one at the end of the lane." Signaling Wire to go right, Marc circled left.

"Okay. Byte, wait for reinforcements, Wire and I will circle the house and find Lightning."

Low, thorny shrubbery placed wide of the structure eliminated possible hiding spots. No telltale pools of crimson marred the front porch floor or the surrounding yard.

Wire would tap his mic if he encountered a problem. Though Lightning clearly held hopes of a relationship with Dani, Marc didn't want the man's blood spilled in protecting her.

Thirty yards of clear space between the house and thick parcel of oaks, pines, and birch trees on two sides made him an easy target if someone waited with a sniper rifle in hand. Yet Dani hadn't picked anything up.

She's nervous.

Quick, uneven strides ate the distance along the width of his home to the backyard.

A hundred yards of zoysia grass stretched between his back porch and the ocean's turbulent surf. Large, breaking waves sent large swaths of foam sliding inland to skim the grass border. With proper camouflage, a tango could easily conceal himself and remain in prime range for a shot or snatch-and-grab.

The back screened porch where he spent free time with his dogs accommodated enough furniture for concealment. The electronic dog door remained closed, which meant no one had broken in unless able to hack that code or his home system. Either was a possibility.

A low groan drew his attention to the side just as Wire's low monotone whispered over his ear mic, "Lightning's down but not out. No information yet. Headache."

Shit. How could anyone get the drop on Lightning to knock him out?

Marc hesitated near the back corner. A faint but distinct foreboding made him duck at the same time Dani's warning sounded in his ear.

"Duck."

Vinyl splinters spat in his face as a dart pierced the siding beside his head, the hiss of its passage kissing his forehead. Judging by its angle, the shooter hid in the stand of pines closest to the beach.

"Marc, Wire, run in the back of the house and come out the window on Marc's side. Hold your breath while in there. Whatever you do, don't breathe that air. It'll knock you out. Hurry. Marc, your shooter is on the move," Dani's whisper trembled over the mic.

What the hell?

As Marc rushed across the porch, another sharp *psssht* of a rifle echoed in his mind before he heard Wire's expletive.

"Wire?"

"Dani, is Wire out?"

The quiet *"yes,"* in his ear bud meant they were down a second man.

Damn it!

Marc's thumbprint unlocked the door as he took a deep breath. Once inside, fifteen seconds saw the alarm disabled and him heading toward the dining room windows to exit.

"Has Byte gotten a position on that bastard with the rifle?"

"Yes," Dani whispered over her mic.

"Are there more than two here?" Marc prayed Dani remained calm and picked up his thoughts.

"Three," again, whispered.

"Are two approaching the back from Lightning's side, and my shooter going for you and Byte, thinking I'm down in the house?" It's what he would've done in a similar position.

"Yes."

"Okay, Dani. Keep your head down."

"Done."

"Byte, head for the woods and circle round to greet the shooter heading your way. I'm coming out the side window now."

Successive clicks through his ear bud acknowledged the plan.

"Dani, when you feel the two others closing in from the back, hiss. I'll pop out and take them down while Byte gets the last of them in the woods. Cough if you understand."

She did.

Slipping to the back corner of his home, Marc waited for her signal. Quiet, even breaths marked his time while thoughts of how one bastard had hurt Dani fueled his rage and augmented the need to destroy his enemy. Disabling one of them could gain valuable information.

Since Dani had warned him to hold his breath, the air inside must be toxic, which would explain why his shepherds were in the yard.

Were they poisoned or chemically knocked out?

Seconds ticked by.

When Dani's soft hiss echoed in his ear, he poked his head around the back corner. Two men wearing gas masks approached, one reaching for the back porch door.

The gun bucked in Marc's hand four times. The first two rounds knocked the distant intruder off his feet with blood spurting from his neck and spilling over his mask. His lifeless husk blocked his partner's exit.

The next two shots found their mark in the leader's left leg and gun arm.

"Drop the gun or die, asshole." Marc keyed his mic while circling the porch. "Byte?"

Another shot signaled the shorthand answer. "Third man down and out," Byte whispered.

With his rifle dropped to the floor and hands in the air, the first assailant hunched over in pain. "How'd you know the inside was toxic?" The bulky mask muffled his words.

"Take it off, asshole. I want to see your face." Marc nodded to the gas mask. "My man that's down..."

"Just knocked out." Another groan from the thug elicited no sympathy in spite of the crimson rivulets draining from his leg wound. "I was just following orders."

When the chin piece cleared the thug's forehead, Marc recognized the intent written in the lowlife's expression, kill or be killed. "Yeah. I definitely want a piece of you. Several, in fact. My girl's not for the likes of you."

"She's a slut, like the rest of the double X population."

In the distance, engine noise diminished then roared as if vehicles turned into his lane. "Are they Colonel Kenson's men?" Marc asked into his mic, not wanting to identify to whom he spoke.

"Yes." Dani's tight voice issued in a high squeak.

"Okay, sit tight." Marc's mind whirled with possible scenarios.

He wanted nothing more than to shove the gunman down a deep well. "Let's go. Step lively if you want to survive this."

"Marc, he's got another gun tucked under his jacket. He'll go for it when he reaches the bottom of the steps." Anger dominated fear in words obviously spoken through clenched teeth.

"If I don't see both hands on your head in three seconds, I'll give you two more nonfatal, but very painful, wounds. Tell me, do you ever fancy diluting the gene pool with your little mercs?"

An instant if astonished response accompanied the hatred in the gunman's glare.

Shoving the sadistic bastard in front of him, Marc edged the stumbling thug to the front of the house and shoved him against the hood of his vehicle. Byte stood by the passenger door while Dani sat inside, still hunched over.

"Hey, sweetheart, you did real well. You holding up okay?"

The barest of nods answered his unspoken question. Byte's shadow created a light veil obscuring the panic in her stiffened shoulders and unblinking gaze.

"Wire and Lightning?" Byte asked as his gaze roamed the perimeter.

"Lightning is sleeping it off. Wire's with him. We'll collect them in a minute." Marc surveyed Dani again. "We're through the worst part. Just a bit of cleanup, and we'll be on our way."

Her expression of subdued rage was the only outward sign of their ordeal.

"Byte, I'm gonna go greet the colonel and give you a minute alone with our new friend here. See what you can find out. You'll find cuffs in my glove box."

"I'm not telling you all shit. Boss has more men at his disposal than you could ever survive. You got lucky this time, but it won't happen again." Pain etched his features, but the bravado faltered when his gaze swiveled to see the arrival of reinforcements.

"Then we'll take him out."

Three black SUVs sent dirt and small stones flying as they skidded to a halt in front of Marc, who stood tall in the middle of his driveway. Before the engines quieted Colonel Kenson had hopped out of the lead vehicle. "What the hell's going on? Where's Dani? Where's your team?"

Not knowing what type of gas filled his home meant he couldn't let the colonel's men walk in without a warning. He also couldn't think of a good lie to keep them out.

"Lightning and Wire were tranqed along with my dogs."

"Which means you sent Byte in search of tangos and left Dani alone and vulnerable? What's going on, soldier? You know better than to leave an asset in the open. There's no way you could've known how many intruders were present. Or, am I wrong on that count?" The commander always thought on his feet.

"I'd never leave Dani vulnerable." Marc needed to sidetrack Kenson's line of thought, fast. "House is full of some type of gas. Don't go in."

"You said the dogs and your men were tranqed outside, how'd you know to not go inside? If the dirtballs were savvy enough to accomplish that much, they'd use something odorless." Colonel Kenson adopted that infuriating frown which bore into his prey.

"My dogs are well-trained. They wouldn't leave the house unless necessary." The lame excuse didn't appease his ex-boss, but Marc wouldn't go into further detail.

Dani's next statement over his ear bud nearly dropped him on his ass.

"Marc, the front door is set with explosives. They used the back to come and go. And more men are coming."

"Shit." Nothing like raising more suspicion. "Colonel, I assume you're gonna want to go in my house."

Kenson arched a brow in response.

"Yeah, okay. Don't go through the front door. They rigged it with enough explosives to ruin your day. Those bastards knew we'd go in and check it before taking Dani inside."

"Yet you avoided the gas. How'd you know about the explosives?"

"We don't have time for that now. More assholes are coming."

"And you know *that* how?"

"No time now, sir."

"All right. Take Dani and go, but we're not done with this conversation. We already have the moron who was waiting by the road in his pickup. We'll clean up this mess and get Lightning and Wire out to you once cleared. Take one of my vehicles. They're well-equipped and were swept for bugs this morning."

"Fine. But I'm taking my dogs now."

Minutes later, Marc drove Dani and Byte along the seldom-used, four-wheeler trail through the woods. Graceful boughs of pine trees slapped the vehicle's top and sides as they bumped along the worn path while sharp holly leaves scraped out thin, high-pitched *eeks*, repudiating the goal of silence.

"Kenson's gonna love the new detailing." Dani's giggle lightened the mood. She'd insisted on riding in the back seat. Darius lay on one side, Pete on the other, each with their head on her lap.

Marc chuckled. "We'll have about five miles of wooded cover and then intersect with Station Rd. From there, we have a convoluted route through back roads and woodsy paths until we reach my place. The truck will be properly striped by the time we stop." Marc silently thanked the vagaries of fate for the abundance of low, heavy clouds that would blind electronic eyes in the sky.

"What about Callie and your brothers?" Byte's gaze met Marc's before scanning his surroundings.

"I called Conner. He'll see to them. They have a similar plan to get Callie and Nate home without a tail."

"It's great that they'll be staying close." Dani's unsteady tone seemed to stimulate his dogs' need to offer comfort. Bucket seats granted a wedge-type view of Darius and Pete rubbing against her thighs at the same time their tails thumped against the doors.

"Nate's place is on the other side of the mountain, so to speak. Whisper and the team are building cabins surrounding him." Amazed at how well the shepherds tuned into Dani's emotions, he commented, "Amazing, they always seem to know what you're feeling." Darius whined and pawed at her chest.

"Yeah, it's an empathetic type of thing, not communication as such." Dani stroked each dog's head, cooing and speaking softly to them.

"Dani, you probably saved our lives today. Thank you." From the front passenger seat, pride and acceptance laced Byte's tone. "It'll be great to combine efforts with Nate's squad. We'll have a nice protection detail. All we need is a secure method of communication between the two groups, sort of an early warning system." Byte's voiced intentions couldn't have come at a better time.

"Already working on it." Marc smiled, his plan coming together as his mind's gears spun thoughts through worn meshed cogs in forming a multi-faceted plan. Integrating Dani with the team would yield the added bonus of boosting her confidence.

Four hours passed in relative silence, each lost in their thoughts. Dark sections of woods secured privacy under interlocking canopies of mature oaks, hickory, and ash trees. One wooded corridor after another marked the vehicle with limbs' clicking along the sides, mud splashing from narrow streams, and rutted bumps. By the time they reached their destination, the sun had begun its descent into the distant horizon.

"Okay, folks. Here we are." When Marc designed the getaway, he hadn't thought about a woman's particular taste or perspective, nor three hulking additions.

The circular drive hosted a shifting patchwork of light and shadows, their give and take imitated his understanding of Dani's life on many levels. Tall oak branches interlocked overhead while large pines and holly trees bordered the shadowed space. A few yards away, two squirrels scampered back and forth in a frolicking dance before darting up the closest tree.

Several pinecones hanging from a low branch slathered with peanut butter and covered with birdseed drew a variety of cardinals, blue jays, and chickadees. Seclusion equaled sanctuary from day-to-day living since his last tour of duty. A sense of peace emanated from the surroundings to calm his mind and soul amid memories of death and destruction.

"This is beautiful. How often do you come here?" Surprise etched her tone.

"Frequently on weekends. Julien and Conner also have cabins within four-wheeler distance. We helped one another in the building process. There's ATV trails crisscrossing everywhere, which means we don't have to travel main roads in bad weather." They'd inherited the land with their father's death.

Inside, he'd designed the two-story cabin with the goal of comfort and relaxation in neutral and earthy tones. Casual and sturdy, it provided relief from the constant turmoil of hectic life.

In the back of his mind, he wondered how long it would take Ray to find them.

Chapter Twenty-Two

Dani settled on the plush, leather sofa in an emotional swathe of comfort. If only Marc could feel her contentment the way she felt his.

"So much change, so fast." An hour spent listening to the men discuss assignments drove home the reality of her new future.

"True, and we still have work to do, but we'll get there."

Over lunch, he'd explained his map, grid lines, patrols, and boundaries, making sure she understood the layout.

The next two hours of testing her psychic limits yielded surprising results. Thinking back, she should've practiced, even embraced her talent. The current freedom and encouragement filled her with anticipation for whatever lay ahead.

Multiple participants combined with Marc's distractions exceeded her ability to focus at times, but he wouldn't relent until a headache etched her brow.

Meals provided time to discuss and assess different aspects of the training amid jokes and suggestions for distractions until Marc curbed their teasing with a glare.

"Can you still feel Byte's presence on the south ridge?"

"Yes. He's picking his way to the crest of the mountain, but his thoughts are growing vague as he moves away."

Marc keyed his mic. "Byte, change course, move lateral."

"I understand why you're testing me. I'm just worried I'll fail at a critical moment." She'd found that the longer she concentrated, the easier it became to recognize the specific energy of each individual.

Southern drawl flavored Byte's thoughts and made him distinctive. Lightning's thoughts often drifted to a ranch in the Midwest and working with horses. Wire worried about the team and ending their threat.

"Don't worry about that. We're not counting on you as an alarm. I just want to see where we stand and test your limits."

She smiled at his thoughts.

On so many levels.

"The colonel's third team is maintaining a perimeter. They'll be coming and going, taking shifts and interacting with Lightning's group."

"The other team is wondering why Byte is roving aimlessly. They think he's a bit *touched*."

"Not a problem. Crofton tactics are synonymous with unorthodox maneuvers. They're probably still trying to figure out the fiasco at my home."

"What happens when this is all settled?" She had no idea what she'd do after achieving a new *normal*.

Though Marc wanted her to remain with him, she still had to piece her life together and figure out where and how she fit. A relationship with him equaled a fairy tale but not if stemming from responsibility or simple lust. She needed more.

"Depends. Let's give it some time and see how you feel when the dust settles."

"I'd like to go back to school if it's safe, study wildlife in their natural habitat."

"That's a great idea. We can discuss it in the coming days."

"Do you think the team will fully trust me?"

"You mean *after* you saved our lives yesterday? Oh, hon, they already do. You really don't invade others' thoughts for personal gain or curiosity, do you? Amazing self-control you have."

"They wouldn't have been in danger if it weren't for me."

"That's their job. It's what they do. No doubt they'll take any help they can get. You heard Byte wanting to make this a permanent assignment."

"That doesn't mean they'd want me in their midst as part of them instead of being sequestered. I didn't invade his mind to find out."

"Kudos to you for integrity. We'll discuss it once Lightning and Wire get here, okay?"

"All right. One thing might help them, working on erecting mental barriers. It might make them more comfortable around me if they knew I couldn't pick their brains."

She smiled when realizing he'd already achieved that goal. "Oh. You've already done it. Is it difficult to do?"

"No, just a little concentration. I can't imagine how hard your life has been, hiding your talent and inviting no one in yet working to keep them out."

Years had passed since anyone accepted her as a human with feelings, hopes, and desires instead of a monster.

Beside her, Marc said, "I don't think I'd like the thought crossing your expression. Explain."

"What?"

"You heard me. Explain the frown that just crossed your face."

"I was just thinking about what one foster family used to call me. It was after my adopted parents died and before I fell into hard times. They were kinda nice and I thought they'd accept me, but they wanted someone *normal*, not a freak."

"They learned what you could do?"

"I never told them specifics. As soon as I'd started to explain, they freaked out and said I was an abomination. They told the social worker I was evil but wouldn't explain why. I guess they figured if they did, they'd never be allowed to foster other kids."

"When did you end up with the Tuckers?"

"They took me in after another family found me *unacceptable*. How is it you read me so well?"

"A lifetime of developing the skill, plus you're pretty much an open book."

"Do you think Ray or the Tuckers will find us here?"

"Eventually, yes, which is why we'll stay prepared if we don't find them first. Can you still feel Byte?"

"Yes, he's circling but maintaining the same distance. He's hungry and wants me to learn how to cook."

"Figures. I think you've had enough for now. I'll call him in."

Quiet conversation filled the next hour. Listening to Marc's calming voice added a peaceful layer to her soul and enveloped her in his warmth even while he extracted past hurts and painful memories.

Outside the bay window, evening pulled its cloak over the landscape in muted casts of ash and charcoals to contrast the few glimpses of purples and pinks through budding branches. It'd become her favorite spot.

Marc's acceptance came without conditions. She'd felt and discerned men's desires in the past, always wanting to take. Marc's approval came with a gentleness that told her he'd be there regardless of the circumstances and provide whatever he could. She'd never existed as somebody's top priority, not in a good way.

She couldn't stop her fingers twining in his hair to pull him closer when he brushed his fingers over the top of her collarbone again.

He tapped her temple with his index finger. "What pictures are forming in here now?"

She startled at his perceptiveness. "I was just wondering about your life."

"And?"

"Were you ever married?"

"No, never made it that far. It's part of why I followed Conner into the military, to learn everything I'd need for the path I'd chosen."

She closed her eyes and let out a low moan of pleasure.

Dani? Still with me? Jesus, I've never seen such responsiveness."

"I've never felt so relaxed."

"Well, in the coming days, let's see what we can do about that." His dark chuckle wiped the figurative cobwebs away instantly.

"Hell. I've never wanted anyone as much as I want you now."

"I wish you could feel my thoughts, what I feel right now. It's like a mirror image of yours."

"This is bad timing."

"I don't care. Life is too short."

"Dani?" Amazement tinged his voice as he stood, scooping her up and heading for the stairs.

"Yes." Her entire body tightened but couldn't look away from his fierce intensity.

"It's time." The smile hiking up one corner of his mouth spoke of seduction and carnal knowledge only imagined. "I want this first time to be slow and thorough." At the top of the steps, he headed for his bedroom.

"You're always thorough." Her breasts felt tight, chafing under the lace and flannel. "I've never asked if you've ever brought..."

Light washed over the room of warm and neutral colors. A stab of jealousy snarled her thoughts. This would be her first time with her man, in his bed. But, how many others had lain there before her?

Nudging the door shut with his foot, Marc pressed his lips together as if understanding the bent of her thoughts. "This cabin is my sanctuary. I've never brought another woman here. You are the first and will be the last. The one for which I've prepared."

When he lowered her feet to the floor, she wasn't sure she could stand. His gaze never left hers as he tugged down the bedcovers then returned to stand face-to-face.

Of their own accord, her feet shuffled a half step forward as her arms wrapped around his waist.

By the time she raised her gaze to meet his, her whole body trembled. He brushed her lips with his own, snaring her body in a vise of desire. When his tongue traced the seam of her lips, she opened to welcome him, heart and soul. The warmth of him delving inside opened her mind, wanting him with every cell, every thought, wanting him to hold her, consume her, wrap her in the inferno that was Marc.

"I want to take my time undressing you." He slipped his hands from her hips and began unbuttoning her shirt. Each button slipped free while his fingers grazed the sensitized skin beneath. Her mouth opened and closed several times, but no words could pass the parched interior.

"You know, a person frequently speaks at a rate of a hundred to a hundred and twenty-five words per minute. Thoughts travel about ten times faster. At this moment, I'm surprised you aren't bursting into flames." He chuckled as he pushed the shirt from her shoulders. It drifted to the floor in a jumbled heap, just like her hopes of making intelligible sounds.

"I want this, Marc. I want you." The graze of his burning touch over her lace-clad nipple ignited a firestorm of sensations shooting through her breast.

"I'd have never guessed. I see you're embracing the lace. Did you have seduction in mind when you dressed this morning?" Slipping his fingers under her waistband, he caressed her lower belly before opening the garment to view her quivering muscles. His gentle touch followed the jeans as they slid down her thighs and calves.

"Um, yes, but I wasn't sure how to go about it." Heat spread from her core to encompass her abdomen and chest. Bra and underwear soon topped the pile of clothes.

"Please don't torture me." Her entire body trembled by the time his gaze consumed every inch of her en route to meet her eyes.

The mattress gave under her weight as he lowered her with gentle hands. Still, watching him undress kept her senses in a state of hyperawareness of cool sheets underneath her and the slight air currents nipping at her body, tight with need.

"Don't take your eyes off me, not for a second." After removing his shirt, he unsnapped his jeans, the sound reverberating in the room.

Commando.

"Now, we begin. I've waited so long for this." Reaching into the wallet he'd set on the dresser, he retrieved two foil packets.

Her gaze jumped to his face.

"It's a start. We have the rest of our lives together." The possessiveness in his tone said she'd never be the same again and be glad for it.

As a young girl, she'd dreamed of a man like Marc. When she'd started reading romance novels, she'd wondered if a lover's possession would feel this overpowering, all consuming.

Leaning over her, he nuzzled her neck before trailing kisses along her jaw then nibbled at her mouth. One hand cupped the back of her neck, holding her in place as he took what they both wanted. He used his other to tease her, mold her breasts, and make her writhe in wanton abandon. When he feathered light caresses down her abdomen and through her curls, her thigh muscles clenched.

By the time he settled in the cradle of her body, tears leaked from the corners of her eyes from denied pleasure. Still, she kept her gaze zeroed in on him, seeing the depth of his desire and listening to his thoughts as he opened his mind."

"*I want you forever in my arms even as I demand your total surrender and walk the edge of your limits. I will always love and protect you. And I'll put your happiness and welfare above my own.*"

He would design a piece of jewelry just for her. Though the scar around her neck didn't faze him, he'd make sure it didn't show, in consideration of her feelings.

"Please."

Their connection was affirmation of all she'd wanted, all she'd ever need. In her mind, she heard his primal roar.

"Mine."

Not once did either look away. In the depth of his gaze, she saw exactly what she'd always wanted and would forever cherish.

When her heart rate and breathing slowed, she was able to focus again. Of all the times he'd sent her world skittering every which way, nothing compared to having him detonate inside her. Little by little, he relaxed, his weight a welcome reminder of his possession even as their bodies remained locked together.

"I'll move as soon as I can, hon." His words were muffled by her hair as he nuzzled her again.

"No, please. Stay like this." With her arms around his shoulders, she tightened her hold, hearing the smile in his groan.

Minutes later, he pulled away and lay beside her. "I think you're gonna be the death of me, sweetheart."

"And I thought you'd split me in two." According to what she read of his thoughts, the soreness would grow to an ache before nightfall, but she'd have no regrets.

"I've always read that the man is the one to complain of exhaustion afterward, but I'm worn out." Not a complaint, she didn't want to miss one second of his attention.

"Close your eyes, Dani. I'll still be holding you when you wake."

"I will always hold you while you sleep." The last thought whispered through his mind and tore through the remnants of her defenses. Though it made him vulnerable, he'd needed to share the intimacy of his mind and let her know what she meant to him.

Dani woke later to Marc's soft snoring in her ear. When she raised his arm a fraction to slip out, he grumbled, awakened, and tightened his hold.

"Where're you going?"

"Um, I'm hungry." The soft stroking down her back gave her other ideas...

Chapter Twenty-Three

"Wire, you're late." The soft click of the back door echoed in the quiet kitchen. Marc's admonishment radiated tension, each man debating the optimal approach in their planned assault.

Conner, Byte, and Lightning sat around the table as bright morning sunshine streamed through the kitchen window. Each soldier portrayed his stress differently, his own *tell*.

Conner drummed his fingers on the table while Lightning toyed with a quarter, rolling it over the back of his knuckles. Byte's lips pressed together in a slight grimace.

"I'm sure he has a good reason." Dani never thought of herself as the middle child or peacekeeper, but it appeared to be her destined path.

She'd slept well last night in Marc's arms, the deep languidness still holding her in its thrall.

"Hey, like sex, I'm never too late." Wire pulled a chair back from the oak table and spun it around before straddling it.

"Somebody's been playing with his tweezers again, no wonder it took him so long to get here." Lightning sat on the other side, shoveling another forkful of scrambled eggs in his mouth. "This is good, Marc. You make it?"

"No, Dani did." Marc's arm circling her waist openly acknowledged his possession. "That reminds me, with the colonel's extra five helping, we're gonna need supplies."

"I'd love to go shopping," Dani spoke up. The thought of simple domestic tasks gave her a sense of belonging in a personal way she never thought to experience.

"Might not be such a good idea unless you need to buy a dress or something." Lightning's mouth curved into a half smile when Marc scowled. "I'd love to help you with that, darlin'."

"Dresses are fun. Lightning wears them all the time, off duty." Wire grinned as Lightning shook his head.

"Come on, Marc. She should have a chance to feel feminine. 'Sides, it's not like Lightning's asking her to spend a night with him," Byte, quiet until now, chimed in.

"Guys, let's keep this rated for those whose diets consist of jellied salad," Conner's warning settled them.

Concentrating on each man's thoughts, she understood they were trying to bait Marc. For what purpose, she couldn't tell.

"Knock it off, he's not stupid." Conner grinned sympathetically at Marc before adding, "'Sides, Dani needs to be with a man who's not a hound dog."

"Then you best not take Lightning shopping. Folks get pissed when animals pee on the fire hydrants. Plus, he's color blind," Byte added.

"No, I'm not. I feel colors with my hands." Lightning again smiled, his mind full of mischievous possibilities.

"Nice try, but it's not gonna work." Marc leveled a stern look at each of his tormentors in turn.

"Hey, it's fun needling a stick in the mud. You're as bad as Nate and Julien." Wire's curiosity lingered. "Anyway, Byte, you'd be out. She wouldn't want to be with a computer."

"Hey, I'm a man." Byte puffed his chest out with a chuckle.

"No, you were hatched in a lab. They had to fill your head with ones and zeros to give you substance," Lightning retorted. "We're still hoping you'll find a woman someday, as in the 3D type.

"Lightning, you say that as if you're a real person," Wire grumbled.

"Look, we need to discuss something, seriously." Marc rubbed his forehead before groaning.

"Hey, we're serious," Lightning shot back.

"Then stop thinking about putting moves on my new little sister." Conner's remark halted the morning's wake up nonsense.

"Can we get down to business?" Marc asked.

Each man looked to Dani then stifled a grin. Byte's shoulders shook with suppressed laughter.

"Freaking troglodytes." Marc snorted in disgust.

"Okay. On to our latest problem. Marc, I've checked the updates to your security system. Nice job." Conner lifted the briefcase he'd set by his chair and placed it on the table.

"What's new?" Wire's ever-present short length of gnarled lines twisted around his fingers.

"Colonel located Tucker's wife for one. They're still up to their old tricks, minus Dani's assistance.

"One of the colonel's men had a talk with the missus yesterday.

Tucker and his sons have split and left the woman behind. He took his boys to continue in his footsteps. She said her husband was obsessed with Dani and getting her back, hasn't seen her men in days... or so she claims." Conner sighed before continuing.

"We still don't know who sent the bastard to Ambrosia. The prick just referred to a boss, and we can't let Dani have a crack at him without tipping our hand to the colonel."

"Shit. If only time hadn't been so limited when they ambushed us at the beach house." Lightning rubbed the back of his neck as he looked to Marc. "Sorry, man, but this has been bugging the shit out of me. I gotta ask." His gaze swung to Dani, an apology written in his expression. "Hon, did Tucker or one of his sons give you that scar?"

Dani immediately covered her neck, heat sweeping upward from her chest until her face flamed. It was the first day she'd worn a normal neck sweater. "Um, yeah, one of his sons. Tucker stopped him from killing me."

"Don't worry. They won't get another chance." Marc pulled her closer.

"Can't wait until—" Lightning's determined statement stopped with Marc's sharp look.

"He's mine, Lightning. All three are mine." Marc slammed his fist on the table.

"Fine, but we get to *talk* to them first." Lightning's nod replicated in agreements from each man, his sideways challenge acknowledged.

"We'll see," Marc relented, his thoughts denying the possibility.

Dani felt each man's frustration like a solid knot in her chest. They all wanted a piece, any piece of a Tucker.

"Found any connection between that misbegotten family and Ray?" Wire asked.

"No, how about you, Conner? Did the colonel find anything different?" Byte took a final sip of coffee before taking his cup to the sink.

"No. None," Conner replied. "Neither has Callie."

Dani knew neither Marc nor Conner would bring up the colonel's comment about someone in Ray's warehouse tracking Lightning.

From Lightning's thoughts, she'd felt his sincerity and dedication to keeping her safe, the need to conceal her secret, and his gratitude for helping save his life.

Images of each man tolerating the colonel's medical team searching them for implanted bugs had equaled a necessary indignation. She'd revealed their experiences to Marc, knowing his concern.

"All right, another piece of business." Marc captured her gaze, his silent question seeking her assent before continuing. "Dani is gonna train *with* us as part of our team."

"What? No." Byte's disbelieving snort wasn't the only one.

"Did she not save your life? Matter of fact, all of our lives? You know they would've damn well killed us to get to Dani. They were too well prepared and equipped."

Each man grumbled over Marc's comment, willing to admit her value but wanting her safe and protected.

"You mean, like in the background, the way Callie helps Nate and his team?" Conner asked.

"Yes. Exactly like that." Marc's thoughts were already defining how she could help them.

"Dani, this is our job. It's what we do. Risk is part and parcel but..." Lightning's faltering admonishment confirmed his indecisiveness.

"And I'll be the sequestered assistant, helping from a distance," Dani added. "Speaking of jobs... since I've told Dr. Carari I wouldn't be back, I no longer have one."

A moment of quiet ensued as a result of each man mulling over his thoughts and expectations before accepting her participation on a trial basis. They'd always want her in the background but realized the valuable information she'd provide could save lives.

Her entire life had derailed from the moment he'd asked her out. Yet, knowing Marc and now, being with him, she wouldn't have changed a thing.

With the grudging decision made, the rest of the day progressed in spurts of assorted tests to judge her endurance and limitations amid jokes, crude remarks, and Marc's grumbling when someone got too close or she blushed due to their suggestive thoughts.

Marc tested her in the cabin with music and TV blaring as well as outside using his favorite form of distraction, kissing her. Standing under the branching systems of interlocking great oaks, she smiled when he wrapped his arm around her waist.

They'd measured distances with and without obstacles. Byte's theory that her brain waves worked similar to a radio and solid objects slowed down or blocked her abilities was disproved, much to everyone's delight.

The only deterrent to her uncanny listening included Wire hiding deep in a fox den, which started another round of jokes and visual distractions.

When they continued with Marc by her side, he deprived her of first one sense then another, and then combinations. Nothing else made a difference in her ability to discern and understand projected thoughts.

Equally important, one after another, they learned to whitewash their minds and block her intrusions. Each man learned to clear his head. Lightning through meditation, Byte and Wire choosing physical movement to release built-up energy. Practice increased proficiency.

The entire time, Pete and Darius stayed by her side, their tails thumping her legs when she rubbed her temples with the overload of spent energy.

"Enough, guys," Marc commanded over his mic. "Time for a break."

"Should we let the colonel's third team in on this?" Dani asked Marc once inside again.

"Not just yet. The fewer people who know about you, the better." Marc framed her face with his large, calloused hands. "Headache?"

"No, just tired. I'm not accustomed to thinking and searching so much." She pushed forward and buried her head on his shoulder, inhaling and reveling in the masculine and woodsy scents.

"Dani, can you feel someone's presence even when you can't detect their specific thoughts?" Wire asked as he brushed by.

"Sometimes. It depends on how close they are. It's kinda like listening to the buzz of the TV when there's no programming."

"What if they're psychotic? What do you get then?" Byte followed his teammate inside.

"A headache and confusion."

"All right. Let's call it a day. You need to rest, hon."

Dani studied Marc's face in an attempt to discern his intentions.

One side of his mouth quirked up as he rubbed her back. "You'll have to try harder than that, sweetheart."

"Can you feel me?"

"Not as such. It's more of an itch between the shoulder blades kind of thing, like the breeze of butterfly wings in my mind."

Daytime maneuvers and dry runs gave way to peaceful evenings with warm conversations and thoughtful expectations. Each day, the team found new and different ways to challenge her, extending her ability. At night, she enjoyed the luxury of Marc's cocooning warmth.

Each man relinquished his doubts over her effectiveness but refused to consider direct engagement with an enemy. She would always remain limited physically, always in the background, and always sequestered. Still—respect shone from their eyes and radiated in their voices.

Normal life had never been a realistic expectation. She saw no sense in wishing for chicken when she had steak. This new life entailed something much better, fuller, and richer. She prayed it would last.

"Time to get that beautiful ass out of bed, sweetheart, before I take advantage." Marc stood beside the bed, dressed in jeans and flannel shirt—walking sin. Waking up to him equaled an adventure in itself. It was disappointing to rouse and find him already up and dressed.

"I'm really tired this morning."

"Sore?"

"In a good way."

She gulped at the expression crossing his face.

"Come on, sleepyhead. We have a big day planned. My brothers are here. With Lightning, Byte, Wire, the colonel's other team coming, and Callie's squad, you'll have more of a challenge. They're going to be moving fast, in different directions, and changing sides. We'll be divided into two teams initially, and you'll have to detect who is where. Should be very interesting."

"You think I'm ready for all that?" As much as she'd like to wait and see what he'd do, Dani sat up and grabbed the robe at the foot of the bed.

"Absolutely." Pulling her close, he nuzzled her neck. "Hop in the shower then come on downstairs. We'll talk over breakfast."

She could barely stand, much less concentrate enough to hold a conversation. Tired muscles protested as she gathered clothes to take into the bathroom. Perhaps she'd get her strength back with the warm water drumming on over-sensitized skin.

Opting for one of his flannel shirts as a light jacket, she wasn't doing herself any favors, but the urge to be encased in his scent proved more than she could resist. Thick socks kept her feet warm and provided extra padding in the heavy boots she'd adopted as normal wear.

The light thud of her descending steps announced her presence to the group below. On the last step, she halted, foot suspended midair, panic draining the previous heat from her face.

"Dani? What is it?" Lightning, attuned to her movements, stood and started toward the stairway.

Marc brushed him aside en route from the kitchen. "What, Dani? Where?" His awareness manifested in a solid grip of her elbow.

"North ridge."

"Not one of ours?" Marc asked.

"No. Tell Wire to turn west and hunker down."

Each of the men jumped up and checked their weapons. Callie, standing next to Nate in the kitchen, looked to him for direction as she checked her Ruger. Lightning and Byte started for the back door.

"Wait. Dani, can you pick up anything from the asshole's intentions?" Marc asked.

"Yeah. He's leaving. Going back to his boss to report our location and numbers. He knows Callie is here."

"All right," Conner said. "Let's see where he goes and converge on him. We can end this and figure out how he found us."

Grumbles of agreement sounded as the men paired up.

"Dani, you and Callie stay with me. I know you haven't trained together yet, but you'll be safer that way. Let's move out. The dogs will stay here." Marc took her hand as they headed for the door.

Chapter Twenty-Four

Ray would miss the farm more than anything else in the States. With confirmation the two women he hunted were in close proximity and reachable, he'd move against Marc and Nate Crofton amid gaining his objectives in one fell swoop.

It felt like an eternity since he'd headed up the work in Minnesota, shut down with Callie's escape. Ray's boss had cut him loose, ending that chapter of life. Hence, it was time to move on.

As it stood, he was lucky his employer hadn't decided to tie up loose ends with a bullet. Yet.

"Boss, Dirk's back with the intel." Frazier sat in the chair indicated.

"Good. Did he keep his distance as ordered?" The view framed by his office window provided a sense of serenity found nowhere else.

"Um, as far as I know. You told us to watch the roads coming and going, along with a healthy perimeter. We've been monitoring electronically, seems kinda paranoid." Frazier leaned forward in his chair, blushing as if realizing he'd just insulted a man who'd kill on a whim. "You gonna call the foreign bastards? Enlist their help?" His gaze shifted away uncertainly.

"No. I don't trust them worth a damn. We'll meet those bastards some place a bit more public after we have the women."

"When do we meet?"

"Tonight, with their extra men and the girls in the house, we'll plan accordingly. I've had good reason to keep our distance. From what our *guests* have told me, Dani is even more special than the little Callie bitch. Time to give our mercs specific orders. We're about to have the biggest payday of our lives."

"I've called them. They'll be here within the hour. I've wanted a piece of the oldest brother for years. This is gonna be sweet." Frazier rubbed his hands together.

"Just make sure everyone else is dead first. No survivors after we get the girls. How are our visitors doing, by the way?"

Ray sent the email informing his contact he'd have Callie tonight. Since he wouldn't be in the country afterward, he no longer cared what weapons her genius mind conjured.

"Crazier than a loon when you mention anything supernatural." Frazier shook his head. "The sons seem just as bad. Talking about computer geniuses and spooks... as in the after-death type."

"Still insisting Dani can communicate with ghosts? The fact they've been killing Dani look-alikes has played nicely into our hands. That stupid ass, Kenson, won't be able to pin the rest of the disappearances on me. Which means, I won't spend the rest of my life looking over my shoulder because of their deaths."

"What are you going to do with the Tuckers?" Frazier frowned as he toyed with the zipper of his jacket.

"Leave them at the scene. Unfortunately, they'll perish at the hands of the Crofton men." Ray shook his head in mock solemnity.

"Which is why we haven't been allowed to play with them."

His subordinate's sadistic streak came out at every turn, and seemed to be a common trait among his men.

"Exactly." Ray smiled. Soon he'd be rich and free of any obligations.

What an awesome combination.

"Fine. At least I'll have Conner." Frazier smiled in anticipation.

"Were you able to identify the others on Dani's team?"

"Yeah, some of them. Your long-range iris scanner is a thing of beauty. We got three of them during their patrols. Do you want us to collect it when we attack?"

"No. That's why you showed it to our guest after wiping it clean. Now, it's got Tucker's fingerprints all over it." Ray tilted his head, trying again to sort out Dani's unique situation.

Though fanatical about the girl, the Tuckers seemed to have it together otherwise. It led him to believe maybe he should identify how Dani's talent worked. Perhaps he could benefit from a bigger cash prize in selling her.

"But they'll know he's not smart enough to obtain, much less use, equipment of that sophistication." Frazier bit his lower lip, as if worried he'd be set up to take a fall.

"Doesn't matter. The foreigners are, and it'll confuse the hell out of Kenson and the Croftons. I just want a bit of distraction until I'm outside U.S. borders. After that, I don't care." Ray hated obstacles, and finding Dani had proven a colossal pain in the ass. He couldn't wait to get his hands on her.

"Oh, before you go, secure the tunnel." Ray turned his laptop around so Frazier could observe their guests on video circuiting the bedrooms and inspecting lamps and furniture for hidden devices.

"Paranoid bastards, aren't they?"

"Yeah, but they sure jumped at the opportunity to get their hands on Dani. As if I'd leave her with the likes of them before finding out the girls' connection," Ray retorted.

"Get them some more books on ghosts and paranormal bullshit. That'll keep them busy until tonight."

* * * *

Dani glanced at Callie in the back seat of Nate's SUV. Anger furrowed the telekinetic's brow, but no fear shadowed her face.

"You've been through this before, Callie." A statement more than a question.

"Yes." Callie's expression softened in sympathy. "And we'll end this a whole lot easier than last time."

Her tone exuded the same determination found in the set of her jaw and precision of her movements as she rechecked her weapon.

Dani wondered if Marc would teach her how to shoot. Unlike the others, she'd never trained in self-defense and couldn't physically protect herself. "Wish I had your talent." Hating guns didn't mean she wouldn't learn to handle one. She put it on her mental to-do list.

Scattered, late morning light filtered through the intertwined branches overhead, the stroboscopic effect cutting the road before them into changing swaths of moving light and shadows. Marc's frustration burned in her mind. He didn't want to bring her anywhere near this fight but couldn't risk leaving her behind.

"And I wish I could read thoughts the way you can. Though, I can see how that might be unsettling at times." Callie glanced at Nate.

"Marc said when this is settled, he and his brothers will help find our biological parents." The thought of family warmed Dani's heart after seeing the way Marc interacted with his brothers.

Marc, sitting in the front seat, blocked her from reading his intentions. She almost wished she'd never helped with that endeavor.

"Anything, Dani?" Marc asked.

Although she picked out the location of the farm when their intruder filtered that thought through his mind, she hadn't obtained much other relative information. "No. If he hadn't spooked and lit out so fast, I'd know more. I'm sorry I didn't pick him up sooner, guess I was distracted." Heat blossomed on her face as she turned to look out the window.

"The fact he avoided our trip wires tells us he's well-trained." Marc frowned as he touched his ear mic. "Conner says he's called the colonel and told him we're on this dirtball's trail. We don't have much farther to go. It's gonna drive Kenson crazy that we found these morons first since he's thrown everything he's got at it. He's damn good at what he does."

Dani grimaced at the thought of further piquing Kenson's interest. "At least this will be over."

"Nate, go over the layout and surrounding area one more time," Marc urged his brother.

"Okay. According to the records and satellite images, it's a one-story rancher with what looks like an office built off the back. Trees are scattered around the perimeter. About thirty yards of clear space surround the house. A covered porch extends the entire front."

"Are the trees suitable for sniper setup?" Marc asked.

"On three sides, yes, but not the front. That's just open rolling farmland."

"He's got to have some type of bolt-hole. He's too clever to not have thought this through." Marc retrieved his cell and relayed the information to the colonel. When he slid his phone in its carrier, gone was the tender and loving man who'd nurtured her, gained her trust, and educated her in the subtleties of strategic warfare. This man manifested full combat mode in a battle he intended to win.

"I'll keep her safe, Marc." Callie leaned forward to briefly squeeze Marc's shoulder.

Nate grumbled in protective possessiveness.

"Nate… we're family." Dani's heart swelled with pride. She'd never belonged to a group where each defended the other. No one had ever desired her for herself as opposed to her talent.

"There's a turnoff two hundred yards ahead. Satellite pics show narrow dual tracks leading through the woods adjacent to Ray's farm.

Maybe from a four-wheeler. We'll use it to get closer. The driveway is a quarter-mile farther along this road." Marc slowed the SUV near a tiny clearing.

County road workers had installed a culvert in preparation for making a driveway, but the land remained undeveloped. "I don't know how far this path goes... looks overgrown and not used in a while."

Three SUVs followed them off the narrow road and, like Marc, found temporary cover among the woody maturity of budding dogwoods, northern cedars, birch, and maple trees along the woods' edge.

"Dani, you and Callie will stay *inside* the vehicle. If things go south, take off. Julien's gonna wait here at the entrance for the colonel's men. ETA less than thirty. Virus and Whisper will stay and help him cover the front. The rest of us will follow this dirt trail as long as it travels parallel to the house.

"Lightning will guard your perimeter while we take up positions around the house."

As he spoke, Julien, Virus, and Whisper exited the last of their caravan, spread out, and began picking their way through the woods.

"Dani, you picking up anything?" Marc asked.

"Not much, just grumblings."

"Okay, then. We've got sufficient distance," Marc replied.

Each bump and pothole along the overgrown path tightened Dani's nerves. Pine branches and pointed holly leaves screeched along the vehicle and lent an ominous apprehension to sharpen her fear. No shortage of damning phrases came to mind for embroiling Marc and these men in her trouble.

Tenacious conviction in Callie's expression mirrored Nate and Marc's profiles. If only she shared that confidence. Heat generated from collective anger combined to create an environment fit for an Amazon tribesman with her perspiration providing humidity to complete a jungle-like atmosphere.

Dani's hands ached from clenched fists. In thinking back, she found nothing which could have avoided this moment short of fleeing that Saturday morning at the Schutzhund trial. Marc's determination would've landed them in this place, in this moment, regardless of which way she'd turned.

Fate would not be her master today.

"Okay, boys and girls. Looks like the path ends here." Marc cut the engine in front of a large pine tree standing sentinel to the remaining forest. "Girls, you'll stay in the vehicle. No questions asked."

"I can pick them up now, Marc. Ray is in there, along with his men." Dani concentrated on the Think Tank administrator's thoughts.

"Figures it'd be him. Good. How many?" Nate asked.

"Not sure. At least twenty. It's too jumbled to tell."

"All right. We'll take our places and sit tight. Lightning is gonna stay here. If you catch any of Ray's men approaching, just whisper over your mic, and Lightning will get you out of here." Marc's mouth tightened when speaking the other man's name.

Two other SUVs pulled up among the shrubs beside them. Men poured out of each, silent as night, gathering in a loose circle around Conner. Marc and Nate exited, each stepping back and opening their rear door. Marc's serious expression melted, his obvious need to hold her strong as he released her seat belt and tugged her into his arms.

"Dani. You and Callie are first priority. You take care of her and yourself. If necessary, you do anything you have to in order to stay safe. If I could've stashed you somewhere—"

"I know, Marc. I know. We'll be fine. Nobody's gonna sneak up on us. I'll pick up anything that approaches on ground or by air." Slipping her arms around his neck, she reveled in his embrace, the hard muscles pillowing her chest, the warmth of his hands sliding under her hair to caress her back.

When his lips brushed her own, images of what he wanted to do crowded her mind and caused a flood of warmth in her belly. Then, cool morning air brushed her face and neck as he pulled away. The vehicle now felt more like a tomb.

Nate nuzzled Callie's neck before kissing her and stepping away. Neither man glanced back as they left.

Minutes passed by with the return of birdsong and occasional aircraft far overhead. Both girls had lowered their windows several inches to hear an enemy's approach.

Dani felt Lightning's presence, different from before when they'd trained, his light, teasing manner ditched in favor of cold, hard determination. If not for ear mics and recognizing his protective thoughts, she might have panicked when he slipped into the woods to do a perimeter check. He didn't roam far.

"How soon before the colonel's men arrive? Can you still feel Nerd?" Callie looked around, anxious. "I'd feel a lot better if we weren't inside here. It's too confining. We're sitting ducks."

"Well, we could lower the back tailgate and sit on it..." Dani glanced at her watch. Marc had left twenty-five minutes prior. "Our guys are in position around the back and other side. Spirit and Blade are with Nate. Wire and Byte are with Marc. Everybody's off the ground at the moment."

"Is Lightning okay?" Callie asked as she opened her door with a soft *snick*.

"Yeah, he's fine and close." Dani's restless gaze searched the woods for unseen enemies as she circled around the back.

"Good. Let's park our butts here." Callie raised the upper glass hatch before lowering the tailgate. They sat side by side, facing the path to the road.

Callie jumped when Dani stiffened, "Oh, shit. The Tuckers are here, too."

"Good, get 'em all at one time." Callie slashed the air with her hand in a dismissive gesture.

"The colonel's just arrived. He's brought... I can't count how many men. I think about two dozen, maybe. They're getting ready to spread out to attack from all sides." Dani grimaced as she sought Lightning's comforting presence.

"I'm glad the colonel's here even if he does give me the creeps. It's like he can see into my soul. He's always prying..." Callie hopped off the tailgate and stood beside the vehicle.

"Well, now he wants more on us both. I wish him luck on that count. Nate is as protective of you as Marc is with me." Dani wrapped her arms about her shoulders to ward off the late morning chill. "Lightning is coming, gonna update Colonel Kenson."

If she hadn't felt Lightning's presence, Dani's knees would've buckled. The man made no noise whatsoever in sneaking up beside her.

"Marc and Nate wanted you two *in* the vehicle." Six-foot-four inches of solid muscle towered over the women.

"Come on, Lightning. We were sitting on the tailgate. That's kinda in the vehicle." Dani could feel his indecision.

Shaking his head, Lighting relented. "All right, but it's your asses on the line if they find out."

"Way to get someone's attention. You do understand I need to concentrate now, yes?" Dani stood her ground.

A light rustling from her left brought Dani's attention back toward the road. Gone was the older gentleman in flannel and jeans. Today, Colonel Kenson had dressed every bit the commanding officer. He nodded to Lightning before using hand signals to split the squad into smaller groups, each branching out as they headed deeper into the woods. Mouth pressed into a firm line betrayed disapproval over the women's presence.

Dani grinned at the frustration swirling inside him. His fondest wish of having the girls semi-alone, and he couldn't afford the time to question them. A missed, golden opportunity.

"Ladies. Nice to see you each in one piece. To be honest, I'm surprised you're here." He held out his hand in greeting, first to Callie then to Dani.

"There wasn't time or a safe place to put us," Callie spoke first. "If we hadn't followed the intruder, we wouldn't have found Ray's base of operations. We really didn't have another option."

"Well, I look forward to speaking with you later about the particulars of that." Though uncertainty filled his mind, the older man pivoted to make his way with the others.

"That went smoother than I expected. He wore his cross-examination face. You girls sure do get under his skin. And even I can tell he didn't buy the nonsense about us following the dirtball here." Lightning grinned before melting into the background. "Stay close to the vehicle, ladies."

Considering Ray's penchant for command, Dani had little difficulty in picking out his energy despite the others present. "Ray is gathering his men to set up a strike on Nate and Marc. He thinks we're still at the cabin."

"Surprise, surprise. What I wouldn't give to be in sight of the house. I'd love to mess with those bastards." Callie's tone carried a need for revenge. "That monster held me prisoner for most of my life."

"I'm sorry. I really am." Dani moved to stand close, tentatively sliding her arm around Callie's waist. Affection came easier when someone returned it, honest and sincere. She thought of Callie as a sister, after a sort.

"Hey, not your fault. Just part of life." Callie returned the light hug.

"Oh, hell. Ray knows the men are here." Dani gulped as her arm tightened around Callie. "One of the colonel's soldiers tripped a security wire." Dani flinched with the sound of gunfire in the distance. "They're coming out the far side. Some are heading toward the back." Dani paced to the front of the SUV, leaning on its hood for support. "A few are exiting the front, too."

Callie rested her palm on the butt of her gun. More popping noises sounded like the crackle of nighttime fireworks.

"I hear the Tuckers. Someone mentioned something about a tunnel."

"Damn it! I should be helping." Callie paced back and forth in front of the SUV, absentmindedly using her telekinesis to sweep a pine branch out of her way with each pass.

"Can you stop a bullet?" Dani asked, surmising the truth but wanting to soothe her friend's ire.

"No, it's too fast. But with you keeping an ear out for who's approaching, and me throwing them against something hard, we'd be unbeatable."

"It'd probably work, but if the guys see us, they'd get distracted—or worse." Dani sympathized with Callie's frustration.

More gunfire erupted. Thick underbrush and dense woods denied them a specific origin while a maelstrom of fear, anger, and frustration emanated from Callie in a wall of blazing determination.

"What's happening now? Do you still feel Ray? Is he dead?" Callie's fists balled at her sides.

Deeper in the woods, rustling sounds indicated the fleeing of anxious squirrels and other small animals while overhead, a hawk's chirping alarm scattered the avian community.

"No. I don't feel Ray or the Tuckers. They're either dead or unconscious." Dani blew out a sigh. She'd waited so long for the evil psychos to receive their due. Now, she just felt exhausted, tired of being hunted, tired of feeling like a freak, and tired of being alone.

When all became quiet, Callie looked to Dani for confirmation. "The only people I sense standing now are our guys and Colonel Kenson's men."

"Extent of our injuries?" Callie asked.

"Marc and Nate are fine. Virus has a shoulder wound. Blade took one in the leg. Both are getting medical attention. Julien took a round in the vest. His chest hurts." Dani rubbed her temples to alleviate the pain.

"Means he might have a broken rib," Callie added.

"Did they find Ray yet?" Now that their men were safe, Dani felt Callie's mind fill with the need for vengeance.

"No. Not yet. There're a lot of bodies. Some are wounded. Too much confusion for me to concentrate. Our guys are taking it slow and cautious." Dani groaned. "Ah... sensory overload. It's too much."

"Ease up. It's over. Relax." Callie paced back and forth along the SUV's side.

"No, something's wrong. I feel it but can't define it. There're just too many people, too much pain."

Without a sound, Lightning appeared by their side. "What's wrong?" Shouldering his rifle, he stood close and met Dani's gaze. "What is it, Dani?"

Before she could answer, Lightning's body jerked forward at the same time a loud crack filled the air. His blood spurted over their faces before he dropped to his knees, crimson seeping from his shoulder. With his good hand, he applied pressure. "Fuck."

Chapter Twenty-Five

"Why, hello, Penny. Or should I call you Dani, now? Long time, no see." The raspy voice broke into soft chuckles. Familiar, cruel, but older sounding, Tucker had finally found her as promised.

"Oh, God, no." Sudden nausea coincided with bile burning the back of her throat as Dani reached for Lightning.

"Nuh-uh. Touch him or move again, either of you, and I'll put a bullet in his brain. I've waited years for this, you little whore."

Tucker held a pistol, his hand shaking with rage. Both his sons, who'd enjoyed endless hours taunting and tormenting her, stood by his side.

Senior never allowed them to rape her, a thought that remained foremost in the younger son's mind. Both were grown men now, still harboring sadistic tendencies. With a gun aimed in her direction, she knew Callie wouldn't risk reaching for the Glock in her back waistband.

"It wasn't my fault you killed those people."

"Of course, it was. If you'd just hacked the computer as I'd asked, I wouldn't have shot them. It wasn't their money anyway. It belonged to the dead codger." Tucker waved the gun back and forth, his internal debate wavering on whether to kill Lightning and Callie.

"Who'd left it to his son and his family, college funds for their kids," Dani retorted.

"All you had to do was ask the ghost for the information, and I'd have let the family live. I sure as hell wasn't gonna wait for some lawyer to unseal the accounts. That would've taken months."

"I wasn't going to help you steal anymore, not even after you killed them."

"Never understood why not. Ghosts have no use for material things. The family had enough of their own without the inheritance. All you had to do was ask the spook nicely, get the passwords, and obtain the account numbers. Surely, the old spirit would've given the information rather than watch his family die. Even so, they never felt a thing since death was instantaneous."

"Hey, Dad." The oldest son leered at Callie. "I'd like to enjoy the blonde for a bit."

When his eldest started forward, Tucker halted them both with an outstretched arm. "Not here, not now. They'll be time for that later, boys. For now, sit tight and shut your mouths."

"How'd you sneak up on us?" Dani thought of all the commotion and confusion during the past half hour. If she'd maintained concentration, this wouldn't have happened. She'd vowed no harm would come to Lightning or Callie, regardless of what she had to do.

In her mind, she reached for Marc, could feel him coming. He'd heard Lightning cuss as he went down but had stayed silent.

"Ray sent us through an underground tunnel from the house to a hidden exit nearby. He has more equipment than you could imagine, detecting heat signatures and the like. I just couldn't pass up this opportunity. I've been looking for so long. You can thank Ray for helping me."

"Where is he?" Callie asked.

"Heading for the road, waiting for us to bring you two. Apparently, he doesn't like to get his hands dirty or take risks."

"You've been killing the girls who look like me."

"Yeah, so what? You've grown a lot since I saw you last. I had no idea what you looked like now. Figured you'd keep your hair long. Surprised you dyed it."

"Bastard." Dani looked to Callie, hoping she'd catch on quickly. "As scared of ghosts as you are, I'm surprised to see you here. This place is full of angry ones, old battleground and all that. Didn't you realize they helped me escape back then? They've kept me hidden all these years."

"We have one more job to pull. Then I might leave you be, bitch. After I've spent years searching, they can't begrudge me that much. Sides, if you want to keep your little blonde friend alive along with this one, I suggest you warn your ghost buddies against any mayhem."

Jeez, still loony.

"All right, all right, I'll come with you."

Behind him, a thunderous crack coincided with a large pine branch breaking. When Tucker and his sons pivoted to look, the limb swept all three off their feet. Tucker's gun skidded among decaying leaves and broken twigs to land near his son. Before he could retrieve it, the gun rose from the ground, lifted by unseen forces until the oldest redhead stared down its barrel.

"I suggest you don't try to touch it. They will shoot you." Callie's assurance brought Tucker's attention to her, searching for cracks in her confidence.

"You, too? How can you both be protected by them?"

"You've lost again, but this time, no one will die, unless you piss off the ghost holding the gun." Dani smiled at the thoughts going through his mind.

"Way to go girls," Lightning said, pushing to his feet while cradling his arm.

Tearing off part of her shirttail, Dani applied pressure to the injured man's wound. She prayed they got the situation under control before the colonel or his men returned.

Marc, where are you?

Callie was thinking the same, her jumbled thoughts ricocheting between fear over discovery and anger that someone threatened them. Her anger surged as she stepped forward and grabbed the gun. "Move one inch and I'll open fire on your egg seekers. Judging by the slope of your forehead and dull glaze of your eyes, I'd be doing the collective gene pool a favor."

Both Tucker and his two boys looked mutinous. "Fucking chit, should've known she'd find a like kind."

"Shit." Dani tensed.

"What?" Callie looked around, ready to shoot anything that moved. Lightning pivoted to face whatever approached.

"It's Ray. He *has* circled around us and is headed for the road but suspects our men are waiting for him. Tucker wasn't lying." Dani grimaced when Lightning alerted Julien, Virus, and Whisper to block Ray's escape.

The slight distraction provided Tucker with a window of opportunity. He scrambled to his feet and darted into the woods, leaving his sons dumbfounded.

"Oh, shit, Callie. Don't let him get away." Dani hissed. "Look!"

Before Tucker gained ten feet, a thick, holly branch swooped down and flung him against the trunk of a solid oak tree. The satisfying *thunk* of his skull against wood presaged his falling in an unconscious heap.

"He's out. I'll know when he regains his senses," Dani assured them.

"The other couldn't move if their lives depended on it." Callie's conspiratorial smile reflected Dani's own thoughts.

The oldest boy glared at his brother, anger and confusion written in their slackened jaws as they remained sprawled on the ground. "Shit, she really does control the ghosts. And they talk to her. I can't budge an inch!"

"Tell them to let us go, you little whore." The eldest brother struggled against invisible bonds, his face a mask of hatred.

"Damn ghosts talk to and do these bitches' bidding." Pure evil beamed from the younger's expression. "Hell, all this time, I thought Dad was batshit crazy. Fuck, Dani. We should've killed you when we had the chance."

Chapter Twenty-Six

Lightning groaned as Dani tied the pressure bandage in place. "I'm so sorry, Lightning. I'm so very sorry."

"It's okay, hon. I'll be fine. If not for you two, I'd be dead. Again." Lines of pain bracketed the corners of his eyes and mouth.

"Callie, I don't know what else to do. Marc's on his way. I feel something else, too, but it's weird." Dani studied the woods all around her.

Callie gripped the pistol, her knuckles blanching white. "If you can't get a fix on the location, Dani, maybe someone else is coming through the tunnel."

Dani closed her eyes and concentrated. "*Ah*, got 'em. It's the colonel and some of his men. They just popped up above ground, I think." Seconds passed. Dani waited, praying Marc would move faster.

Seconds later, Colonel Kenson raced around the large pine, gun in hand, surveying the scene before him. Gray hair and long of limb, he hustled with no signs of age slowing his movements.

"Fascinating conversation you girls have had. I've enjoyed it immensely. Ghosts?" Kenson's men followed, all with weapons at the ready. Several took custody of the sons while two more carried Tucker from the woods, unconscious. All three were dragged toward the road.

Dani stood rooted to the forest floor in fear, frozen as an oak tree bound to the earth, expecting the colonel's words to cut her down like a lumberjack harvesting a prized specimen. Her mouth opened and closed like a tiny bird, yet no sound emerged.

"Lightning, how bad are you hurt?" The colonel examined the wound after loosening the makeshift pressure bandage to examine the wound.

The injured man groaned when the colonel checked his back, then retied the bandage.

"Through and through. Lucky thing neither of you girls were hurt." Kenson nodded to one of his men who took over Lightning's care.

Oh, shit. Callie, please say something because I can't.

"Uh, where'd you come from? We didn't hear your approach." Callie's face had paled but she inherently understood Dani had lost the ability to function.

"You mean your non-corporeal friends didn't tell you? How rude."

From the corner of her eye, Dani watched as several strings of cobwebs dislodged from its pine needle base and floated against the breeze to land on the back of Kenson's head.

The commander ducked and jerked around to counter any strike, one that didn't come. Wiping it away in disgust, he pivoted to consider the two women.

Dani strangled a chuckle behind a cough, somewhat relieved Callie took the lead to let her mind thaw enough to concentrate.

"Little early and inappropriate timing to be hitting the sauce, isn't it, Colonel?"

Kenson matched Callie's grin with one of his own. "If you'd like to humor an old man and join me for a drink, I'd love that."

"I'll talk to Nate. We'll see," Callie replied.

Baiting a predator had never ended well in Dani's book, then realized Callie's ploy was a diversion.

Kenson retrieved a small mic he'd nestled in a pine bough left when leaving. He'd heard every word spoken. She thought back to their conversation about ghosts and telling Callie to not let Tucker escape when his body had landed ten yards away, shielded by holly and pine trees. Neither she nor Callie had moved.

Oh, shit. No wonder Marc wanted us to stay inside the vehicle.

"Actually, I knew you were special, Dani, but I'm just having trouble wrapping my head around it. I'd love to sit down with you two over a beer and enjoy a little chat. A ghost whisperer or telepath, and what, a telekinetic?" He hesitated as his gaze swung between Callie and Dani. "I swear we can keep it just between us and your men."

Dani's legs gave way as Marc and Nate rounded the pine tree. Marc caught her, supporting her weight. "You okay?" His pivot to stand between Dani and the colonel blocked the latter's sight of her. Pulling her in close, he nuzzled her hair.

"Don't say a word, okay?"

She nodded against his shoulder.

"You're white as a sheet." Marc held her tighter.

"Her color didn't change until I inquired about her *other* friends. Imagine that." Kenson stowed his mic in his shirt pocket.

"Damn, I wish this had video, too. You girls like to explain how Tucker ended up unconscious in the woods, out of sight, and heading toward the road? All the while, these two boys remained frozen and unable to move. Not to mention the fact my highly trained Special Forces soldier is shot, and the girls are unscathed," Kenson continued to put pieces together.

"Tucker wouldn't have left without you, Dani, and he must have had the gun in order to shoot Lightning. Yet, now Callie is holding the gun. Very interesting. I didn't hear signs of a scuffle. What I *did* hear was the most fascinating, earnest conversation ever witnessed."

Nate moved to stand face-to-face before Callie, relieving her of the weapon. "You all right, babe?"

Callie wrapped her hands around his waist, her muffled assent against his chest accompanied by a nod.

"Want to explain why you're spying on my girl, Colonel?" Marc's tone was controlled yet pleasant.

"Hey, you left them here with just one man. I wanted to make sure they were safe."

"Obviously, they've been training also. You remember hand signals? We taught the ladies to use them. Hence, they communicated and remained unharmed." Marc rubbed his hands up and down Dani's arms.

"Oh, I heard their communication. And that doesn't explain what I've learned or how Callie got Tucker's gun after he shot Lightning, or why Tucker ended up unconscious and out of sight." Kenson indicated where Tucker's sons had lain. "Or how they kept Tucker's sons immobile..."

The soldier mentally salivated.

Glancing at the colonel, Marc murmured, "I've been waiting to meet these sadistic maniacs. I'd be glad to escort them and their father to wherever they're going, sir. Seems I owe them quite a bit." Very gently, Marc fingered the scar around her neck.

"Sure, I'd appreciate that. You and Nate transport them while I take Callie and Dani back to your cabin. I'd be more than happy to keep them company." Colonel Kenson arched a brow, a small smile playing about his lips.

"No!" Marc and Nate barked at the same time.

Marc was furious, the desire to kill on her behalf strong yet tempered by the need to protect her secret.

Shaking his head, Kenson added, "Marc, Nate, you know I can protect them better if I know what's going on. I am concerned, also, about how these bastards found your cabin. It occurred to me, we checked the men for bugs at your house. Did you check your dogs? It would've been easy enough to chip them." Stepping to Marc's side, Kenson leaned forward, his gaze boring into Dani.

"I won't ever betray or let harm come to you. You girls can *trust me."*

"Don't worry, sir. We'll take care of that detail," Marc said as he tugged Dani toward the SUV. "I'll call you after the girls are settled.""

Nate guided Callie to the back and Marc fastened Dani's front passenger harness, both men taking a deep breath. "It's time to go home." Nate updated Julien and Conner as he slid into the front passenger's seat.

"The colonel knows, Marc. He knows things about Callie and me. He thinks either I'm telepathic, or I talk to ghosts. He knows Callie is telekinetic." Dani worried her lower lip between her teeth.

"He may suspect, but he won't ever be sure without confirmation. He's a very *prove-it-to-me* kind of guy, relies on his five senses," Marc started the vehicle.

Nate murmured as he removed his ear bud and neck mic. "It'll be a while before we talk about confirming it. I, for one, am not ready to let him into our circle. I'd trust him with my life, but until he retires, he has to answer to superiors."

"Agreed," Marc said, confirming the topic closed.

Long after Marc dropped Nate and Callie at their cabin, Dani still couldn't get a read on Marc's thoughts. He'd remained closed off. Was he angry about her disobedience? It amazed her to think of any place as home after years of living day-to-day, hiding, and always looking over her shoulder.

"What's going to happen to the Tuckers and Ray now?" Her frustration grew as Marc's face remained a mask, giving nothing away.

"Black site seclusion. None of the survivors will see the light of day or talk to a lawyer." Marc's hard façade fractured for just a second. His look of compassion acknowledged her fear and uncertainty.

"Don't worry, even if Kenson didn't suspect your ability, he wouldn't take a chance on Callie's safety and let his prisoners see a normal prison. Knowing him, I'd say he'll take equal safety precautions with you." Again, Marc's mental wall went up. "I suspect one or both dogs have been chipped. I'll check as soon as we get home."

"You have all my secrets, Marc. I'm not hiding anything."

"All right, but realize this as your only warning. Omitting a truth is the same as telling a lie in my book. Once our commitment is firm, if you withhold anything, anything at all, we will have problems."

"I understand. I won't hold anything back."

"I'm sure Callie won't get off so easy."

The rest of the silent ride allowed Dani's mind to chew over Marc's talk of commitment and warning.

Never in her life had Dani felt so energized yet relaxed at the same time. She snuggled deeper into Marc's embrace while lying on the couch. Amorphous shadows frolicked along the oak floors, given freedom and energy by the strong breeze outside.

Marc set his cell aside. "Okay, here's the scoop in case you weren't eavesdropping. Ray, Tucker, and his sons have been dealt with, no phone calls and no lawyers. We won't hear from them again. Conner's gonna bring Pete and Darius out in a bit.

"Dr. Carari removed a GPS chip from Pete's shoulder. He's gonna be fine. Your ex-boss said she misses you, by the way. Conner gave her just enough information to let her see the gravity of your situation. She understands you not being able to give notice."

"It's hard for me to believe my years of hiding are over."

"We'll still have to be careful. From what Kenson has learned, neither Ray nor the Tuckers informed anyone about your *uniqueness*. Which doesn't mean someone out there isn't looking, having obtained information from Holland Freeman. We still have Ray's boss to deal with."

"Holland Freeman, the head of it all."

"Plus, Kenson thinks there's at least one more Think Tank holding a prodigy of some type. We'll deal with that later."

Dani smiled at Marc's thoroughness in wrapping up a nasty situation. "You want to talk about us."

"I want you in my life."

"Is that complete honesty?" She arched a brow. Waiting.

"Look, when I was a kid, my girlfriend was in one hell of a horrendous situation. I promised to help get her out of it, and I failed. She ended up paying the ultimate price."

"And that's why you haven't married. You're worried you won't be able to protect what's yours." Regardless of what lay before them in the days ahead, she wanted Marc to be part of her world. She willed him to understand the commitment in her gaze even as the pain in his own took her breath away. "Relationships are two-way streets. We take care of each other."

They'd each shared the worst of man's horrors yet still craved the freedom to love without reservation. There would always be threats of some kind, either man-made or through nature, but they'd weather them together, holding on and taking comfort from each other.

"Jesus, Dani." His caresses became bolder, filled with the resolve to have it all.

"We've discussed everything we need to for now. I want this. I want you." Dani twined her fingers in his hair, the silk contrasting with the hard man who held her.

"Sweetheart, you had me months ago at the vet's office." He cupped the back of her neck, immobilizing her head.

"The men are out on perimeter checks so we have the house to ourselves for a couple hours." In one lithe movement, he stood and held her cradled against his chest.

She was exactly where she wanted to be.

* * * *

Thank you for reading Shadow Guard.

Callie and Dani have gained their freedom. They've honed their talents, vowing to find others held prisoner and set them free. Follow their journey in Whispers After Death as the Crofton men band together to hunt the predators preying on their women.

“Kendra Lea Bower, ’bout time you got your scrawny ass down here. You been helping Father McKinley at St. Marks again?” Daeron’s rhythmic foot tapping signaled his pre-performance adrenaline rush, complete with an all-too-familiar hand gesture asserting, ‘today would be nice’.

“Yeah. He’s still ragging on me to stay there.” Kendra darted up two steps at a time, her beloved and battered acoustic guitar thumping against her back and snagging her hair.

Though the source of trepidation eluded her, a wary foreboding sandwiched between hope and confidence dampened her mood.

“Maybe you should pray for patience, Daeron.” Their band manager, Wes, indicated this might be a good break for them, but remained stingy with details except that it would be a short night, more like an audition.

Money equals food in our stomachs.

Jutting up from the serene landscape, immense castle-type walls portrayed a primeval struggle between the virtuous and immoral, the results determined by each individual passing through the remote gate to hell.

Deep-set windows on either side of the arched, wood-plank doors beckoned the intrepid to press a curious nose against the smoked glass and bear witness to the activities occurring within the darkened interior. Wes had also warned them this club was like none other, his ironfisted grasp of the details something no one could dislodge.

“If I prayed, it’d be for the strength to toss your sorry ass in the sea.” Slightly crooked front teeth gleamed white against Daeron’s sun-coppered skin to give him a certain backwoods charm. Aside from the worn threads, no one would suspect him to number among the teaming homeless.

Impatience stiffened his solid frame as he stood by the massive door, willing to tempt the fates that tossed enough curves to enforce a demeanor exceeding his nineteen years yet failing despite the effort. A soft wash of silvery moonlight filtered through the adjacent oak leaves to add a layer of mystery to her protective friend that could be neither defined nor unraveled.

"Wouldn't hurt you to stay there, you know." A lopsided smile softened the admonishment.

"Hey, you won't, so don't hassle me. What is this place anyway, a special retreat for the lost dregs of the Earth? How'd Wes get our first gig in a medieval joint like this? It's making my skin crawl." Kendra hesitated at the top step, doubt and curiosity warring for dominance.

"Wouldn't say, but its five hundred bucks. A hundred for each of us this first night, less thereafter, but it's steady work, which means a steady supply of food if you don't keep giving half of it away." Daeron yanked on the iron door handle to reveal a wide antechamber lined with assorted jewel-toned tapestries, each draped over tightly mortared blocks behind gleaming silver suits of armor.

Lifelike armored figures silently dared the stouthearted to enter, lest some dark prophecy from within awaken to subjugate their will. "Unless you want to sleep in a condemned building or at the church tonight, you sing." Inside the door, a bull-necked man in black jeans and t-shirt nodded a greeting as they passed.

Focusing on music lent clarity of purpose despite her world having plunged into hell in the aftermath of her brother's death. The band members touting her a strong-minded street rat belied the paradoxical evidence of her heartbeat resembling castanets flavoring Spanish music. Stoicism was a trait not yet perfected and, like any art, needed practice.

"Yeah, yeah. Just so they're not sacrificing virgins..." Three men in dress slacks and pressed shirts stood near the end of the vestibule, each turning to give her a brief head-to-toe perusal that quickly morphed into blatant interest.

Of the three, the closest broadcast a curiosity understood all too well, a shark sensing prey in murky chum waters.

"Not likely, asshats." Words mumbled under her breath didn't catch the predator's attention.

"Ha! I knew it. That's why none of the guys have put any moves on you." Daeron's innocent comment drew intensely inquisitive looks, like heat-seeking missiles locking onto target, her incrementally swelling anger.

"As if I'd fall for one of my own rat pack." Her playful biceps punch drew a round of silent chuckles from the sudden admirers. "I prefer a man, thank you very much."

"That's our girl. Just chafe in that chastity belt 'til you find the one." Daeron exchanged greetings, scowling in the face of the men's appreciative grins.

Taking a deep breath, she let her gaze warp around the room, taking in the walls of draped satin, couches lining the perimeter, and tables in the center bearing candles.

"Fuck me sideways. What is this place?" She didn't belong in the building, much less on its stage. "What the hell is Wes playing at?"

Understanding came too late that she'd walked into a trap with no clear escape. Daeron's second rule came to mind. Never walk into something without first knowing the exit.

As if sensing her next move, Daeron reached back and grabbed the arm securing her guitar. "We need to eat, Kendra, unless you want to sell this, which I know you don't."

Reily's Books

Romantic Thrillers

McAllister Justice Series

Tender Echoes

Digital Velocity

Bound By Shadows

Inconclusive Evidence

Carbon Replacements

Shattered Reflections

Remnants of Evil

Moonlight and Murder Series

Shifting Targets

A Critical Tangent

Pivotal Decisions

Seeds of Murder

An Unlikely Grave

Deadly Interception

Love You To Death

Bayou Murders Series

Perfect In Death

Psychic Thrillers

Mind Stalkers

Bending Fate

Silent Depths

Shadow Guard

Whispers Beyond Death

Mind Hunters

Paranormal Romance

Immortal Lovers Series

Unholy Alliance

Blood Union

Standalone paranormal romance

Tiago

About Reily

Reily Garrett is a writer, mother, and companion to three long coat German shepherds. When not working with her dogs, she's sitting at her desk with her fur kids by her side.

Author of chilling suspense and snarky romance, her stories span the distance of romantic thrillers, paranormal romance, and erotic romance. Regardless of genre, each book delves into a dark and twisted imagination yet is tempered with romance and a touch of humor.

Reviews by Kirkus Reviews, San Francisco Bay Review, and BestThrillers.com best describe her work:

"This could be James Patterson, Lee Child, and Tess Gerritsen rolled into one, but the dark, twisted methods used by the serial killer could surprise even those readers…" - San Francisco Bay Review

"…steamy, seductive police procedural…" - BestThrillers.com

"…well-researched thriller that remains romantically genuine throughout." - Kirkus Review

Prior experience in the Military Police, private investigations, and as an ICU nurse gives her fiction a real-world flavor. Find Reily below.

Published by Reily Garrett

Made in the USA
Columbia, SC
15 August 2024

40453299R00126